SUPER

PAUL HORRELL

ISBN 978-1-5272-7280-4

For my own girls, B & L,
who didn't exist when all this started.

1

DOCTOR

'Superpowers are *not* real.'

For just a moment, Michael thought he'd said the words himself. He hadn't, this time, although it was certainly the kind of thing he would say, and had needed to say all too often recently. But this time, it was one of the junior doctors across the ward who'd felt it needed saying.

Their chattering grew closer.

'I'm not saying I could do it,' a male voice said. 'Well, not right now, I mean. But I reckon I could with practise.'

Michael knew from those few words exactly what they were talking about. They were well-educated young professionals, but apparently that didn't stop their conversation from being decidedly lowbrow.

'I can already hold my breath for, what, I don't know, I'd say maybe three minutes,' the same voice said. 'Probably longer.'

Michael could just about see the small group of young doctors, despite their best efforts to remain tucked away in a veiled corner of the ward.

'Three? They said the world record is something like twenty minutes,' said a female voice at a raised volume.

'Keep it down, Toni.'

'Sorry', said Toni.

'You're so bloody loud.'

'Alright, Shaun, you're one to talk.'

'Anyway,' continued Shaun, 'I meant four. Four minutes, if not more.' He was the shorter of the male doctors, and he seemed eager to dominate the conversation. Despite his stature, he spoke down to his peers, especially the women. 'So, I'm right, then. Twenty minutes. Yeah, I remember now, reading that in the paper. So eight minutes is nothing, really.'

'You read that in the paper?' asked a different woman.

'Yep.'

'Okay.'

'Okay, what, Jess?'

'Which paper was it in?' asked Jess.

'What? I don't know, I can't remember.'

'*I* didn't read it, Shaun, and I'm betting you didn't either,' said Jess. 'It was on the Winnies the other night. Friday, I think. You *read* it? No, you *watched* it. Stop trying to sound clever.'

' "Stop trying to sound clever!" ' he repeated, in a high-pitched mimicking tone.

Michael found him obnoxious.

Jess whipped out a small tablet, or perhaps a large phone, Michael couldn't tell. His daughters would know the difference. Within seconds, the show from Friday was loaded and playing.

'Wait a sec, I'll just find it…' She squinted at the screen and moved her finger back and forth. 'Here we go.' The junior medics huddled around the flickering screen. Music blared out at full volume. 'Shit, shit.' She fumbled to find the volume button.

'Jesus Christ, just mute it, woman,' said Shaun, snatching at the device.

'I'm doing it.' She pulled it back from him and found the required button. The music quickly ceased and the doctors looked around to make sure their cover wasn't blown.

Michael looked around too. He knew they had nothing to worry about; there was no one here who might question them. They were safe in their bubble, for now at least.

'There you go,' said Toni, pointing at the screen. 'Twenty-two minutes.'

'But he's a kid,' said Jess, 'not an athlete who's trained for, like, a decade. There's no way he could... Nah, I'm not buying it.'

Michael turned away and rolled over slightly. His chest still hurt. Not like it had, nothing like that hell, when it'd been all-encompassing. Now, it was just a reminder.

'Oh, *you're* not buying it?' said Shaun, taking the tablet. 'Well, that's that, then, I guess. She's not buying it, folks. So, I guess that's case closed.'

'Shut up, Shaun,' said Jess. 'You're a tosser, you know that?' She held out her hand, requesting the device.

When she eventually got it after a lengthy death stare, she tapped away at the screen and loaded something else. *Someone* else. Michael wondered who it would be. He thought about those people, the special ones, who were dominating the conversations of his family at their dining table as much as they were those of junior doctors in shadowy corners of hospital wards.

'Oh, yeah,' said Toni, 'this is the minibus guy. His son forgot his lunchbox or something.'

'Yep.'

'He chased down a bus,' said Shaun. 'So what? They go, like, I don't know, like, really slow. They're, like, the slowest things on the road. Give me a break.'

'A school minibus, Shaun, not a double-decker. Hang on a sec,' said Jess as she searched for the details.

'What'd he do, overtake a tractor too?'

'It was going thirty, Shaun.'

'Thirty miles an hour?' asked one of the taller men.

'Why, is that *fast*?' asked Shaun.

'It's the speed limit.'

'Yeah, on minor roads, when you have to go *slow*.'

'Well, let's see, shall we?' asked Jess. She spun the tablet around to show a buffering video.

'Wow, that's fast,' said the taller man, and Shaun sniggered.

'Shut up, Shaun.'

'What? I didn't say anything. It was *him*.'

The video loaded and played.

Michael couldn't see the screen now, but from the sound alone he knew exactly what was playing. Usain Bolt, Berlin, 2009. Over in nine and a half seconds.

Michael remembered it well. Anyone who'd seen it would remember it, but Michael had a special reason to. He closed his eyes and pictured an empty seat a few rows behind Mr Bolt. Michael had been given tickets to the World Championships, including the flagship event that was the 100-metre final, to ensure his attendance at an otherwise avoidable conference in the German city. But, in the end, he didn't attend either event. His girls, particularly his eldest, Carissa, had needed him more. A nasty bullying incident at school meant he was needed at home, so he'd skipped the conference and missed the athletics too. No Bolt. No problem. His girls came first.

'Which one is this?' asked the tall man.

'It's his Olympic gold medal.'

'Yeah, but which one? Hasn't he got, like, ten or something?'

'No, it's not the Olympics. It's the Worlds.'

There was no way Michael could see the screen from his bed, yet that empty seat of his behind Mr Bolt was as clear as day in his mind. What a race to miss. Not just a world record, *the* world record. Smashed. It could stand for a very long time, especially with Mr Bolt now in retirement. What a race to miss. But Carissa had needed him at home. That was more important. Besides, Michael Richards didn't do regrets. Important decisions were part of life. Occasional mistakes were therefore inevitable.

The doctors sniggered.

'Hey, what's so funny?' asked Shaun. 'I can't see it.'

Neither could Michael, until the screen was lowered for Shaun. Even then, it was hard to make out what was happening. It sounded to him like the same Berlin video was playing.

'Is that McCann?'

'Yep.'

Michael, squinting, could just about see it now. In the outside lane, previously empty, was Jack McCann, the man who'd supposedly chased down a thirty-mile-an-hour minibus.

'Who made this?' asked Shaun.

'I don't know. Someone.'

'Someone with too much time on their hands.'

'Give it a rest, Shaun, it's just a bit of fun.'

'It's well done, too,' said Toni.

'If you say so,' said Shaun.

The video showed McCann speeding past the athletes and winning the race in nine seconds flat, followed by Bolt's bemusement at losing.

The junior doctors chuckled.

'The point is,' said Jess, 'Usain Bolt hit just over twenty-seven miles an hour that day. This is the fastest human ever, running in the fastest race of all time…'

'…and McCann was faster.'

'If it's true, three miles an hour faster.'

'Oh, well, now I'm convinced.'

The taller man clicked on a suggested video. This one, of course, had been taken even further; squeezed into Lane 10 was not only the hero McCann but also the school minibus itself. Michael remembered Rachael watching this one over and over on the family tablet and laughing hysterically each and every time. A nine-second win by McCann, who was then followed shortly afterwards by the minibus, Bolt and the rest of the sprinters. Again, the reactions made the video. Bolt's infamous lightning bolt hand gesture took on a whole new meaning as he appeared to signal for the minibus to stop and pick him up.

'Okay,' said Shaun, 'that's not bad. I mean, you know, nobody sticks their hand out to catch a *minibus*, but yeah, otherwise… go on, let's see it again.'

They watched it again and laughed, Toni especially. She let out a louder-than-planned yelp before attempting to stuff it back into her mouth.

'Ssh,' said the others.

They looked around anxiously again, expecting the added volume to have finally blown their cover. But nobody was the wiser and so they returned to their entertainment.

Michael turned away from them and sighed. He knew who McCann was. He knew all about the minibus chase. He even knew about the underwater kid and how he'd saved his sister from drowning. He knew exactly what they were talking about.

It'd been impossible to avoid it all, even this early on when the actual awards were still about three months away. Like Christmas, the Winnies buzz seemed to start earlier each year. But especially so this time, since the dramatic events of last year's awards.

When Michael's gaze returned to the group of young doctors, they'd moved on to reading about the young girl who'd supposedly understood a radio warning about an incoming snowstorm and warned her mother about it. Simple enough. Except that the family were on holiday in Shanghai and the warning was communicated in Mandarin Chinese.

'She's nine,' said Toni. 'She barely speaks English, okay?'

'Slight exaggeration,' said Shaun.

'Also, she'd never been abroad before.'

'What difference does that make? Nah, sounds like a con to me.'

Michael felt that way about all of these so-called superheroes.

'That's putting it mildly,' added the tall man. 'Who does that leave? Did the burning building guy make it through?'

There was a time when the burning building guy would have reached the final. But not anymore. Not since last year. Not since Damo.

'Who?' asked Shaun. 'Oh, him. No, obviously not. Come on Jim, why the hell would *that* get through?'

If Michael had had the energy, he'd gladly have got up and given the obnoxious kid a slap. Well, a few choice words, anyway.

'Can't believe we missed it,' said Jim.

'Yeah, maybe medicine isn't for me after all. It's getting in the way of more important things,' said Jess, and Michael really couldn't tell if she was joking or not.

Michael, on the other hand, had seen the whole show. It had been on the ward TV, so he'd had little choice. There was a part of him that had wanted to watch it, at least at first. That feeling quickly left him, though, as the burning building chap got knocked out and the finalists were announced.

'Don't tell me the human X-ray machine made it through,' said Toni.

'Hang on, let's see.'

The tablet operator took back control and loaded up the show's website, or one of the tabloid newspapers, or one of the social media outlets; Michael wasn't sure. They all looked the same, one hundred per cent Winnies. Besides that, when it came to technology, Michael was out of his comfort zone. He was a reluctant digital immigrant, or, as his native daughters would describe him, a 'dinosaur'. He wasn't convinced it was progress.

'No way, I don't believe it.'

'Oh my God, the British public are so gullible.'

The screen had loaded to show five faces: the three they had discussed and two others.

'Stupid, more like.'

'I can't decide which is more ridiculous,' said Toni.

'The X-ray guy clearly,' said the Shaun.

'I don't know. A granny with a force field? What, did she use her brolly?'

They all laughed.

'I'm not saying that's not stupid,' said Shaun, 'but, come on, Toni, you're a doctor. Well, kind of…'

She glared at him.

'Hell, I'm all for it being real. Save the service a ton of cash,' said Jess. 'You know, each of those scanners cost, what, 50k? That's reconditioned, not new. God knows we can't afford new.'

Jim began reading from the screen.

'Evan Sykes was on the tube heading home from work. He liked the solitude of a quiet carriage. He was therefore understandably annoyed to see a thickset middle-aged banker slouch down in the seat one away from him, which, thanks to the man's girth, also meant on the seat directly next to him. It was especially annoying for Sykes as there were so many seats further away to choose from. He tried to ignore it but couldn't, so he got up to sit elsewhere. He turned to the man to deliver a parting glare. But when he looked at him, he saw something truly unexpected. He saw pain. He saw evil inside him. He saw a tumour. It stopped Evan Sykes in his tracks. He had to say something. "Excuse me," he said. The man turned to face Evan. As their eyes met, Evan realised he had no idea how to break the news. "You need to go and see someone." The large man just looked at Evan. "I mean, a doctor, you need to go and see a doctor." The confused man told Evan he'd just been to his GP. She'd sent him away with a prescription for a migraine. "No," Evan interrupted. "It's not a migraine." He hesitated. "It's more serious than that, I'm afraid. You have something, something going on. I can see it." The banker stared at him, open-mouthed, saying nothing. "Tell them…" Evan didn't know what terminology to use. "Tell them to look…here." He stepped forward and very gently tapped the man on the left side of his head.'

'Okay, okay, that's good,' said Jess. 'But listen to this.' She read out loud an account of Miss Geraldine Adams. 'The blast radius reached over three hundred yards while the family and Miss Adams, 72, stood barely fifty yards away. When asked how she did it, Miss Adams replied, "I just did what came naturally. I knew, in that instant, that I had the power to do something. So I did." Scorch marks on the ground showed a perfectly circular zone that had been protected from the gas explosion. Even the grass within the circle was untouched. When pushed further for an answer, Miss Adams simply said, "I'd rather be asked why than how. It doesn't matter how I did it, just that I could do it. What matters now is using my gift to help others." Both Mrs Jacobs and her son Liam were completely unharmed in the explosion. Miss Adams had scorch marks on the fingertips of both hands. She claims she used her hands to repel the energy into a force field around the three of them. Odds on Miss Adams have recently been slashed in the wake of Tuesday night's interview with Damo.'

'Okay, enough of that rubbish,' came a loud, authoritative female voice. 'Hand it over and listen to me.'

The tablet was dutifully handed over and the doctors stood to attention.

'Okay,' said the new voice, 'this one's for Shaun, and only Shaun.'

'No worries,' said the annoying little man. 'Bring it on, doc.'

'A father and his son are involved in a serious car crash. The father is killed instantly and the boy is rushed to hospital in a critical condition. It's not looking good for the lad, and the staff wait anxiously for the chief resident – a gifted surgeon – to arrive. The surgeon makes it to the operating room but, upon seeing the boy, stops cold and says, "I can't operate on this patient. He's my son." Now, Shaun, how can that be?'

Michael smiled to himself. It'd been a good few years since he'd heard this riddle. He didn't remember who'd first told it to him, but he was sure it was someone a lot older than this doctor.

She'd appeared in his line of sight and, to him, looked like a junior herself.

'Wait a sec,' Shaun said. 'What was that last bit?'

The doctor sighed. ' "I can't operate on him because he's my son." '

'Oh, that's so obvious,' said Jim.

'Yeah,' said Jess, 'the doctor is–'

'Uh-uh, it's just for Shaun. You can't help him with this one.'

'Who says I need help?'

'Go on, then.'

Shaun stood with his eyes looking up, searching for the answer.

Nothing was said for a minute. The other junior doctors shook their heads and covered their faces.

'Wait,' said Shaun finally. 'Say it one more time.'

There were groans.

'You can have this back,' said the doctor in charge, holding up the tablet, 'when Shaun has worked it out.' She walked away.

'What's the answer, Toni?' asked Shaun, quietly.

'Ha ha, no chance.'

'Come on.'

'Nope.'

'You know I was only kidding before. You're a great doctor. Come on, at least tell me the riddle again, eh? I really didn't hear it first time, anyway.'

'Fine. Father and son in a crash, father dies, ambulance brings boy to hospital. Surgeon walks into theatre, sees boy, says "He's my son". Simples.'

'Walks in,' said Shaun to himself, 'sees lad, says "my son".'

Toni's grin stretched wider and wider.

'Got it. Stepdad. Easy. It's his stepdad. Just didn't hear it first time.'

'Nope, no stepdad.'

'I meant, two dads, the boy has, you know, two dads.'

'Like that 80s sitcom?'

'Eh?'

'Never mind. You mean a gay couple?'

Shaun swallowed hard. 'Yeah, I guess, I mean, I don't know about that sort of thing, you know, but yeah, gay chaps.'

'You're straight,' said Toni, 'I get it.'

'So, I'm right?'

'Sorry, nope. You're missing the obvious, Shaun. What if I said the word "biological"–?'

'Or, or,' said Shaun, interrupting, 'how's about this? Yes, I have it. Here we go. It *is* the son's father, but it's his spirit, because, you know, he died in the crash, and this is the moment when he realises that he's dead.'

'Shaun,' said Jess.

'Yeah?'

'You owe me an iPad.'

The young doctors laughed as they walked away, and Michael very nearly chuckled too.

The elephant that had crashed down on to his chest a week ago had now sat up and moved on, but, boy, could he still feel its impact. The doctors had called it an episode, his wife a warning. In layman's terms it was a heart attack, albeit a mild one. Now here he was, laid up in a hospital ward, with just a hangover of intense chest tightness as a reminder that it wasn't all a bad dream. Decades earlier, he'd felt something similar while on a road trip through Indonesia. The questionable water quality of Bali's Kuta Beach. He couldn't resist the water and the waves. Not to mention the escape from the scores of replica watch sellers. A day later, his stomach felt the brunt. But by day three it had spread to his chest. Pain like he had never experienced before. It had felt like the end. But he was young then. A mere boy. He could shake it off and keep travelling. Not these days. Middle-aged recovery was a longer road. This episode had taken its toll, and not just physically. Michael Richards was a different man now.

He'd reached his mid-fifties with a good amount of grace and dignity. That said, recently the salt in his hair had overtaken the pepper, and the wrinkles that had once framed his charming features were now more prominent than the features themselves.

Michael leant back on to his hard, functional pillows and stared up at the ceiling. He flicked his eyes around the stale ward. The doctor and her students had moved on. As annoying as they'd been, at least they were living. Their departure meant there wasn't much of that remaining. Monotonous electronic beeps pierced the otherwise deafening silence. Michael closed his eyes for a couple of seconds, perhaps longer.

'Good morning, Michael.'

It wasn't immediately clear where the voice was coming from.

'My name is Doctor Reyes. I hope you're up to visitors?'

When Michael attempted to sit up the pain spiked through his chest, forcing him back into a prone position. His dry throat cracked as he failed to reply.

'Just a few minutes, mind.'

Michael summoned the strength to shuffle up a few inches. He saw the doctor from before, who'd returned sans students. She was standing, measured and purposeful, at the foot of his bed.

He realised he recognised her. He knew her, although not personally. Reyes. He'd read about her. In just her early thirties, Olivia Reyes was the one of the youngest cardiologists in the country. With more than a fleeting interest in neurology, she'd studied both simultaneously, such was her intellect, but had ultimately decided on the heart over the head, which, he'd read, was somewhat ironic considering her professional approach to all aspects of her life. She was famous among her peers for her straightforward motto – Work harder – and when the press attempted to tell her story, the closest they got to the real Olivia Reyes was the quote: 'I'm driven by two things. The strength of my mother and the weakness of my father.'

'You still need plenty of rest.' There was an air of superiority about her, and the intensity she brought to her job was written across her harsh but not unattractive face.

Michael's reserve of strength could last only a few seconds before giving out. He collapsed back on to his stiff bed. His exhale filled the silence.

'Your lovely family is here,' she said.

If ever there was a phrase to give Michael the strength he needed, it was that one.

Susanna was over a decade younger than him; while that meant little now, at the time of their meeting it very nearly did. Barely out of university, she was smart and well read, but with little life experience.

Doctor Reyes helped Michael perch himself high enough for him to see his family approaching.

'Susie…' whispered Michael, '…my girls.'

'You're a very lucky man.' It wasn't clear whether Doctor Reyes was referring to Michael's medical state or the gleeful smiles on the faces of Susanna, Carissa and Rachael.

Twenty feet away, here they came, full steam ahead. The smallest engine led the way, her bigger sister not far behind. Bringing up the rear was the love of his life, trying desperately to keep up.

The doctor's supportive arm gave way and so did Michael. He hit the bed again and saw the same ugly ceiling. This time, though, a smile broke out across his face.

'Wait for me, girls,' called Susanna.

Michael's smile grew wider. He was alive. He shifted his weight to one side and stretched his neck beyond its usual comfort. There they were.

'Dad!'

'Daddy, we missed you.'

'Rach, don't push.'

His beautiful daughters, arguing as usual.

'Daddy, I missed you loads.'

'We all did, not just you.'

And then, following closely behind, wearing no make-up and all the better for it, his soulmate. The woman he'd fallen for the moment he'd seen her. He shot her a smile. She returned it, and they locked eyes for the briefest, purest of moments. But then pain returned – a thud against his chest. This time, though, it was just his youngest in all her enthusiasm. Even a warning from both her big sister and her mother didn't stop twelve-year-old Rachael from squeezing her father with all her youthful might. Carissa was more measured, but no less passionate. She wrapped her teenage arms around her dad's neck and kissed his forehead.

Susanna propped herself on the edge of the bed and clasped her husband's hand between hers. 'Hey, come on, girls,' she said. 'Go steady.'

'It's okay,' said Michael, barely audible.

'How are you, honey? Are you okay?'

A whisper of a response was all he could manage. 'I am now.'

The family embraced in a cocoon, but the privacy of the ward was limited. As Susanna reached over to close the curtain, Michael watched Doctor Reyes using her mobile. The curtain now around them, Susanna beamed a smile at Michael. They looked at each other like they had on their wedding day. Her smile was the same. Michael was instantaneously transported back to that wonderful day when he'd looked over his shoulder to see his young bride-to-be approaching.

2

PATIENT

I could remember her face, but nothing else about the day we married.

I hurt. I had a dull, aching pain everywhere. It had been dark for what seemed like a lifetime, but now there was a bright white light. It took a few seconds for my eyes to adjust. A doctor's penlight. Click. It ceased and the darkness returned. And it was most welcome.

'Patient is awake,' said a clinical voice.

For the briefest of moments I thought I recognised it, but before I could think who it might be another voice interrupted my thoughts.

'Patient wakes 10.47 a. m.'

My eyes settled and I saw the two figures: a doctor and a nurse.

The nurse took a pen to my chart. She seemed a little shifty. Not exactly hiding my chart, but definitely treating it like it was her private property.

I looked around as best I could. There were about eight beds, most of them empty, and from my spot next to the ward entrance I could see down the corridor to where there were countless more wards. Doctors, nurses, admin staff – all of them walked briskly about their business. It was a hive of activity out there, yet there was a staleness to the whole place. The air hung heavy under its history of sickness and the threat of the end. I sensed I'd always hated hospitals, although for some reason I couldn't actually remember if that was true.

'Where am I?' I asked.

'You're in hospital.'

Stupid question. 'No, sorry,' I said. 'I mean…why? What happened?'

The doctor stepped in closer, blocking out the harsh fluorescent light from above. Again, my eyes adjusted as best they could, but, like everywhere else on my body, they throbbed with pain.

'I'm Doctor Reyes,' she said. 'You were in an accident. You took quite a hit.'

She was young for a doctor. Young-looking, that is, but otherwise wholly a doctor. Maybe it was just the uniform, or my eyes trying their best to cope, but she had a reassuring familiarity about her. Not that her bedside manner was anything to write home about.

'When *will* people learn to cross the street properly? Luckily for you, we have decent paramedics in this city.'

Ouch. Still, she at least seemed to know what was going on and what had happened, which was more than I knew. And then it hit me. Not only couldn't I remember the accident, I couldn't remember anything at all. I should've panicked, but I didn't. I didn't know who I was, and yet, I wasn't scared. It made no sense, but, somehow, felt normal.

'I don't remember,' I said. 'I don't…holy shit, I can't remember anything.'

She looked at me with an expression of both pity and, strangely, pleasure. A silence followed. And then her bedside manner reared its head again. 'That's unfortunate. You probably hit your head. There might be some confusion.'

If she was trying to reassure me, she was doing a lousy job. But I sensed she wasn't trying to. Or, at least, she wasn't trying particularly hard.

'Tell me what you do remember,' she said. 'And, please, take your time.'

Again, the words came with no warmth. I thought hard, which also hurt. I closed my eyes. There was darkness everywhere I looked. The past was blank. But then there was something in the back. I searched the shadows. I had glimpses. Three figures, three faces. But not faces, not people, just feelings. Three feelings. Love. I couldn't see them, but if I looked hard enough I could feel them. I could feel my wife and two children.

But nothing else.

'So…tell me, where are we?' she asked, waking me from my trance. I heard the question and was working out a response, but I obviously took too long to answer. She repeated herself. 'Do you know where we are?'

'I'm sorry,' I said, not really knowing what I was apologising for. 'I-I…well, I think I-I…' I was a stuttering mess.

'Calm down, sir, please,' she said. 'There's no hurry. Please just take your time.' Her cold tone didn't match her kind words.

'Hospital,' I blurted out.

'Okay,' she said.

'I-I mean…'

'Hospital, yes, and… What else?'

I felt under interrogation. 'I don't know.'

'Okay, tell me about your family. You must remember your family.'

I turned my head to the large window. It looked out over car parks: three, four, maybe more of them. They were all full. Car after car, squeezed in. And then more cars, creeping around, waiting for somebody to leave so they could score a valuable space. Visitors being overcharged for visiting their loved ones at their most vulnerable moment, their hour of need. My eyes went beyond the metallic colours and eventually, up and away, they found some real greenery. Trees, woods, what looked like a stream tucked away among them.

'Your family?' she asked again. 'Anything at all.'

Her words brought me back. Back from the stream, through the trees, across the multicoloured metal roofs. Back through the window, across the ward and into my bed. Her eyes searched mine but I had nothing for her.

'Your name?'

Nothing.

'Your job, maybe?'

Nothing.

'Nothing at all about your family? Often patients who have... Patients in your position, they remember family first.'

I closed my eyes. The feelings returned. 'Yes. Yes, my family.'

'You're married?'

My God. My wife. Yes, I was married. More than that, my wife was my life. 'Yes,' I said. That was sufficient.

The doctor flashed me a look of satisfaction.

'We have children. Two,' I said enthusiastically, but then instantly lost confidence. 'Two, I think.'

She came at me, slowly and methodically. Her fingers felt my pulse, and the whole time her eyes were locked on mine as if she could diagnose me purely through vision alone. Next, her stethoscope chilled my chest. She was clinical at every touch.

I scanned the ward. Nothing was happening. Opposite were two elderly patients, their respective families awkwardly exchanging pleasantries about the weather and whatnot. Nobody wanted to be there.

The doctor finished her checks. 'Okay, that's good. Well, I can't see there being a problem with you seeing your family really soon–'

Before I could tell her how wonderful that was, the moment was interrupted. The short, tired-looking nurse who'd been hovering at the end of the bed cleared her throat in an embarrassed and exaggerated fashion to cut off the doctor's sentence.

When the doctor gave her a puzzled stare, the nurse held out my medical records. The doctor skimmed through the papers, looked at the nurse, then at me, then at the nurse again, all without muttering a word.

Just as I was about to break the silence, she spoke. 'You were in a serious accident, sir. Your vital signs are good...' she paused, almost long enough for me to ask about my family, '...but you must rest if you're to make a full recovery.'

Something didn't add up. Her demeanour. Her eyes, for the first time, avoided mine, while the nurse simply looked down at the chart.

'Are my family here?' I asked.

No answer.

'Were they in the accident?'

Her response was no help. 'Right now, I need you to rest. That will help your recovery and help your memory to return.'

'Are they hurt?' I asked. 'I need to know, please.'

'Sir…'

'Oh God, please, no…'

'Sir, it's fine, they're…' She glanced at the nurse, who still hadn't looked up. Finally, with no reason given for such a long delay, she delivered the news I needed to hear. 'You're the only one injured, sir.'

I sighed. I smiled. *Why did I have to plead?* 'They're all right?'

'You were the only one in the accident.'

And relax. Thank God. I stopped worrying. My memory was shot. I was in a hospital bed for no reason that I could remember. My world was upside down. But, but, my family were okay. She'd said so. *I'm the only one involved.*

'We can discuss visitors soon.'

I was so relieved, so happy, that I only heard the 'visitors' part, not 'soon'. I nodded like an idiot, missing the point that she was delaying my visitors, my family.

'Right now, you must rest.'

When I snapped out of it and realised I needed more information, it was too late. The doctor was out of the ward almost before her sentence had ended. The nurse scuttled away as well. As my eyes followed her, they were met with a framed photo on the table next to my bed.

I picked it up. My God, they were beautiful. My family. My gorgeous wife and perfect kids. I'd never truly understood how I could be so lucky – she was out of my league, and the kids were thankfully full of their mother's genes. The result was a family that looked too good for me. I picked up the framed photo, kissed it and then held it to my chest.

I tried to imagine what that day must have been like. I must have taken the photo, capturing that magical moment, one that summed up everything that mattered most to me: my beautiful wife, radiant, handing our new baby to her big sister for their first-ever cuddles together. I wished so badly to remember it. I closed my eyes and told myself I would remember, I could remember.

And maybe I did, because the vision came to me within seconds. I could see them.

3

DOCTOR

Michael Richards sat in his favourite armchair. It was brown leather and in no way matched the bright, modern decor of the living room.

A voice came from behind him. 'I still don't quite know how you did it.'

'Did what?' asked Michael.

'You know what,' said Susanna.

'I do?'

'Well,' Susanna said as she perched herself on the chair arm, 'firstly, how you convinced me to buy this damn thing.'

'Hang on, hang on.' He put his arms around her and pulled her closer. 'That's not what happened and you know it.'

'Isn't it?'

'You just want me to tell the story again, don't you?'

'Hmm. Maybe.'

'Just to remind me of how lucky I am?'

'Maybe.'

'How lucky I am, and how wonderful you are?'

'Keep talking.'

'Well,' Michael said, squeezing his wife around the waist, 'the memory is a bit hazy, so please correct me if I make a mistake…'

'I will.'

'Ha, I'm sure you will. So, let's see, it was a good few years back, I was a young man, in the prime of my life.'

'Some of us still are,' said Susanna without missing a beat.

'Ouch.' Michael held his chest.

'Sorry, cheap shot. You were saying?'

Michael recounted the story of the chair, which was actually a story of two chairs, the one he and Susanna were currently sitting on and the long-lost one that had preceded it decades before.

It looked less upright, maybe, and the stitching was a different colour, but otherwise it was identical. Michael walked over to the chair while a heavily pregnant Susanna tried out multiple sofas for comfort. He drew his finger along the blue (not brown) stitching. He squeezed the arm. The memories came flooding back. It wasn't the same chair. Still, emotions ran high.

'You okay?' Susanna appeared at his side.

'I'm being silly,' he said.

'What's new?'

Michael didn't bite. He was too busy reliving his past.

'Why don't you try it out?' asked Susanna.

Michael turned away. 'No, no need for that.'

'Try it out,' she said, no longer asking.

'It's okay, I don't need to–'

Susanna gave him her 'I'm pregnant' stare. He stopped arguing.

He continued to trace the line of stitching with his finger until he found himself positioned and ready. Ready to slide back into that old friend he'd left behind. And if, somehow, it felt like it looked, like that old friend, there was no way, this time, he was leaving without it.

It wasn't the same chair. It was better. The reclined design felt to Michael as if his old friend had aged and relaxed, matured and tired, just like he himself had over the years. Michael closed his eyes for, he swore, a few seconds and no more. And yet, when they opened again his wife was walking back towards him having already secured the deal.

'Delivery is Wednesday.'

'What *was* I thinking?' asked Susanna.

'I guess you were thinking just how much you loved me.'

'No, that wasn't it.'

'Charming.'

'This is what happens when you let pregnant women make decisions.'

'I'm glad you said that, not me,' said Michael.

'But that's not what really puzzles me.'

'It's not?'

'No. What I really want to know,' she said, wrapping her arms around her husband's neck, 'is how it is still, even now, here in my otherwise perfect living room.'

Michael smiled. Driving home from the furniture shop, Susanna had made it very clear where the new addition would live: the study. At first it had, but then came Christmas and it was brought into the living room to accommodate their visitors. It stayed there throughout Boxing Day and remained for the New Year's Eve party the Richards often held for their neighbours. And now, many years later, it somehow remained, stubbornly defying the tasteful decor Susanna had worked so hard to create all around it.

Decades ago, when he was a student, he'd had a chair that was almost identical.

That original one was a pleasant, welcome accident, left behind by the previous occupant of Michael's new flat. It was tatty even then, so, after much use by Michael, it was truly on its last legs by the time he left university. He had spent hour upon hour working in that chair. So attached to it did he become that he decided to take it with him when he left. First though, he took it to a carpenter and then an upholsterer, who, between them, had brought it back to life. He spent more time and money on it than he should have. However, when the day eventually came to leave, Michael realised that the chair had to stay. It belonged there, in that flat. And so he left it for the next occupant. He even decided to write a message and attached it to the chair as a welcome for the future owner. Something to let them know what they were inheriting and how lucky they were. He sat and wrote, as he had before countless times, in that chair. But the words didn't come. They didn't flow. They felt forced. *Perhaps the chair knows what I'm writing*, he joked to himself. Multiple screwed-up notes filled the rubbish bin before he realised he should just stop, sit there and enjoy the moment. Enjoy the chair, for one last time.

Susanna had disappeared into the kitchen, leaving Michael sat in his chair. He picked up the framed photo from the side table. It depicted the happiest day of his life. That was a bold statement; Michael's life was full of days almost any one of which most people would gladly call their happiest.

Travelling around Europe as a young twenty-something had given him many wonderful times. Memories of meeting interesting people and getting into adventures were made all the more special now by way of his rose-tinted glasses. Another contender was that magical, if blurry, evening when he first set eyes on his soulmate Susanna. The effort it took, not just to get her to talk to him but to even drag himself to that party in the first place. There was the morning Susanna came out of the bathroom with a huge, beaming, nervous grin on her face. He didn't even need to ask, he knew what it meant. She went to him and he cupped her navel. Without words, they lay down and held each other for an hour. Then there was the evening Carissa was born; the horror and, ultimately, ecstasy that followed. She took her time, stayed inside her mother as long as she could. Even now, as she approached her potentially awkward teenage years, her connection with her mum was rock solid. Her little sister, on the other hand, was a daddy's girl if ever there was one. Which brought him right back to the photo he held so tightly. Baby Rachael brought home and passed to big sister Carissa. The joy in Carissa's face matched only by the smile the memory brought to Michael's own face now, over a decade later.

There were highlights in his psychotherapy career too: being the first of his family to attend university, building his own practice from scratch, being successful with incredible, outlandish, controversial treatment techniques. Even getting his golf handicap to single figures meant a lot to him.

But these all paled in comparison to his family. Of all the things Michael was, he prided himself on being a family man.

He stood and walked over to the window, looking out across the well-kept gardens of their detached home. The weather was warm for the season and the girls were taking full advantage. The water fight had been an even affair, with each sister having similar ammunition. Carissa's extra strength was countered by Rachael's playful bodyguard Ginga; the four-year-old Beagle belonged to the whole family but followed Rachael everywhere, including, most importantly today, into the heart of battle.

Michael was just glad they weren't on their phones or glued to Winnies coverage. Outside was good, and the generous space behind the house was one of the reasons he and Susanna had chosen it as their family home. The sight of his two daughters enjoying themselves was everything he had hoped for and worked for.

Michael turned the frame over to read what was written on the back of the photo.

Hours old, I dressed
This person, whom I knew not
Yet loved forever.

He looked up again. Before either of the girls could win the war of the water pistols, the beating sun had defeated them both. It appeared, for short a while at least, that a peace treaty was in place. It was, however, shaky. Carissa lazed by the patio furniture while Rachael slumped on the grass. Even Ginga flopped to the shaded ground in relief at the temporary ceasefire.

'It's all fun and games at the moment, but we both know what's coming.'

Susanna had her arms wrapped around her husband's shoulders before he even knew she was there. It felt good. She always did. He had friends who had to pretend, act or convince themselves. Not him. He loved her even more than the day they married.

'One day, it won't end in tears,' he said.

'Yeah, maybe you're right,' she said. 'Maybe one day. But not today.'

'Maybe today.'

'The perpetual optimist.'

'Well, it beats being a pessimist.'

Susanna leaned in. 'I prefer "realist".'

He felt her breath on his neck. 'I'm sure you do,' he said, bringing his mouth close to hers.

'Here…' said Susanna, as she leant back, holding out a mug of tea. The smell hit him, but before he could complain she was on the offensive. 'It's called kombucha and people swear by it.'

Michael inhaled the pungent aroma; he was far from convinced. *What people?*

But again Susanna was ahead of him. 'Jackie put me on to it.'

He took the smallest of sips before retracting in exaggerated disgust. 'Jackie?'

Susanna rolled her eyes.

Michael knew why; he had developed a habit of not remembering Susanna's friends, or at least their names. Her recounting of the dinner and dance party from three years ago, where he had supposedly got so drunk with Jackie's husband Simon that they were asked to leave the private function, did little to help. Of course, if he had been as drunk as she claimed it was understandable that he wouldn't remember. The truth was Michael didn't really care for friends, and in particular new friends. He had three, maybe five close friends whom he had known his whole life, and, crucially, who had a similar attitude towards friendship to him. His closest and oldest friend, Conner, had moved abroad. Four years passed with barely any contact between them. Upon Conner's return, he and Michael had picked up exactly where they'd left off, with a pint and a handshake, a joke and an update. No need for nonsense, not with real friends.

'Anyway,' she said, 'Jackie swapped coffee for kombucha after Simon had *his* heart attack.'

Michael tried another mouthful, his third now. The truth was he was starting to enjoy it, not that he'd give in that easily. Coffee was at stake here, after all.

'I didn't have a heart attack. Not a real one.'

Susanna took a step back as if the words were a physical attack. At first, her reply wouldn't come out; it was stuck in her throat. Michael realised then that he'd been too flippant, but it was too late to take it back.

'Excuse me?' said Susanna. 'Not a real one? I don't know how real it felt to you but I can tell you it damn sure felt real enough to me!'

Michael was already regretting what he'd said. 'I'm sorry. I didn't mean–'

But Susanna wasn't done yet. 'Not real? Michael, this is as real as it gets. It was a warning to change, to slow down, and the doctor, the doctor said if you don't take it seriously then you're going to…' Her anger became upset; tears formed.

Michael put his tea down. He went to comfort his wife, who at first held him away but very quickly gave up the fight. He apologised and they embraced.

'Okay, okay, you're right,' said Michael. 'You're right, honey. I'm sorry.'

'Words aren't enough, Michael.'

He stood up straight and puffed out his chest. 'Okay, okay,' he said. 'You want action? Yeah? Okay, you got it.'

Michael picked up the kombucha tea and downed the rest of it in one swoop, burning his mouth in the process. He coughed and spluttered a little. 'There.' Michael plonked the empty mug down, catching his breath. 'This shit just got real!'

This broke Susanna's resolve and she couldn't help but let out a little smile and a chortle.

The moment was just an instant old when a deafening screech from outside penetrated the double glazing. Michael and Susanna looked at each other and smiled. He turned to see that Carissa had taken advantage of the momentary truce, sneaked up on her younger sister and completely soaked her from head to toe with a huge bucket of ice-cold water.

'Mum!' screamed Rachael as Carissa fled the crime scene. The French doors slammed open and a dripping-wet Rachael came in and screeched again. 'Dad!'

Susanna attempted to calm the situation. 'It's okay, Rach, it's just water.'

Michael couldn't help himself; a snigger escaped him, much to Rachael's annoyance. She looked at her parents before shrieking once more and stomping her way through the living room towards her bedroom. Ginga, of course, followed faithfully behind.

'See, a realist,' said Susanna, as though she had just placed a winning hand on the table.

4

PATIENT

I woke up to find the photo of my family gone.

I didn't remember who I was, but I remembered them and I remembered holding the photo to my chest as I drifted off yesterday. It wasn't there now. I looked around the bed as best I could, assuming it had fallen, but I couldn't see it anywhere. I'd fallen asleep with their faces searching my soul and I'd dreamt about them. And now I was back here, in this hellhole, without them, and without their photograph.

'My photo is gone,' I said to nobody and anybody. 'Who moved it?'

There was a nurse opposite me, attending to an elderly man. I guessed it was her or one of her colleagues who had been 'kind enough' to put the photo away somewhere safe or had simply returned it to the table next to my bed, to my left, just out of sight, maybe. I looked up at the flickering fluorescent light and took a deep breath, preparing to roll on to my side, which would certainly bring with it pain. But it would be worth it, if the photo was waiting there.

I rolled on to my right slightly, and then again, to build up a little rocking momentum, and then I leant on to my left side to see the table. There was a vase of flowers – tulips – desperately in need of water, a couple old lifestyle magazines and a George Orwell novel. But no photo.

The nurse was fussing. Sorting the old man's pillow, rearranging his items. It went on and on. Forever. Every second felt like an eternity.

With a croaky, quiet voice I called out for her attention. I watched her stow away the old chap's belongings into his bedside cabinet. *That's where it must be.* My cabinet.

I raised my voice as much as I could. 'Excuse me, nurse?'

She didn't reply, didn't even turn around. I was sure I'd been loud enough that time. I suddenly felt like I was being ignored. She continued attending to the man as if I didn't matter. I did one of those obviously intentional coughs for attention, and she finally acknowledged my existence.

'I'll be with you in a moment, sir,' she said, without looking up from what she was doing.

Her tone was a little rude, I thought, considering our roles. Or, if not rude, then certainly cold. I very nearly apologised for interrupting her duties. But I didn't. I stopped myself in time.

It must have been five further minutes before she was done with him, although the faulty clock on the far wall made it hard to know. She had said 'a moment', not 'a minute', but I supposed nobody literally meant a minute when they said that anyway. I was being unfair, I thought then. She was just doing her job, a difficult job at that, for low pay. I felt guilty for my thoughts towards her and quickly smiled as she came across the ward. She returned my smile as she walked straight past my bed and towards the ward exit. My smile vanished as quickly as she did. I called out but it only won me a finger – not that one – indicating that she would just be a minute. Or a moment. I felt less guilt about my earlier thoughts.

The old bloke opposite had a big grin on his old weathered face, and was pointing it right in my direction.

'All right?' I said.

He didn't reply. I was starting to feel invisible. I looked back at the clock. The battery, like everything else in the place, was nearly dead and the second hand seemed incapable of performing its sole purpose. I stared at it and went into a trance. Although I was far across the ward, if I concentrated solely on it, I thought I could hear every faulty tick.

That moment of near peace was shattered by the nurse's abrupt return. 'Now…' She seemed put out. 'How can I help?'

I took a moment. By this stage, I'd gone back and forth in my opinion of her. But then I realised that didn't matter and focused instead on what did matter: my family.

'My photo is gone,' I said, more bluntly than I'd planned.

She said nothing, just stood there staring at me.

I repeated myself. 'My photo, it's gone.'

'I'm sorry,' she said, 'what photo is that?'

This both confused and then really worried me. 'My photo,' I said. 'Look, last night there was a photo right here on the table next to me. In fact, I held it as I fell asleep. I may have dropped it, but I've looked and I can't see it anywhere.'

She nodded in an unconvinced manner.

'It means everything to me,' I said. 'It's a photo of my family. I haven't seen them yet, not since the accident.'

The nurse offered a slightly sarcastic 'Okay,' before looking around the bed and table area as if the photo was right there next to me and I was blind.

I was starting to think I'd done something to piss her off, especially after seeing her treat the old chap so nicely before.

'Hmm, that's strange.' she said. 'I'll speak to the night-shift nurse. She might know where it is.'

I sighed loudly. Then, realising she might take offence, I quickly thanked her for the offer. 'Oh, and it had writing on the back…'

But then it dawned on me. *What am I doing?* The photo wasn't important. That wasn't the point. That wasn't what this was about. I was missing the point, and so, therefore, was she.

It'd been three days now. Three days since I came in after the accident. Three days with no visitors. My family hadn't been in to see me. No visit, and no word from them either. Not only that but every time I asked the doctor about it, about them, all she talked of was resting.

'Right now, just rest.'

'You need to rest.'

'You must rest, David.'

Each time I got to bend the ear of a nurse, they repeated that my memory would return.

'It'll come back.'

'Be patient.'

'You need rest, David.'

It didn't make sense. 'Actually, forget the photo.'

The nurse stopped fishing around in the cabinet.

'It's not important,' I said, as her confused face met mine. 'I mean it is important, but, but…'

I could see that any patience she'd had was evaporating rapidly.

'What I mean is,' I composed myself, 'rather than the photograph, that's not important itself, it's the people *in it* that I need to see.'

I realised this was the longest I'd had the attention of anyone since coming in. The nurse made as if to speak, probably to say something about resting, but I wasn't going to miss this opportunity. 'It's been three days now,' I said. 'Three days, and for some reason my family haven't come in to see me. I'm sorry, but I need to know what's going on. Please, if you know anything, anything at all, please tell me.'

The nurse looked at me. Before answering me, she scanned the ward and reception area beyond. 'Look,' she said, 'I'm sorry, I wish I could help, but I don't have the answers you need.' I felt frustration build inside me. Before I could respond, she put her hand on my leg and continued talking. 'However, I can tell you that I did see a family here, earlier on, like.'

I couldn't believe it, and didn't know how to feel. Ecstatic, to know that they were okay, and that they'd been to see me, and yet, heartbroken, massively heartbroken, that I'd missed them. Missed holding them. Missed touching them. But then I realised how good this news was. The positive emotion won out, and the nurse could see my relief.

She tried to curtail it. 'I can't say who they were here to see, I'm afraid, but it *was* while you were sleeping, that much I know.'

The frustration from before reared its head again. 'I can't believe nobody woke me. And please, please don't mention having to rest or doctor's *bloody* orders.'

The two of us looked at one another, unsure of how to proceed. I started to apologise for being so snappy. She touched my leg again. 'Listen,' she said, 'next time I see them, I'll give you a nudge…' she looked around again before finishing, 'no matter what the doctor's orders.'

I nodded, and she flashed me a wink before going about her duties.

'Sir? Wake up, sir.'

It sounded like the same nurse. I felt groggy. I must have slept for a good while. I wearily opened my eyes to find her stood at the end of my bed. My eyes refocused and I could see she was smiling.

'I hope you're up to visitors.'

I had a rush of adrenaline. This was it, my family was here. Finally, I'd see them, I'd hold them, I'd squeeze them, I wouldn't stop kissing them. I was sure they'd always been my entire life, but this was literally the case now that I could remember nothing but them.

I must have smiled at the nurse.

'I'll take that as a "yes",' she said. She skipped to the side of the bed to reveal three figures approaching.

Here they came.

I watched them.

They had smiles, huge smiles.

My heart sank.

Something was very, very wrong.

They were men.

Three men. The first one was a big guy, overweight, obese. The other two were slimmer, but looked no less unfit. In jeans and shirts, which didn't look clean on today, they surrounded the bed, they surrounded me. I felt under attack, yet they looked so very happy to see me.

The overweight man spoke first. 'Hey, man, how're you doing?'

I didn't respond.

'It's really good to see you. We was worried. Right, lads?'

'Right, right,' said the skinniest one.

'Oh, yeah. Shit, yeah,' said the other. 'When I heard, I was, like, what the fuck?' He looked around the ward, perhaps realising the company he was in, and then more softly said, 'I mean, what the fuck?'

The skinny man, sporting a big goofy smile, nodded away in complete agreement with his associates. 'It's great to see you, Dar.'

I looked them up and down. I looked into their eyes. They seemed genuine, but there was nothing I recognised. The men squirmed at the lack of conversation; they were just as uncomfortable with the silence as I was.

'You look great,' one of them said, I don't know which one. 'I mean, considering, you know, the accident an' all.'

'Yeah, I mean, you look like hammered shit,' said another, 'but what's new?'

I think that was a joke. I said nothing.

'Oh, come on, mate, I'm just joshing with you.'

I couldn't continue with it any longer. I had to say something. 'I'm sorry, who *are* you?'

More silence. They looked at each other, clearly concerned.

'Come on, mate,' said the big guy. 'It's us: the four musketeers!'

The phrase struck something in the deepest, darkest corners of my shattered memory. I'd heard it before, that phrase, it held some meaning.

'You remember, right, Dar?' he asked.

I wasn't remembering, but I *was* listening now. 'You know me?' I asked.

'Know you?' asked the overweight guy. 'You were best man at my goddamn wedding!'

I was shocked. I took time, took stock, and then realised they were probably telling the truth. I couldn't remember anything, after all. *Who am I to doubt them?*

'Best man?' I said. 'Listen, I'm sorry, my memory is completely shot. I remember my family, but that's about it.'

They understood, they said, constantly telling me how it was okay, that they were there to help me remember. 'The four musketeers,' they kept saying. 'Dar' was short for d'Artagnan, Porthos told me, reminded me. They were nicknames we'd assigned ourselves, Aramis, or perhaps Athos, added, following our mutual appreciation for the 1998 movie *The Man in the Iron Mask*.

'Completely underrated film.'

There was a lengthy back and forth between the men on the merits of the movie, along with a passionate exchange about the performance of Leonardo DiCaprio.

'How he plays the twins so different, but, you know, er, like, especially when they're both on screen, you know, awesome, just awesome. No Academy Award, not even a – what do you call it – er, nomination. Not even a fuckin' nomination.'

'He won a Razzie for it.'

'He did? That's something, I guess.'

'No, you fuckin' moron, that's a *bad* thing. Nobody wants a Razzie. It means you're crap.'

'Yeah, wasn't it "worst screen couple" or some shit?'

'Fuckin' disgrace, that is.'

Their chat – which had now turned to DiCaprio's subsequent career – seemed genuine enough, but they talked and acted like single men. I was married with children. Something didn't add up. I felt uncomfortable, and then a little suspicious. It made no sense. I decided to test them. I had no choice; I needed to know what was happening here. I addressed the overweight man.

'I was the best man at your wedding?'

'Oh, yeah,' he said, nodding slowly like the dog in the insurance adverts. 'Threw me one helluva stag too.' He turned to his friends. 'What was that stripper's name? Daisy?'

'No, no, er...it was...Dolores!'

'Dolores!' they all yelled in unison.

It rang no bells.

'Ah, Dolores,' the overweight man said. 'You've got to remember Dolores, mate?'

'I was your best man,' I said again, half question, half statement.

He just smiled back at me. The others made positive comments about my memory returning.

I cut them short. 'Were you mine?' His face told me he didn't understand so I elaborated. 'Best man. Were you *my* best man?'

The obese chap looked at his pals for help, but there was none on offer. They shrugged their shoulders.

'You weren't, were you?' I asked. 'None of you guys were, am I right?'

Nobody answered.

'Well, am I?' I asked.

The overweight man cleared his throat before answering. 'No,' he said. 'I mean, yeah, you're right. I wasn't your best man, mate. None of us have been, but, but…'

'…but we will be,' said his friend, trying to help his pal out. 'Any one of us will be, we'd be proud. As soon as you meet the right girl, we're there.'

What? The right girl? That's what he'd said. I had to be sure. I asked him to repeat himself, which he did. I felt anger build.

The quiet one chipped in.

'He's right, we'd all be honoured. Me, especially. I ain't had a chance yet. Your choice of course, mate, but I have this great idea for the stag do…'

I chose my words carefully and delivered them with complete calmness. 'How fucking dare you?'

It was a response, an attack, that they weren't expecting. They froze. Silence filled the stale air. The jovial mood they'd worked so hard to create was gone.

'Whoa, hang on, mate,' said the fat man. 'We didn't mean…'

'How dare you make judgement on my marriage?' I said.

'Nah, you've got it all wrong…'

One of the other men tried to help out. '…yeah, thing is, you ain't even…'

His sentence was shut down abruptly by the overweight man's sudden stare, followed by a sharp shake of his head. 'No, no, you're right, man,' he said. 'I'm sorry. We're sorry. Our mistake. We should probably be going, give you some rest. Doctor's orders, right?'

I treated it like a rhetorical question and just stared at him. It was time for them to leave, but they weren't doing it fast enough. 'I don't know these people,' I said, hoping somebody would pay attention. I'd had enough. These were not the people I needed to see. 'Call security!' I said more loudly. 'I don't know these people.'

A gesture from the overweight man and the three of them scurried away down the corridor. He looked back once more.

'Security!' I yelled at him, and they were quickly gone.

5

DOCTOR

The dining table was laid with various Spanish tapas, all home-made by Susanna Richards, with a little help from her daughter Carissa.

'Wow. You've done it again,' said Michael. He sat at the head of the mahogany table and surveyed the selection of delectable offerings. 'I don't even know where to start, it all looks delicious.'

When they'd first met, Susanna hadn't been the culinary whizz she was now – in fact, she'd had an unwelcome reputation for not eating, let alone cooking. In her teenage years, she would go without meals completely if her family wasn't there to cook for her, such was her lack of interest in food. She once went a full week just snacking because her parents had gone away on business. Not now. Now she enjoyed food, both the eating and the preparation, especially if it gave her quality time with their eldest, Carissa. Besides which, she was adamant that her daughters shouldn't have any hang-ups about food or body image. Carissa especially, following a recent incident at school. She'd been picked on by a group of girls in the changing room because she had 'canckles'. This had upset Carissa, but even more so, Susanna. Carissa was a slip of a girl and yet was feeling she needed to lose weight; Susanna was transported back to her own youth when she'd had similar, poisonous thoughts in her head. Susanna's first impulse was to race up to the school, get the addresses of the responsible girls and pay them and their unsuspecting parents a visit. She'd have done it too, if the incident hadn't fallen just before the summer holidays. Thankfully, that meant she had six weeks to calm down, during which time she'd been able to speak to both of her daughters about body image and self-esteem. It seemed to have had the desired effect, as the girls, as usual, filled their plates tonight.

'This is definitely new, this one,' Michael said, mouth still half full.

Michael had acquired a taste for all things Spanish, first, while travelling around Europe as a young man, and then later while working in Barcelona. When he took Susanna to the Spanish city for their first city break away, she had fallen in love with the cuisine along with the culture as much as he had. Upon their return, they immediately made it a weekly event to eat out at one of the city's top Spanish restaurants. Since the girls had come along, that had morphed into a Thursday night home-made tapas feast, which pleased the whole family – nobody more than Ginga, who knew there would always be enough to go round. Moreover, the hands-on nature of the eating meant it was easier for Rachael to get the goods to him unnoticed. He sat under her chair, a good boy, not asking for anything. He didn't have to – Rachael was a constant source of snacks. Although Susanna didn't exactly approve, she turned a blind eye for the sake of a happy family meal. Carissa fired Rachael evil looks. Michael, meanwhile, was oblivious to the extra dinner guest.

Susanna finished setting the plates and bowls, and took her seat opposite her husband.

'Let me ask you a question,' Michael said to anyone willing to answer, or listen, for that matter. 'At what point did pulling a family out of a burning building become not enough?'

Michael was referring, of course, to the fact that the choices for the Winnies final had been made and they were all in some way or another of a supernatural nature. He acted confused, but he was really more frustrated. Especially so as he had felt duped last year when he had done the unthinkable and actually paid to vote for a contestant. Strictly speaking, Rachael had voted for him, but the choice of the recipient for his vote had been very much his own – an off-duty police officer who, no fewer than six times, had rushed into a burning block of flats to rescue people and their pets. A real hero, Michael had thought, and so he'd felt it was the least he could do to vote – six times, one for each of the brave acts – for the man. Especially as it became clear from the bookies that there was a frontrunner, and it wasn't Michael's choice. But it wasn't just the act Michael respected, it was the man too. For him, the very essence of what makes a hero was demonstrated by this man; after he risked his life numerous times he then tried to avoid the media. He didn't want recognition, and, for Michael, that meant he deserved it all the more.

'Dad, you're just upset because Damo beat your cop guy last year.'

Hearing the name did little to temper Michael's annoyance. Damon O'Donnelly. Damo, as the media, and now everybody, called him. Damo had won the third annual Great Briton Awards – or 'Winnies' as they were more commonly known, after Winston Churchill. Mr Churchill's lesser-known nickname, Copperknob, was also sometimes used as nomenclature for the awards show, particularly by those not impressed by it. Michael wouldn't stoop that low, well, not in front of his girls, anyway. Other hopefuls whom Michael had thought more worthy than Damo included the two-year-old girl who had saved her pregnant mother and unborn sister, from something, he couldn't quite remember exactly what. He remembered that she hadn't been able to offer the emergency services a geographical location – she was two, after all – so, instead, at the prompt of the telephone operative, she'd searched around for any clues she could understand. Using her newfound alphabetical knowledge, she'd read out the letters C-A-T-H-E-D-R-A-L from a road sign and added that they were close to a bridge. That was enough. Mother and unborn sister saved. Michael had also voted, but just the once, for the captain and crew of a fishing boat who'd come to the rescue of five holidaymakers who were swept out to sea in their dingy. Leaving their safe mooring, they'd searched in the dark through twenty-foot waves, sub-zero temperatures and eighty-mile-per-hour gusts of wind to find the dingy.

'Don't forget the man who risked his life to jump on to the tube tracks and pull that homeless guy from certain death, either from the high-voltage rails or the impending train,' said Susanna in an overly dramatic, mocking tone.

Michael didn't detect the mockery and held his hands out in smugness. 'You see?'

His daughters found it all amusing. Rachael, especially, was just one of millions who had been won over by the story of Damo.

The first Winnies, broadcast on BBC2 in 2014, were a huge success, especially the big award of the night. There were various additional minor awards given out, but the only one that really mattered to the masses was the Great Briton, the hero of the year. And the reward that came with the award was significant: a very attractive £100,000. But that was barely the tip of the iceberg compared to the lifetime of opportunities and riches that came as part and parcel of the award. An OBE was offered in the first year, which became a CBE in the second year. Last year, Damo became Sir Damo. It wasn't just a moniker. He *won* a knighthood. He was an actual knight. No wonder people like Michael found it distasteful.

Last year started off as the first two did, with stories of everyday people risking life and limb for family members, or even better, complete strangers. Then, in July, news came through of a man who had lifted a 4x4 vehicle off a single mother and her child. Not just news though, actual video footage. And not just footage, four separate mobile phone videos of the same event, all from different angles, all from supposedly impartial bystanders. Experts spent hours trying to debunk the footage as bogus, but to no avail. Within days, there were two camps: those who believed and those who didn't. There were a lot of believers. There were a lot of people who needed something, anything, special to believe in. Damon O'Donnelly himself gave no explanation for his actions, his powers. But he did always claim that what was seen in the footage was completely true.

Those who believed were even more assured by Damo's subsequent chat show appearances, while those who saw only a fake had more ammunition than ever. He was, and is, whatever you want him to be. You either bought into it, into him and into the idea of superpowers being real or you didn't. Sir Damo was suave and charismatic or smarmy and cheesy, depending on your take. He was the world's first real superhero or he was the ultimate fraud.

'How come he never repeats that magical feat?' Michael wondered.

'He can't control his power like that,' Rachael said. 'It came to him in that moment because of the intense emotions he was experiencing when he saw that woman crushed by the big car.'

'That's convenient,' said Michael.

It was an elaborate hoax, he thought, and one that had carved out a lucrative career for Sir Damo. Hosting the upcoming 2017 Winnies, replacing former host and national treasure Stephen Fry, who had publically criticised the crowning of Damo, was just the next step in his newfound fame.

'They're expecting all records to be broken,' continued Rachael.

'I heard twenty-five million viewers in the UK alone,' said Carissa.

'I heard thirty,' said Rachael.

The sisters bickered.

'Nonsense,' said Michael. 'Complete nonsense. There's no such thing as superpowers outside comic books and movies. This insane thirst for them to be real is ruining lives.'

Carissa chipped in. 'Damo's the only real one. The rest are a bunch of wannabes.'

'You're only saying that because you fancy Damo,' Rachael said.

Michael looked at his eldest daughter uneasily. He wasn't sure if it was the fact that his firstborn believed in this Damo rubbish or that she was growing up so fast that she found Damo physically attractive that bothered him. For the first time, Michael noticed that Carissa had dyed her hair dark purple at the tips. She looked like a teenager, not his little princess.

'Shut up!' Carissa shouted at Rachael, who just smirked.

Michael's heart sank more than a little. *Too fast.*

He picked up a newspaper from the side table. The front page was dominated by two stories. The first sported a huge photo of Sir Damo and the headline 'Let's find the next Damo!' and covered three-quarters of the page. The second story, almost tucked away, mentioned a teenage boy who'd fallen to his death jumping off a roof. 'The boy, 16, who believed he could fly…' the story trailed off. 'For more details, turn to page 6.'

'Look at this. This is what I mean, people are getting hurt, dying.'

In the last twelve months, Michael had treated more patients with superhero complexes than in his previous thirty years of practice combined.

The newspaper, having been moved, revealed a letter from the health service. A referral, a new patient for Michael to treat.

Susanna noticed it. 'What's this?' she asked.

Michael hadn't been hiding it, exactly, but he knew it wouldn't go down well after recent events.

'You're meant to be scaling down,' she said, reminding him of his promise.

He reacted as if he didn't need reminding, but the truth was he was already on the back foot. 'I am. *Massively*. If I scale down much more, I won't have a patient left.'

'I dream of the day,' she said, to herself and to him.

Michael looked at his wife.

'We don't need the money,' said Susanna. 'The insurance, honey, it's enough. Or if it isn't, I can get a job.'

'You're getting a job, Mum?' asked Carissa.

'What?' asked Rachael.

'No,' said Michael. 'That's not necessary.'

'Are things that bad?' asked Carissa.

'Things are fine,' said Michael. 'Everything's fine. Come on, let's eat.' Michael had loaded his plate with a number of favourites, along with one or two new recipes which were thrown into the mix each week. As the family ate, he continued talking about the referral. 'It's a really interesting case.'

'They always are, honey,' Susanna said.

'Doctor Reyes put me on to it, actually.'

Susanna rolled her eyes.

'She came across this chap, so confused, so sad.'

Susanna's subsequent sigh was too loud to ignore. The girls looked at each other across the table, sensing that the mood had just changed.

'What?' asked Michael.

Susanna took a sip of white wine.

'Susie, what?'

'You know *what*,' she said, increasing the tension around the table.

Just as Michael was about to ask again, Rachael, without looking up from her plate, spoke her mind. 'She wants you to quit.'

'Rach!' said Carissa, in a half-shout, half-whisper.

'We all do,' Rachael said.

'Rachael, stay out of it. It's not your business!' Carissa said.

Another silence.

Michael put his cutlery down, glanced at each of his children and then finally settled on his wife. 'Is that how you feel?' he asked. 'Is that how you all feel?'

'I think you know how I feel,' Susanna said, between sips.

'I feel the same,' Rachael added.

Carissa kicked her under the table, and poor old Ginga, munching on a tortilla, came a cropper too.

Michael addressed Rachael. 'This is what I do, Rach. My patients need me.'

'Yeah, well, we need you too, Dad!' Rachael shouted. She got up from the table and stormed off, a confused and hungry Ginga following after her. Carissa, while looking at her father, asked her mother if she could be excused. When Susanna nodded, Carissa left the table too.

'Rach, wait!' she called out.

'They'll be okay,' Michael said.

Susanna took her time before responding. 'It's not *them* I'm worried about.' She stood up and followed her daughters.

Michael Richards, not for the first time, sat at a table of delicious home-cooked food with nobody to share it.

6

PATIENT

I dragged around the apparatus that was hooked up to me. The ward was a maze and I definitely felt like a rat. At each turn I found either empty space, a dead end or, it seemed, people promptly disappearing. I was becoming more and more suspicious.

Eventually, I stumbled across the ward receptionist. I didn't hold out much hope. She had never spoken to me before and if there was any sort of conspiracy going on she would certainly be in on it. But then, I thought, I was probably being paranoid. It was more likely there was a sensible answer for everything that had happened so far. *Yep, I'm over-thinking it. Probably something I'm known for.*

I awkwardly yanked the cumbersome equipment across the cold passageway to where she sat in front of a blinking screen. My robe left me with little dignity, but I was past caring about such things.

'And what might you be doing out of bed?' she asked, without looking up from the glare of her screen.

Despite my determination to find out the truth, find out what was going on, find out anything, I was caught off guard and struggled for the right words. 'I, uh, I know, wh-what, you're going to say,' I stammered eventually. 'You're going t-to say 'doctor's orders'. I know, I do, it's just...did I have a-any visitors today?'

"I'm sorry?'

'I know I did *yesterday*,' I said. 'Yesterday, I had those guests. Those men, those three men, but today, I mean.' I kept talking, scared of what she might say if I gave her chance. 'Did anyone come in *today*, when I was asleep, maybe? Anyone at all? Not those men. Anyone else. Well, even them, I guess. You see, I slept pretty much all day, so I'm thinking there's a good chance...'

'Okay, well, I just started, sweetie.'

'Just started?'

'Yes. I just started. My shift, it just started.' That's all she said. She seemed more than content with the silence that followed.

I was not. 'What about the other receptionists?'

'Say again?'

'The others. The others who sit there, doing your job.'

Surely there's a record of visitors? The whole time I was questioning her, she smacked away at her keyboard, half listening and less than half interested. She hit the keys so hard, slammed them home, that she must have been old enough to have once used a traditional typewriter. Maybe that explained her disinterest, too many years in the job. But I wasn't done yet. I somewhat had her attention and that was more than I'd had from anyone else in a while.

I took a different approach. 'When do visiting hours end?'

'Oh, you still have an hour or so,' she said, still without looking up from the monitor.

'Still time, then,' I said, hoping the conversation would continue. When it didn't, I elaborated. 'Still time, I mean, for them to visit.'

She stopped punching the keys and for a second I thought I had her attention. But then she spun her wheelie chair around, collected some paperwork from the desk behind her and turned back to her beat-up keyboard.

She's busy, I get it. 'Yeah,' I said, basically to myself, 'still time.' This was as close to a breakthrough as I'd had and I wasn't leaving without getting something from her. Something to take away, to hold on to, to cling to. Some hope, I guess. If I couldn't get answers, I could at least get hope. 'Think I'll wait around here, if you don't mind. Meet them, you know, as soon as they arrive.'

That worked. She didn't stop her onslaught on the keys, but her tone changed. 'Tell me again, sweetie, who're you waiting for?'

'My family,' I said, with equal measures of frustration and optimism.

'You're expecting your *family*?'

'Yes,' I said, with more frustration and less optimism. 'My wife and children. Not the men from yesterday. They were…*not* my family. It was a mistake.'

'Okay.'

'A misunderstanding, that's what I meant, a misunderstanding.'

'Well, you go back to bed–'

'But I–'

'–and I promise,' she said, now looking directly at me, 'that I'll bring them over just as soon as they arrive.'

I thought about arguing, but she had already returned to her screen. I nodded in agreement, even though she wasn't looking my way. It was probably the best deal I was going to get. At the very least, I had someone looking out for them, for the next hour, anyway.

I'd taken a few tentative steps back towards my bed when I heard them. I heard children. My children, maybe. They were laughing. At first, they were laughing. But not for long. Then they were crying. Crying without their father. Crying for their father. I turned back towards the receptionist. She didn't look up, just kept whacking. Maybe only I could hear them, maybe they were in my head. I closed my eyes and they got louder. Not crying now, talking, moaning, arguing and fighting. They were getting louder…no, closer, they were getting closer. And then a voice spoke over them.

'Sounds like *someone* has visitors,' said the receptionist from out of the darkness.

I opened my eyes. The sounds, the children, weren't in my head, they were real. She heard them too. She heard the voices coming down the corridor. Two whiny, shrill, young ones arguing and one older one – their mother – pleading, demanding quiet.

She looked up from her screen and smiled right at me. Before I could return the favour, a buzzer echoed through the ward loud enough to remind me how unstable I was. I grabbed at the nearest wall. *This is it. My family are here. Thank God.*

In one smooth motion, the receptionist pushed herself away from her desk, glided across the carpet and arrived at the big red security release by the door. Her hand hovered over it as she studied the black and white images displayed next to it. I squinted, as if I had any chance of seeing their faces from so far away. But she was happy, and she hesitated no longer. The lock clicked and the doors pushed open. The muffled voices now filled the ward.

'Get off me, you bitch,' said the first child through the door.

'You get off *me*, scrote,' said the second, as the door slammed against the wall.

'If you two don't shut the fuck up,' said the mother, pausing to build up to a decent threat, 'there won't be no McDonald's after, got it?' The kids had already disappeared down the corridor.

'Excuse me,' said the receptionist, as the mother followed in their wake.

'It's all right, love, I know where he is,' said the mother. Rolls of fat escaped her purple tracksuit with each step.

'No, you need to use the hand gel,' said the receptionist.

The mother stopped, sighed loudly and said 'For fuck's sake,' under her breath, just loud enough for everyone to hear.

The receptionist and I looked at each other.

'You calling me dirty or somin'?' the mother said as she plodded back.

'It's policy,' said the receptionist.

'Yeah, yeah.'

'The children will have to…'

'They'll do it on the way out.'

'That kind of misses the point. You see, it's so that–'

'Look, I ain't getting 'em. All right? They've been little fuckin' toe-rags all fuckin' day so you can go get 'em if you want, but I ain't, right?' And then she noticed me, watching, staring at her. 'What?' she said.

My mouth opened, but no words came.

'You got a problem?' she asked.

'No,' I said. 'I just thought you might have been, for me, here for me, I mean. Visiting me.'

'I'm 'ere to see me old man,' said the fat woman. 'I don't even know you, ya freak.'

'I know that,' I said. 'I meant, before I saw you, I heard you and well–'

She turned back to the receptionist. 'What's he on about? This the fuckin' mental ward or what?' She turned back to me. 'You keep staring at me an' I'll have me old man come give you a fuckin' slap, I will.'

She flashed her clean hands at the receptionist and then trudged away, looking back at us every few steps, until she was out of sight.

'I'm so sorry. Are you okay?' the receptionist asked me.

'What the hell was that about?'

'I can call security if you like, in case she returns.'

'I'm okay,' I said. 'It's fine.'

'Why don't you go back to bed? Get some rest, for when your family come see you.'

My family. Seeing that woman, her kids. And now, as I closed my eyes again, my family, my perfect family. A smile came across my face.

The receptionist must have known what I was thinking. 'I'm sure they'll be in soon,' she said.

'Yeah. It's just, it's been three days, you know?'

'Since they last came in?'

I took a half a step back towards her. 'Since I was brought in. Since the accident.'

I realised then that I should have made it clearer before. This whole situation was bizarre. Abnormal. All I needed was for someone else to see it too. She looked at me properly for the first time. She removed her glasses and scrunched her forehead. She saw it too. It was weird, wrong.

'They haven't been in to see you yet?'

'No.'

She looked surprised, concerned, genuinely interested. A reaction I hadn't experienced up until that point. 'At all?'

Finally. It isn't just me. 'Oh, no, I'm sure they've been in,' I said, 'but every time I've been sleeping. Doctor's orders, not to be woken, you know how it is?'

She looked really confused now, and for the first time it seemed someone understood how strange the whole situation was. *How come I haven't seen them yet? Have they really been in to see me? Have*

I really slept that much? Did they simply turn and leave because of the doctor's orders? I felt a cold shiver. It wasn't that simple. Something else was going on.

'Well, I guess so,' she said, as unconvinced as was possible.

Yep. She shares my confusion. I was getting worked up now.

She could see that and intervened. 'Listen, I'll do you a favour and try to find out when they're coming in next. Okay?'

She had put out the fire within me just before it properly ignited. I thanked her, told her I appreciated it. She smiled, without trying to hide the pity she clearly felt for me.

'Right, that's it, no fuckin' McDonald's!' came a shout from down the ward.

The receptionist looked at me and shook her head. I returned her bemused look. 'But first,' she continued, 'you do *me* a favour. Go back to bed so we don't both get in trouble with the doctor.'

It worked. A wide, real smile escaped me and I walked back to my bed somewhat satisfied that the status quo involving my family had been challenged.

Behind me, I heard the receptionist pick up the phone and, just as she'd promised, ask for information regarding visitors to the ward over the last three days. 'Thanks, Tom, appreciate it. Yep, I can see it here in my inbox. Nice one.'

I felt justified. Vindicated. I slowed my retreat to ensure I could hear what she said next.

'Wait, Tom, are you still there? Yeah, this doesn't quite add up.'

I came to a halt.

'You're sure this is for Ward D? Okay, no, no, it's what I wanted. Tell you what, can you send through *all* the wards? Yep, just so I can be sure. Brilliant. Yes, it's come through now. Thanks again, Tom. Bye.'

I looked back to find her staring at the screen, spectacles back where they belonged, perched on the end of her narrow nose. She noticed my attention and gave me the thumbs up. 'Bed, please!' she said.

I returned the gesture and continued back to base, thinking that whatever was on that screen, at least someone was on my side now. My head hit the pillow and I was out within seconds.

Awake again. Hospital ward again. Alone, again.

The old chap opposite was snoring his lungs out, so loud it was like a comedy snore. Except nobody was laughing. There was a new patient, hidden behind a curtain. I rolled over on to my side and spotted the two of them talking, the nurse and the ward receptionist. I lay still for a short while, partially out of comfort – the pathetic excuse for a mattress had played hell with my back – but mostly because of their demeanour. They kept looking over towards me. I made a conscious effort to keep my eyes closed just enough to fool them into thinking I was still sleeping, but open just enough to see what they were doing. They weren't just generally chatting; they were talking about me. That was clear. In the receptionist's hand was something just out of sight. The nurse shook her head. *What are they saying? What is she holding?* I couldn't quite hear. I couldn't quite see.

I shuffled up slightly, as quietly as I could, to try and catch a glimpse of what was in her hand. I felt a twinge in my back and slumped. Couldn't see. Not enough. I shuffled again, and – *Shit!* – they noticed. They abruptly stopped talking and parted company, heading in opposite directions. That just made me even more suspicious. There was no doubt in my mind now; people in this hospital knew more about my situation and my family than I did. Including those who pretended to be on my side. They were keeping information from me. They were keeping my family from me. That wasn't acceptable.

They disappeared from view. I laid there more frustrated than ever. It was becoming a conspiracy. In that moment, I decided enough was enough. I was going to find out what was happening with my family, no matter what it took.

I didn't have to wait long. The nurse entered the room with the dinner trolley. The old man was snoring away, so she laid him out a meal and turned her attention to the hidden patient. She disappeared from my view for longer than expected. She was in there for ages, behind that curtain. God knows what she was doing. Avoiding me, maybe. Yep. Probably. And then finally, it was my turn. An opportunity I wouldn't waste.

As she approached, I could see that dinner was some kind of spaghetti. Even by hospital standards, it wasn't pretty. No effort had been made to make it appealing, or even to look edible. Just dumped on the plate like it was meant for a dog. It looked like dirt. And it smelt like shit. It was, though, an 'in'.

'Road-kill again, is it?' I was practically repeating myself from last night. And this morning. And yesterday lunchtime. It was an established routine we had going, only this time I was pretending, part of a new plan I was pretty much making up on the fly.

'You need new jokes,' she said, with less eye contact than usual.

'You need a new chef,' I said, with more force than usual. My delivery shocked her, but the words didn't; I was still on script. Besides, the food was disgusting, she could see that as well as I could. 'You know what? I've just lost my appetite.' Still on script, just about.

Her stoic face told me she sensed the undertone. She looked down, continued to set out the meal. 'You need to keep your strength up,' she said. There was a different tone to her voice too. She was nervous. And she was right to be.

I didn't let her get away with it that easy. 'My wife,' I said, 'she does an amazing Bolognese.' We were now into new territory. Off script.

She uh-huhed.

'Do you know what her secret ingredient is?'

She didn't answer.

'Do you know what it is?' I asked again. I was determined, and I played on her nervous demeanour. She just shook her head, low-key. 'Huh?' I pressed her, tested her. I was playing with her like a cat with a mouse pup.

'I'm sure I don't,' she finally answered.

That wasn't enough for me. I leant in towards her, close enough for her to feel my breath. 'It's,' she turned her head slightly towards me, '...sugar. Just a pinch, mind,' I whispered.

She swallowed hard, clearly intimidated. 'I can get you some,' she said. 'Some sugar.'

I stared at her. Said nothing.

'Would you like me to get you some–'

'What I want is for you to take this away,' I said, interrupting.

'Got to keep your strength up...' As she paused, I joined in. '...doctor's orders'. This freaked her out, like I could read her mind. Maybe I could. She was predictable. She started backtracking. 'Maybe I can find something better for dessert? Pretty sure we have some crème brûlée left over from–'

'What do you know about my wife?'

That came out of nowhere. Bang. *Tell me what you know.* No more messing around. I had waited long enough. I wanted answers, and I wanted them *now*. She wouldn't leave me until I had answers. That was a fact. Clear in my mind. She knows something that I don't. Something I should know. I need to know. *She leaves when I know*, and not before.

'Uh…nothing,' she said. 'Well, except what a great chef she is.'

'No,' I said, with a little anger. 'I saw you. I saw the two of you talking.'

She scrunched up her face. She was playing dumb.

'To the receptionist,' I said. I was holding back; I wanted to shout, at her, at them all.

'What, Sara?' she asked. 'Oh, we were just discussing that little boy who saved his sister from drowning. Can you believe that? Eight minutes, I think they said. Now *that's* a hero. He gets my vote.'

I grabbed her sleeve.

'What are you doing?'

I only had her sleeve, not her arm, I made sure of that. I wasn't a monster. I didn't want to hurt her, or anyone else. But enough was enough. She knew something. 'What do you know? Tell me.'

'I've told you already. I don't know anything. Let go of me.'

'I saw you. You know something. Tell me,' I said, more forcefully.

'Tell you *what*?'

I told her I'd seen everything. I had seen them spying on me, discussing me and my life. I'd seen them laughing at my situation, my loneliness. I'd seen them talking about how funny it was that my wife and children were being kept from me. Yes, I'd seen everything. She couldn't deny it. She tried, but she was lying. I had her, and I wasn't letting her sleeve, or her, go.

'Let go of me now!' She'd changed tack. She was more hostile. 'Right now. I mean it.'

It didn't faze me. It made me even more determined. I tightened my grip like a vice.

'I'll call for security!'

I didn't care. 'I won't let go until you tell me. Why won't you tell me?'

'There's nothing to tell. Now, let go–'

'Stop lying to me!' Without realising it, I now had her wrist.

'You're hurting me!' She reached for the emergency alarm. I jerked her towards me, away from it. She was no match for me physically. I hurt her. And then, in her pain, she let it slip. 'I can't tell you anything.'

Can't. That was it. That was enough. She'd said 'can't'. I'd been right all along. She knew where they were. She knew where my family was, my beautiful wife and perfect children. She knew why they weren't able to come and see me. She was part of it, the whole conspiracy. But I had her now, at my mercy. She'd already cracked – 'can't' – and now I'd break her. My family would be mine again. She'd break and they'd be mine.

But for the moment her resolve was holding. 'I just meant I can't tell you because I don't know anything.'

'Don't fucking give me that. You know. You're part of it. I've seen you with her over there, you both know. I'm going to hurt you if you don't tell me. You believe that, don't you?'

Her resolve faded as I dug my nails into her skinny wrist. 'Please, I can't. I can't,' she said, wincing as the tears formed. She kept saying 'can't'.

'Yes,' I said. 'Yes, you can.' And, for the first time, I properly squeezed. 'You can and you will. Now *talk*.'

She tried to scream but no sound came out. 'I can't,' she whispered.

I leant in again. 'Yes, you can.'

'Please, I can't say.'

'Stop saying that! Stop it!'

'But–'

'Why can't you? Why?'

'We're waiting on him…'

'Him? Him, who's *him*?'

'Please…'

'Who? Who is he?'

'I'm not supposed to say. Please.'

'I'm going to really hurt you…' I twisted her arm and she yelped.

'The resident psychiatrist.'

'What? Why?'

'Please, I've said too much. I have, we all have…' And then she said the two words that pushed me over any line I'd perhaps considered staying on the right side of. '…doctor's orders.'

I saw red. Not just figuratively, literally. My nails were long, unkempt, sharp. I hurt her with all my might and claret red soaked through her sleeve. I had no choice now. She'd put me, us, here. They all had. This was their doing, not mine. I'd never wanted to hurt anyone, but the time had come for these people to realise I was serious. I wouldn't take this any more. I wouldn't be treated like this for one more minute.

She went limp and her eyes rolled to the back of her head. She would pass out in a moment if I continued my assault. *Wait*, I thought. I needed her conscious.

I eased my grip just enough to keep her with me. I whispered into her face, 'Fuck doctor's orders.' Her breathing was heavy. I put a finger to her lips – *Quietly, or I'll squeeze again.* 'Now, tell me everything you know.'

'Your wife…'

Finally. *Yes, tell me.*

'Your wife. Your family.'

Yes, where? Where?

She gasped for words. 'They're in, in…'

In where?

'…in…'

Tell me…!

And then, the universe collapsed in on me.

'Your mind.'

What?

'They're in your mind.'

A cold sweat engulfed me. I didn't understand. She was speaking nonsense.

'They're in your mind. Please, let go. Please. Let go.'

I tried to process what she'd said. Obviously, it was bullshit. But why make up such a thing? What was going on here? I didn't realise that my grip was loosening.

'I'm sorry, I'm not meant to tell you, but they aren't real. You don't have a wife. You don't have children,' she kept saying.

'What *is* this?'

'We're waiting for the resident psychiatrist to come and see you. He's been held up…'

She made an effort to escape, but I was too quick. I reacted instinctively by clamping around her arm again and reaching up with my other hand to grab her neck. I was in a trance. She squealed as I started to throttle her.

'Get off her!' shouted a male voice.

'Where are my family?' I asked her again. 'Tell me the truth.'

A doctor came bouncing to her aid. He prised my hand off her neck, but that allowed me to grab and twist the stethoscope around his neck at each end and start choking him. The nurse was free but in no state to help the doctor. She fell to the floor.

The chokehold I had on the doctor allowed me to drag him down to the floor, while, at the same time, I levered myself out of the bed. Other staff members arrived to help him.

'Stay back!' I shouted. 'Stay back or I'll strangle him!'

His legs kicked out and connected with the floor enough for us to keep moving. An orderly appeared from a side door, ready to swoop.

'Stay the fuck back! I mean it! I'll kill this bastard!'

'Okay, okay. Just calm down.'

'I'll fucking do it!'

I was a desperate man. And I'd crossed the line. There was no going back now. So I kept going. I dragged the doctor to the lifts and hit the down arrow, yanking hard again on the stethoscope to ensure he didn't try anything. The lift was waiting. The doors opened and I used my remaining strength to heave him and myself into the lift. I reached up behind my head and fumbled for the button to close the door before collapsing back into the corner. My eyes closed.

I heard him cough and splutter, and then speak with a gravelly voice. 'Why are you doing this?'

Muzak began playing all around me. I don't know if I said it or just thought it. *Why am I doing this?* Before I could consider my next move, darkness seeped in from the corners of my mind and engulfed me.

7

DOCTOR

Michael Richards and his doctor Olivia Reyes sat on a bench surrounded by well-maintained flower beds. The setting was one of serenity and calm. Olivia had just finished recounting the story of David's near escape from the hospital a week ago.

'Your colleague,' asked Michael, 'the doctor. He's okay?'

'He's fine now,' said Olivia. 'The nurse, however, remains on sick leave.'

'And David?'

Olivia hesitated. 'Before we go any further I have a confession.'

'Confession?'

'Of sorts. I've spoken to your wife.'

'What? You what?' He was shocked. The two women hadn't met or even spoken as far as he knew. Directly, at least. All contact had been through him. Now, everything had changed. The two halves of his life had come crashing together. Not only that, but behind his back, without his knowledge. Olivia had spoken to Susanna? Olivia. And Susanna. Speaking. About him. Without him. Michael felt sick. 'You spoke to Susanna?' he asked. *Maybe I misheard.*

'I did,' she said, offering him no further reason or justification.

Suddenly, he wondered why it was that they'd never met, and why it was so important to him. He had nothing to hide, after all. So why had he tried to keep these two women who were key to his recovery apart? Surely, everybody working as a team could only benefit his recuperation. He pondered it for a moment. *Is there a reason I want these parts of my life kept apart? These women?* He realised it was irrelevant now, now that Olivia had taken the initiative to make contact with Susanna. He turned to his doctor and met her stare. He wondered how long it had been since he'd spoken and whether he needed to explain his silence.

Thankfully for him, Olivia spoke first. 'Michael, we are all concerned about you.'

We. Since when had there been a 'we'? The shock quickly became something else. Sure, it was his doctor's job to look out for his well-being. And, of course, Susanna and the girls were worried. But bringing those two elements together, his family and Olivia, was a dangerous cocktail that threatened his plans to get back into full-time practice. That was why he wanted the women kept apart. That made sense. *That's it*, he thought to himself, relieved. He didn't have anything to hide, just as he'd thought.

'She called me because she–'

'Wait. *She* called *you*?'

Up to this point, Michael had assumed it had been Olivia who had contacted his wife, not the other way around. He wasn't sure if that was better or worse, or if it made any difference at all. But it felt different. Like, maybe, he'd been betrayed. Betrayed by the one person he trusted the most. He entertained the thought for a moment before realising just how silly and juvenile an emotional response it was. The thought was dismissed, almost completely.

'Yes, Michael,' said Olivia. 'That's right. Susanna called me.'

Hearing Olivia say her name was just weird. Like they were old school friends, catching up after years apart. They were close enough in age that such a scenario could be true. Much closer in age than he and Susanna were. And again he felt like the outsider. More childish thoughts.

'It was a really interesting conversation,' said Olivia.

He knew what that meant. And, in that moment, all his immature thoughts subsided. He knew why Susanna had called Olivia, and it certainly wasn't to catch up on old times. Susanna had called Olivia because she didn't want him to take on this extra case, this new patient, David. Her heart was in the right place; she was genuinely worried about Michael's health. She didn't want her girls growing up without a dad. He got that, he did. But only he really knew how he felt. There were other people who needed him besides his family, people who had nobody else. People like this David chap whom he was itching to meet. But he wondered if he would get a chance now. Surely Olivia wouldn't have met him here, in the gardens of where David was staying, if she was about to deny him the chance to help. But then, they'd organised the meeting location days ago. That left plenty of time for Susanna's call, and Olivia had probably thought that changing the meeting location would ring alarm bells with Michael.

'She has concerns, Michael,' said Olivia.

She had a briefcase with her. David's case file would be inside. But that didn't mean she would open it and give it to him, not if Susanna had been convincing. The briefcase probably went everywhere with her; it didn't mean anything. He was known for his over-thinking, was Michael.

'Concerns?' he asked, feigning ignorance.

'Concerns regarding you taking on this case, Michael.' Every time Olivia said his name he detected something, but he wasn't sure what. *Over-thinking.* 'She wanted to share these concerns with her husband's doctor to seek assurance that this was a healthy move.'

'I see. Did she say anything else?'

'Yes. She told me that her husband has a habit of getting too emotionally involved in his patients' problems, that he carries those emotions with him back into their home life. That it has become a stress between them, as a couple, and a problem within the family, for the family. That this habit had led directly to this recent health issue, the heart attack. And that it couldn't happen again. That this wasn't an acceptable way of moving forward. For you, and for the family.'

Wow. Susanna had told her everything.

Michael looked up at the dark clouds building above them. It wouldn't be long before these beautifully maintained gardens, with the tulips and roses and other flowers that he couldn't name, would get the drink they so desired.

'I got the impression she didn't like me much,' Olivia said.

Michael looked at those clouds, and a smile escaped him. 'Well,' he said, 'that's probably just because you were the one who suggested David to me.' The moment the words left his mouth, Michael realised what he'd done.

Olivia looked at him, eyes narrowed, brow wrinkled. 'Well, I worked that out for myself,' she said. 'Wait, what do you mean, "probably"? I don't understand. Is there another reason she wouldn't like me?'

Michael wished the heavens would finally open and save him from having to continue this increasingly awkward conversation. He knew there was another reason that Susanna would take a dislike to Olivia, but going into that here and now with his doctor, and now colleague, was the last thing he wanted.

He tried his best to dismiss it. 'No, no, I didn't mean it like that. I just meant…' She didn't have to interrupt him, he ran out of words all by himself.

She stared at him, and Michael could sense it slipping away. His new patient file, which sat right there in the briefcase just feet from him, not to mention David himself, who was almost as close. It was all slipping away.

Michael turned to Olivia. 'Okay, look, it's not you,' he said. 'It's nothing you've done or anything.' He had started the sentence as a lie but somehow it had started to reveal the truth. 'It's Susanna's hang-up, nothing that you've done.'

'She's younger than you, isn't she?'

Michael hesitated, searched for the words to defend his wife, his marriage, his situation, but then just said, 'Yes.'

'How old *is* she?'

'I guess she's, you know,' Michael looked away, 'your age.'

'Ah, I see,' said Olivia. 'She's jealous.'

Michael was surprised at how flippant Olivia was. 'It's not that she thinks anything is going on between us…' Michael stumbled through his words. Olivia wasn't just a brilliant doctor, she was an attractive woman who had been looking after Michael in a way his wife wasn't able to. And then there was their ages being so similar; Michael knew this would have rung alarm bells in his wife's head. Not that he had given her any reason to suspect anything, and not that he had any thoughts towards Olivia that were anything but professional. But that wouldn't stop his wife thinking about it.

Olivia just smiled. Which, rather than reassuring him, made Michael even less comfortable. Maybe that was what she wanted. *Wait, is she flirting with me?* He hoped not. Not that he wouldn't be flattered. He would be. She was so brilliant, so young and so confident. She could have any man she wanted. If she wanted Michael, he couldn't help but be flattered.

He continued with a slightly smoother tone to his voice. 'So…what did you tell her?'

'What do you hope I told her?' she said, still smiling. It had been a while, but Michael was sure this was flirting.

'*You're* going to psychoanalyse *me*?' he asked.

Olivia chuckled and then took a deep breath. 'Well, we had a long chat,' she said. 'In the end, I told her three things. Firstly, I told her that you need David in your life as much he needs you. And I truly believe that.'

Michael wasn't entirely sure what she meant. 'How so?'

'Oh, come on, Michael, this is what you *do*. This is who you *are*.' Eerily, her words echoed his own when he was arguing with Susanna. 'And I hear you're damn good at it. One of the best.'

He pretended to be hurt. '*One* of the best?' She smiled again, and he nodded. 'You're right. This is what I do. I don't know how I'd fill my time if I didn't have my patients. There's only so much golf one man can play.'

'I also told her that you're a changed man and won't make the same mistakes again. I think she enjoyed hearing me say that, although she did ask me just how well I thought I knew her husband, seeing as we'd only recently just met. At the time I didn't think much of it, but now with what you've said about her insecurities…'

'She's not insecure,' Michael said, far too defensively. He calmed his voice. 'She's just–'

'And finally,' said Olivia, 'I told her that I'd look after you.' She winked at him.

Yep, flirting. 'And how did she take that one?' Michael asked, with an equal mix of fear and excitement.

'Well, that was the moment I began to suspect she didn't like me.' They exchanged glances. 'So, did I do okay?'

'You did just great,' said Michael. He looked up to the heavens again. The first drops of rain hit his face. He welcomed the sensation they brought, the coolness of their gentle slaps. But then one hit his eye. He turned away to see Olivia lifting up her briefcase and balancing it on her knees.

'Maybe we should head inside?' she suggested. The droplets were attacking both the briefcase and the bare legs it balanced on. Or were they skin-coloured tights? He couldn't quite tell. Not without staring, anyway.

'No hurry,' said Michael. He saw the dark clouds dominating the skies above but he didn't want the moment to pass. Not until he saw more. Not until he saw the contents of that briefcase.

'You think?' she asked.

'We have time,' he said.

'Okay.' Olivia took another deep breath, and Michael realised that despite all she'd said she still had Susanna's words swirling around her head. Susanna could be convincing when she needed to be. More than convincing. Passionate. Fierce. Ferocious, even.

Michael had to seal the deal. 'It's true that in the past I've taken on too much. Got too involved. If that's what she said, Susanna, I mean, if that's what Susie said to you, she's right. Completely. But you're also right when you say I've learnt my lesson. I really have…' he paused, realising he was starting to beg. 'I'm a changed man, Olivia.' Michael heard the clicks of the case, and knew he was in.

'Okay, then.' Olivia held up David's file. 'Let's do it.'

Michael shot her a quick smile before opening the file and scanning the first few pages. There weren't many details about the patient, not much information at all. But then there was something. Something he recognised from his own past. David had an interest in art. Not much skill, apparently, but a keen enthusiasm nonetheless. Michael was transported back to the early days of his practice.

He'd had a young woman referred to him, a slip of a girl, barely eighteen years old. Jennifer. She was absolutely convinced that she had a daughter, even though all those around her – her family included – swore blind that she'd never given birth or raised a baby. While all the other treatments she'd undergone had focused on trying to convince her of how wrong she was, Michael instead created a world in which her daughter Maisy really did exist. He tapped into Jennifer's passion for music. Using this medium, they were able to make sense of the fact that Maisy could be real within the world of the music even if she didn't exist in the world itself. Michael's ideas were radical and controversial, and, at that point, it was make or break whether his practice would survive beyond his treatment of Jennifer.

The platinum-selling album that Jennifer released a year later brought her huge acclaim and brought Michael's practice financial stability. The songs were, of course, tributes to Maisy. Not just tributes, but stories based on Jennifer's memories, written as lyrics to catchy pop melodies. It was a phenomenal success. Until, that is, Jennifer took her own life within weeks of the album hitting the number one spot. Her parting note, the lyrics to a new song, released posthumously, suggested – to Michael, at least – that the treatment had been a mask. A blanket that didn't actually address the issues once the music stopped. Michael was heartbroken. Some days he blamed himself. He would read those lyrics and see Jennifer screaming back at him. On other days, he convinced himself the treatment had indeed worked and that it was the success of the album that meant Jennifer had stopped working with him too soon, due to the influence of the record label and media conglomerates who all wanted a slice of Jennifer's success. She was dead before her twentieth birthday. It hit Michael hard; he'd invested so much in her and the therapy that he'd developed for her.

A song called 'Unconditional' was a Christmas number one for Jennifer, and so it was often on the radio around the holiday period. Whenever Michael would hear it, he'd not only be reminded of the whole affair, he would also see Jennifer everywhere he looked. The Christmas just past, he'd been driving in the car when 'Unconditional' came on the radio. The lyrics swam around his head. 'Hours old, I dressed / This person, whom I knew not / Yet loved forever'. He had loved those words since the day he first heard them, but it was only since the birth of his baby girls that he really understood their meaning. One Christmas past, when the girls were little, with 'Unconditional' playing loud, he found himself almost subconsciously turning the photo over and writing the lyrics on the back. Now, all these years later and stopped at a red light, a young woman walked in front of Michael's car and in that moment he saw her, Jennifer. There she was, alive and well. Older now, although not much. Not enough. But it was her, so much like her, it had to be her. He went to call out, but instead grasped at his chest. Michael's heart attacked him. And when he woke up in hospital, he found Doctor Reyes taking care of him.

Michael turned back to the first page, and then the third again, cross-referencing in his mind.

'What are you thinking?' asked Olivia.

He didn't answer. His mind was racing with ideas. He thought again of Jennifer. He was engrossed, but he knew it was dangerous. Jennifer wasn't alive. He hadn't seen her. She had killed herself, and he had to live with that. But still, he thought of her as he read about David and his love of art.

'Michael?' His eyes had glazed over. 'Michael, hello?'

He looked up, not at Olivia, but at the clouds that were now ominously filling the whole sky with a dirty grey. 'When can I meet him?'

8

PATIENT

I was a different person now. Admittedly, because I had no idea who I was anyway, that was a strange way to look at things. But some things you know instinctively, memories or no memories. I knew I wasn't the kind of person to ever want to harm another. That wasn't in me, of that I was certain. But they took away the one thing that makes me who I am. My family. Who knew who I was without them?

After the hospital incident I was detained in a few places, all of which were quaint, all temporary. This place was more long-term – although, I hoped, not permanent. It was some sort of medium-stay mental home, and it was lovely and awful in almost equal measures.

At first, they weren't willing to talk about my family. When I mentioned them, they simply ignored me or sometimes even left the room. Since I arrived at this place, there had been a couple of shrinks coming through the door, all eager to help me forget them. Every one of them was a pompous, arrogant tosser; they were all white, middle-aged, middle-class men, and all them a complete waste of time.

And here came another. White. Fifties. Wealthy. Male. Tosser. He stood in the doorway of my room as if waiting for permission to enter. As if I had the power to decide one way or the other. When, in fact, he would enter my living room, my space, my life, whenever he wanted, and I had absolutely no say in the matter.

Doctor Reyes hovered behind his shoulder. She spoke before he did. 'Richards,' she told me. 'Doctor Richards. He's not just an expert in this field, with a track record of ground-breaking ideas, he's also...well, a friend of mine.'

I saw him look at her a little strangely. I turned back to continue watching the enormous flat-screen TV that dominated the spacious yet somehow completely-stifling living room. So, his name was Richards. So what?

'He'd like to speak to you.'

Then why didn't he? Why did she speak for him? I knew he was a shrink, I could spot them a mile off. Their half smiles, their understanding demeanour. Their balanced attire, smart but relaxed. Everything about him screamed 'Let's be friends!' He already had Doctor Reyes as a friend. Why would he want me? He probably had a shitload of friends. I didn't want to be his friend, anyway. I didn't need what he was offering. I wasn't crazy. Of course, watching the TV probably didn't communicate that too well, seeing as it was turned off.

I went on the offense. 'He's not a doctor like you're a doctor,' I said. 'Am I right, doctor?' I was still watching the TV.

'Right,' Reyes said. That's all she said.

Of everyone who had come through that door, Reyes had at least earned a little of my respect. She spoke straight, and, even though I didn't particularly want help, she did seem to be genuinely trying to find me some. I also knew she'd been just as frustrated with the previous shrinks I'd had as I was. I'd heard her complaining about them to the warden. Useless. Predictable. A joke. White. Middle-aged. Male. Yet here she was again, with this Richards guy. He wouldn't be any different. A waste of her time, a waste of my time.

I looked right at Doctor Reyes and asked the one question that mattered. The one that none of them could answer; if they could, they wouldn't be needed and if, when, they couldn't, they'd be finished before they started. 'Does he know where my family is?'

She turned away, to the new guy, her friend. I saw a new emotion in her: embarrassment. I realised that she really cared what this chap thought. He was more than just another shrink, to her, at least. And I'd put her on the spot.

'I don't think…' she said, lost for words. Wow, Doctor Olivia Reyes, lost for words. I'd never seen her lost for anything, especially words. No – especially confidence. If there was one thing Reyes lacked, it was self-doubt. Until now.

I turned away, back to the TV. Same blank screen.

The new chap filled the silence that Reyes had so unexpectedly left. 'No, David,' he said, subtly emphasising my name. 'I don't know where your family is.'

Honesty, at least. But I'd heard it all before. My money was on the old 'We're all in the same boat here, nobody knows where they are' approach.

'But I'd like to help you find them,' he said, before I could respond.

Okay, that was somewhat new, but my bet still stood. 'So you believe me?' I asked, testing him. 'You believe they exist?' His answer would tell me all I needed to know about him, and no doubt confirm my assumptions.

'I believe *you* believe they exist,' he said without hesitation, 'and that's enough for me.'

He was well prepared. Reyes had no doubt primed him for what I'd say and how I'd be. They were close, I could tell. I hadn't looked at him yet, but I could see both his reflection and that of Reyes in the blackness of the TV. They stood together. Touching, almost. I decided to test their friendship.

'They tell me they aren't real,' I said, nodding towards Reyes. 'That they're in my head.'

'That must have been really difficult to hear,' he said.

'*Difficult*? You think being told that my family – the people I live for, who I love with every corner of my heart, my mind and my soul – you think being told that they're not real is *difficult*? Like it's an annoyance? A minor issue? An irritation?' I looked back at Reyes and asked her, 'This the best you got?'

She squirmed a little but I was surprised at how he reacted. That is, he didn't. He stood strong, just smiled and nodded slowly, in what seemed like admiration. This new guy, Michael, she called him, just seemed to brush himself off as if he was still on course.

As if he was completely prepared for this line of conversation. As if he'd seen it all coming.

'No, you're right, David,' he said. 'I apologise for my choice of words. That wasn't what I meant. I misspoke. I didn't mean "difficult". I meant that it must have been–'

'How about *hell?*' I spat.

He rightly shut the fuck up. But it was fleeting. Barely a beat had passed before he was back at me, nodding again, that slow, annoyingly confident nod that a moment ago had seemed respectful but was now all arrogance. A tosser, just like the others.

'Yes,' he said, completely calculatedly. 'Yes, it must have been. It must have been hell.'

The rain was coming down now, and through the one window in the room I could see flower petals opening up to take advantage. There was life out there, there was change. Not like in here. There was no hope here, there was just another bullshit shrink looking to impress hot young Reyes and get her in the sack.

He stepped in closer, into my space, and I felt my defences drop slightly. 'So, if it is indeed hell, David,' he said, stepping forward again, 'let me ask you a question. Why do you continue to tolerate it?'

Excuse me?

'Why do you listen to them?'

What?

'Why don't you do something about it?'

Had I heard him correctly? Had he read my file? He was accusing me of choosing to believe what they told me, like I had a choice in the matter. I couldn't believe what he was asking. The arrogance of the man.

'What choice do I have?' I asked, both disgusted at the question and even more terrified of the answer.

'There's always a choice, David.'

'Oh, yeah? What choice? Tell me. What choice do I have? I fight back and look what happens. I end up here.' I looked around, as did he, to emphasise the point. The room was safe and sad. From the curtains to the carpets, the prints hanging on the wall to the furniture, which purposely had no hard edges. It was pathetic, and it was impossible to feel any other way sat in here for hours at a time.

He stepped in closer again as he spoke. 'Well, I'm sure you'd agree, David, that violence is never the answer.'

He said my name again, as if we knew each other. He didn't know me, and he didn't know where my family was. This was another waste of my time. I just sat there, saying nothing. I thought he'd leave soon enough. They always did.

But he didn't. The silence didn't bother him, it seemed. He just stood there. The rain got harder and the wind picked up, lashing droplets against the window. I was grateful for it; otherwise, there would have been just a deafening hush. I realised that to get rid of him I'd have to say something.

'Okay, you know what, tell me, then, doctor, before you go, tell me, what are my choices? What is the answer?'

'Well,' he said, 'I was hoping we could figure that out together, David.'

Ha. He blew it. That was his last chance and he blew it. A bog-standard answer, Psychiatry 101. I wasn't impressed. I gave him a smirk and a glance and then, I saw it. Left hand, second finger. A wedding ring. Perfect. Time to turn this around and have a little fun.

'I see you're married,' I said.

He looked down and, with his other hand, twisted the ring around his finger as if caressing the neck of the woman it represented.

I continued before he could reply. 'Tell me, doctor, do you and Mrs Doctor Richards have children?'

A smile came across his face. 'We do indeed. Two.'

I chuckled to myself. 'Oh, yeah?' I asked. 'Are you *sure* about that?'

He continued to smile but in a different way. He got my joke. I continued, asking him if he loved his children, if he loved his wife. He told me that they were his entire world, that they were everything to him. And I could see he meant it. He was practically welling up at the thought of them. As if he wouldn't get to see them, hold them, at the end of his day.

'So, imagine if you woke up tomorrow and they were gone,' I said. 'That there was no sign of them, no sign that they'd ever been in your life. Imagine how you'd feel. Imagine if you were then told that they weren't even real. That they didn't exist, and never had.

That they weren't yours. That they were never yours, and your memories and feelings were all made up. Figments of your imagination. Your sad, pathetic imagination. Close your eyes and think about it, doctor. Just for a minute. Because that's my life now. Every minute. Every single minute, every fucking day.'

He closed his eyes as I had asked, which surprised me. The whole time he continued fiddling with his wedding ring.

Like the rain that rolled down the window behind him, I'm sure I spotted a droplet running down his face. This guy was either a terrific actor or he really did get what was going on. And then, most strangely, I felt a pang of sympathy for the guy. He was the one with a loving family waiting at home and I was the one sat here alone. It was bizarre. I was actually feeling guilty about what I was making him imagine.

His eyes were still closed. I turned to Reyes. She nodded at me and I turned back to Richards. 'So?' I asked, and he opened his eyes. 'How would you react, doctor?'

He took a deep breath and blinked, causing another tear to follow in the first's path, bigger and faster. He took a tissue from his inside pocket and cleaned himself up. I wasn't sure what to make of it. I hadn't expected such raw emotion – or such a fantastic performance. Perhaps that was it, maybe Reyes, annoyed by the shrinks so far, had instead employed a thespian to come in and act out this scene with me.

When he finally did speak, his voice was weak, feeble, fragile. Not in any way the commanding voice he'd used just minutes earlier to introduce himself. 'I can't imagine how I'd react,' he said. 'I don't want to imagine how I'd react and I certainly don't want to imagine life without them.'

'Well, I don't have that option, do I?'

He didn't answer.

'You don't have a wife,' I said. 'Listen to me, doctor. You don't have a wife. And you don't have any children. They're figments of your imagination. Not real. You must've hit your head or something. They aren't real, and how you feel about them isn't real. Your love for them is made up. *They* are made up. You made them up, probably to deal with some trauma from your childhood or some shit. Your mother, perhaps. And your beautiful, devoted wife, yeah? She's gone too. Not real. You never met her. You never fell in love with her. You never married her. She never gave birth to your kids because they aren't real either. You're all alone in this world. Unless, that is…you can show me proof right now that they do exist.'

'David,' said Reyes from the back of the room.

'It's okay,' said Richards. 'It's okay, Olivia.'

The spinning of his wedding ring had become more determined; he was trying to take it off, but he was failing. It was too tight around his finger. It had never been removed, probably. How poetic.

'Leave it on,' I said. 'It proves nothing.'

'It doesn't?'

'I wasn't wearing one when I woke up, but I'm married…' my sentence trailed off as I realised that was evidence against my family, not for it.

Richards reached into his back pocket and pulled out his wallet. I knew what was coming. He removed a picture and held it out for me to take.

I didn't want to see it. I looked away. 'Give it to Reyes.'

Michael hesitated, but then walked over and gave it to her.

'They took my photo,' I said. 'They took it while I slept. And now I have no proof. Without my photo, I can't prove my family are real. So, now that Reyes has taken your photo, prove to me your wife and children exist, doctor.'

'I guess that's not an easy thing to do. Okay, let's see. I could tell you their names, where we live, the school my daughters attend.'

'I can't remember any of those details.'

'I guess that makes it a lot tougher.'

'It makes it impossible.'

'A challenge, certainly,' he said. 'Perhaps not impossible, though. You see, I have an idea. It could help. Now, it's a bit out there. But if you're willing to give it a try, I think it could allow you to see your family again.'

'Save your breath if you're talking about hypnosis–'

'This isn't something you've come across before.'

He had piqued my interest, but I wasn't totally convinced. 'So, you wouldn't just accept it, then? People telling you they aren't real? That they never existed?'

'No, of course not.'

'Why not?'

He looked over at Reyes and then walked slowly to the window. The rain was heavy now, and large drops were being fired at the window by the rising wind. 'I know them to be real,' he said, as he looked out at the drenched gardens. 'I remember them. I remember times shared, as a couple, as a family.' For the first time I looked at him properly. 'The idea of not having them is the same as not having life.'

A purposeful cough came from the back of the room. Reyes was trying to interrupt him, no doubt worried I was getting ideas of suicide.

Richards turned to face me. 'But it's not just memories, it's not just in here.' He touched his temple. 'I feel them in here.' He held his chest. 'I know the love I have for them is real, and so I know *they* are real.'

He was convincing. A superb actor, well-rehearsed. Probably. But if not…

I gestured for him to take a seat. He nodded at Reyes to leave us alone. She seemed apprehensive, but she left. Richards sat down opposite me. 'Let's find them together,' he said, having no idea just how right he would be.

9

DOCTOR

Michael worked closely with David to lay the groundwork for the therapy that would come. He felt that progress was being made. Although David's future was still unclear, Michael was certain a move away from his current institution to a place of his own, with independence, was needed. That was the main reason Michael had called the hearing two weeks earlier than was standard. But also, he disliked hearings like this; they always made him feel he was standing on trial, and he was happy to get it out of the way.

He sat before a panel of four hospital board members, two of whom he knew. They were at least thirty foot away from him, and elevated. They were literally looking down on him. He had come prepared to speak on David's behalf and prepared to argue if necessary.

In the middle of the panel was Deborah Howe. When he'd seen on the paperwork that she was named as chair, he knew he'd need to argue. Next to her was a fresh-faced junior, Jeff something. At the other end was another board member, whose responsibility this day was little more than taking minutes. Finally, there was Doctor Reyes. David wasn't present.

Michael wasted no time in recommending that David be released.

'Under your supervision, Michael?' asked Olivia.

'Yes, under my supervision,' he replied with complete assuredness and zero delay.

The junior member of the board wanted more details about what that actually meant. Michael outlined the support he'd provide for David: twice weekly visits to his flat, a private mobile phone number that David could call in emergencies and treatment plans and additional support as required. Michael reeled it all off.

He also pre-empted questions about merged, false and even implanted memories, all hot topics within the world of conditions such as David's, since the work of MIT started playing around, somewhat successfully, with the minds of mice.

'Excellent, Doctor Richards,' said Jeff. 'Very impressive, thank you.'

Deborah Howe was not so easily convinced. She shot her inexperienced colleague a look of disappointment and Jeff squirmed in his seat. It was clear Jeff saw her as a role model, but so far his embarrassingly obvious attempts to impress her had failed.

'Yes, yes, all well and good,' she said. 'Tell me, doctor, is it therefore your opinion that the patient now accepts the fact that his wife and children are figments of his imagination?'

Michael could sense the disapproval in her words. He had expected it, and had prepared for the worst. She was known for being a stickler for the rules, but beyond that he knew she would make it as difficult for him as possible. This was nothing to do with the case, but because of differences of opinion that had surfaced between them over the years, sometimes in an ugly manner. They were not Michael's proudest moments, but that was all in the past, as far as he was concerned, anyway. Whether Deborah Howe felt the same way was less likely, and it seemed highly plausible to him that she'd chosen to chair this hearing when she saw his name attached to the case. Olivia, of course, was there for David. And for Michael too, he liked to think. He was grateful for her presence, made possible only by a serendipitous series of events, involving other professionals dropping out at the last minute. Whatever the various motivations of the panel, Michael was determined to do what was best for his patient.

'I wouldn't say that, exactly,' he said. 'It's not that straightforward.'

'I'm sorry, I don't understand,' said Howe. 'You've been working with this patient,' she checked her notes, 'for over three weeks now.'

'Almost a month,' her young apprentice said, at which she flashed him an annoyed look.

'As I was saying, you've been working with David every day, for a substantial amount of time. Surely, by now, with all your experience and,' she paused, 'expertise, you can ascertain whether he believes in this fictitious family or not. So, in your professional opinion, which is it?'

She was questioning his professionalism. He wasn't surprised; he knew why. She had never forgiven him for the time he'd embarrassed her in front of her peers at a conference.

'I'm sorry,' said Michael. 'I don't think I can answer that question with a simple yes or no.'

Howe scoffed.

'Excuse me,' said Olivia. 'Sorry, Doctor Richards, could you elaborate as to why that is, please? If only for me?'

'Of course, yes.' Michael perked up. 'You see, David still believes in his wife and children, that they existed, that they were all together as a family at some point in time…or space.'

'So, clearly, he remains delusional–' Jeff began.

Michael spoke over him and continued to direct his answer at Olivia. 'Over time, he has come to accept that perhaps they don't exist here, in this reality.'

The panel leant in to discuss.

They were too far away for Michael to hear what was being said, but the flailing arms and head shaking from the chairperson told him all he needed to know about how she felt. He braced himself for the onslaught. But then her demeanour began to change. Olivia was talking now, and whatever it was she was saying, it was doing the job. For a woman who happily admittedly she lacked the natural bedside manner of her colleagues, right now she nevertheless had the panel eating out of the palm of her hand. It was mesmerising. Michael found himself desperate to know what she was saying. Finally, they broke rank and looked back at him.

'Doctor Reyes, here,' said Howe, 'speaks extremely highly of you...and your work.'

And your work. So she'd spoken about him as a person, first and foremost. He thought about that for a second; he liked it. Olivia thought highly of him as a person, not just as a doctor. He knew he was focusing on an irrelevance, but he couldn't help himself.

Howe cleared her throat and he was back in the room. 'I'm just not sure that's enough to convince me,' she said.

In his younger days, professional insecurities would have resulted in a juvenile response. Like it did that day more than a decade ago now. A conference, one of so many. Doctor Deborah Howe was on the panel then too, and had been very outspoken about, well, everything. Michael had always felt that everyone was entitled to their opinion and he certainly didn't expect to agree with everything that was said, but it was the manner in which Howe had delivered her opinion – like it was fact, like no other point of view existed, let alone had any value. She was obnoxious, and back then he was arrogant enough to let that influence him.

So, by the time she started piping up about something he knew a whole lot about and she evidently did not, despite what she thought, he'd had enough. She made claims, gave outrageous opinions. And he made notes. Lots of notes.

When she eventually stopped, he casually, condescendingly, raised his hand, stood and one by one told her just how wrong she was on each bullet point he'd made. At the ninth point, he held his hands out to the packed auditorium and declared, 'I could go on, but I think we're all ready for lunch, don't you?' and promptly walked out of the room. Although, perhaps, he'd been in the right, he still shuddered when he thought back to how he'd handled the situation. Challenging the points as they arose, perhaps, rather than compiling a list of attacks would have been better. Suggesting another seminar in which to discuss the issues because he felt he had something to offer on the topic – yes. Approaching Deborah afterwards to talk, maybe over lunch – definitely. But that wasn't possible. Deborah Howe didn't appear in the dining room. She didn't appear at all. Later, Michael heard that she'd been so horrified by what he'd done that she'd left immediately, meaning the afternoon session she was to be involved in had to be cancelled. Yep, not his proudest moment.

But, as if to emphasise how pointless that moment had been, Deborah Howe's career had gone from strength to strength. She'd climbed the corporate ladder and now here she was. And here he was, needing her to be kinder to him than he'd been to her.

'I don't wish to second-guess the panel,' Michael said, 'but I imagine there's a specific question that you need answering?'

The junior member, Jeff, was bemused. 'I'm sorry, what?'

Michael wasn't addressing him, but he rephrased nonetheless. 'Doctor Howe. Deborah.' He wanted to connect with her, apologise maybe. For David's sake. And perhaps for Olivia, too. She deserved it. She'd been amazing. 'I know we've had our differences,' he said, speaking quickly to ensure there were no interruptions, 'but I know that's only because, as I do, you care so much about the people we treat and you have strong opinions about how to best help them.'

'Doctor,' said Jeff, thinking he was part of the conversation, 'you're not making any sense.'

Michael didn't respond. He was waiting for Howe. Olivia leaned over and whispered something into her ear.

Howe cleared her throat. 'Thank you, Doctor Richards,' she said. 'You're right, there is one pertinent question that needs answering. So, I ask you now, is the patient safe?'

Michael smiled. Partly at her, to make amends. And partly to himself, for it always came down to this one question.

'Okay,' he said. 'Yes, David is safe. That is, providing he has an outlet for his memories. If he has that outlet, then, yes, I believe he is *completely* safe.'

'To the public?' she asked, by the book.

'To the public and to himself,' Michael said, by the book.

'And to you, Michael?' asked Olivia.

Michael paused. She really cared. He felt guilty, suddenly, for his thoughts. 'Absolutely,' he said.

There was a silence. Everyone was immersed in their own thoughts. Michael's were of David, mostly. And a little about Olivia, if he was honest with himself. He was so grateful to her. And obviously, he thought of Susanna and the girls. Everything was for them, ultimately.

The members of the board, each with their own agenda, leant in and discussed the issue once again.

This time, Michael took the initiative and spoke up. 'You have to understand that David has nothing.'

The board parted.

'Actually,' continued Michael, 'he has less than nothing, because he believes he once had something very meaningful. In fact, he had everything. Everything a man could ever want: a beautiful, devoted soulmate and two children to dote on. And now he's left with nothing.' Michael thought of his own wife and children; that's who he pictured when he thought of David's phantom family. As David had asked him, how would *he* feel? He took a sip of water and composed himself.

'Go on, Michael,' said Olivia. 'Please.'

Her words, her voice. They gave Michael the confidence he needed. 'David once had everything,' he said, 'and whether he really did or didn't – to us – doesn't matter. Because as far as he's concerned, he did. So, he needs to be able to remember *that* 'everything', and he needs to not be judged in any way.'

'What do you recommend?' asked Olivia.

'Art.' The word stuck in his throat. He couldn't help but think of Jennifer and her rise and fall, *his* rise and fall. Although the specific details of her treatment were officially confidential, the controversial treatment was known within the professional community, and Michael worried how much Deborah Howe, in her search for revenge, may have dug up. Or perhaps Jeff, in his search for Howe's approval and his own promotion, would have somehow found out and would use this opportunity to bring it up. Just the thought that it might raise its head, that Olivia would find out. *Shit.* That single, wild thought sent Michael's mind racing and so he spoke without thinking.

'Now, before you say anything, this is a completely different situation to any that have come before. Different patient, different problems and a different solution.' He barely took a breath, for fear that a question might be squeezed in. 'On the face of it, I can understand why you might be reminded of past treatments. But I assure you, there's a world of difference.' Michael had gone from giving as little information as possible to verbal diarrhoea. He calmed himself. 'David has a keen interest in art. Sketching, in particular. He will draw anyway, that's for certain. So my plan is to utilise this. I recommend encouraging it as a form of therapy. You see, if David can recreate his memories as sketches and paintings he can escape from the torment of having them trapped within his mind. He can bring them into the physical world, in the form of a canvas. He can bring them into this reality in which they don't exist, and yet should, according to these memories that continue to haunt him.' He was aware that he was starting to repeat himself. He directed a question at Olivia, hoping desperately that it might minimise questions from the others. 'Doctor Reyes, you know David. Your professional opinion?'

Olivia looked surprised to have been asked, as the only non-psychiatric practitioner in the room. During the moment that Deborah and Jeff looked at each other in dismay, Michael made eyes at Olivia as if to say 'Help me out here'.

'Yes. Yes, I like it,' she said. 'I think David would respond well to art.' She looked at him as to say 'Sorry, that's all I've got.'

There was a delay, but then Deborah spoke. She spoke to the room without looking up from her paperwork.

'Hmm. So, it's recommended, with some reservations on the part of the board, I may add, that David be released with immediate effect, under the direct and complete supervision of Doctor Richards. Doctor Richards, could you please confirm that you understand the terms of the release?'

Michael was lost in thought.

'Doctor Richards?' said Deborah.

'Michael?' said Olivia.

Her voice snapped Michael back into the room. 'Yes. Yes, I understand. Thank you.'

The board members looked at each other. Olivia looked only at Michael, who rushed to collect his papers and promptly left the room.

10

PATIENT

Doctor Richards came through on most of his promises. He'd said that if I committed to working with him, as he put it, I'd get out of that place and into my own. And, here I was, barely a month after first meeting him, sat in my own flat.

Of course, there was one promise he was yet to come through on: the big one, the only one, really. Finding my family. He always said 'find' as if it was a foreign word, like its meaning was open to negotiation. And yeah, his interpretation of 'finding' had been different to mine in the beginning. But now, I'd come round to his way of thinking. I didn't care what 'finding' meant, I just wanted to see them.

He'd called me on the phone that morning to say he had an idea that would allow me to see them again. But now he was saying 'see' in a strange way.

It wasn't a bad place, this flat, it felt like home, I guess, but then I couldn't remember home beyond a few blurred colours in the background of my family. It was about midday and all morning the sun had been streaming through the windows, bouncing off the walls and making the place seem bigger than it was. Until an hour ago. Now, the dark clouds were descending. The view was good, especially for a ground-floor flat. No sweeping meadows or panoramic seafronts, but it was a stark improvement on a hospital ward or that wretched halfway house with its overly manicured flower beds. My God, everything so perfectly in place it made you lose your mind. In contrast, I had my own little flower bed. The three tulips I'd bought from the local florist were doing well, considering I'd had no idea how much water they needed and was undoubtedly over-watering them. He'd be here soon, sat opposite me, talking as if we were friends. Like he'd popped over for a coffee.

'Don't tell my wife about the coffee,' he'd say, every time. Every single time. And I would smile, every single time.

A package had been delivered an hour before, but on the phone Richards had asked me not to open it until he got there. It was big and bulky with all of the packaging. It sat on the kitchen table; a corner of the packaging had been ripped in transit and it was just begging to be prised opened.

An idea that would allow me to see them again. Was this package it?

I pulled at the broken cardboard just slightly. Even if I couldn't repair it, I could tell him it came that way. That was the truth, I wouldn't be lying. It did come damaged. I only needed to pull it slightly more open to see what it was. I pushed my finger in and eased the corner slightly. It held. It was well packed, apart from this damaged part. The courier must have properly smashed it down on to its corner. That meant whatever was inside could be damaged too. Even more reason to open it. I went to the cutlery drawer and pulled out the sharpest knife I had, which wasn't sharp at all. They didn't trust me with anything that could puncture human skin, or an eggshell for that matter. *Wait, the bread knife. Serrated.* That would be better.

The tape held firm for a good while before snapping. I attacked the second strap. When that also fell, I was able to ease the package open. I could see that it was made out of wood. The clouds outside were darker now, which didn't help me see inside the box, and the still warming-up energy-efficient light bulb that hung above it was of even less help.

Did I own a torch? Probably not. Unless one was left by the previous resident. I looked through the kitchen cabinets, on top of the wardrobe, in the little electricity meter cupboard, nothing. No torch.

Idiot. I searched again, but this time for my mobile phone. Richards had organised it for me, and his was the only number saved in it.

The living room was tidier than usual. I'd made an effort to spruce it up in advance of the doctor's visit. But that fell by the wayside as I searched high and low for the phone. I eventually found it stuffed down the side of the leather armchair. The built-in torch app worked a treat. I could see that I'd been right. It was made of wood – oak, a light, white oak. Some metal parts too, plates, screws. *What is it?*

'David?' I spun around to see Doctor Richards peering through the window. 'Can I come in?' he asked.

I didn't know how much he'd seen, but it was too late now to tape it back up. 'Doctor, yes, of course, please. It's open,' I said, meaning the door, not the package.

He sat down at the table and I put the kettle on, while slipping the phone into my jeans without turning the app off, and discreetly sliding the bread knife back into the cutlery drawer.

'I'm afraid it's been damaged in transit. Just the packaging I think, though.'

He took a look. 'Should be okay. They wrapped it well, thankfully. Have you guessed what it is?'

I shook my head. Richards smiled and said we needed more room to open it up. He picked it up and carried it into the living area.

'Oh, and bring the bread knife with you,' he said, without looking back.

The easel stood four-foot high and held the accompanying canvas and pencils proudly. There were a bunch of additional canvases, a couple sketchpads and various other materials too. Everything a budding artist could want.

'I guess I've mentioned sketching a few times, huh?'

'Just a few,' he said, with a smirk.

I thanked him and asked who'd paid for it. When he said it didn't matter, I realised he'd dipped into his own pocket.

'I'll pay you back, doctor, you know, as soon as I'm–'

He shook his head. 'No need. My pleasure.'

We both stared at it for a moment and then Richards sat down in the armchair. Despite my best efforts, it was once again covered in clothes, which he didn't bother to move.

'Okay, then, why don't you have a go?'

'I don't think so,' I said.

'Why not?'

'I can't draw. Not really.'

'That doesn't matter. Have a go.'

'I don't want to waste the canvas…'

'There's an unlimited number of canvases. Just call the number on the back there and they'll deliver however many you need. Paints too.'

I smiled and picked up one of the pencils. But nothing came. I felt pressured. 'I'm sorry, I–'

'Don't worry, David. There's no hurry. Actually, there's something else, something that should help. I've set up some lessons. Art lessons, for you to attend, at the local community centre.'

No. My plan had been to teach myself one day. Get a book from the library. Maybe get one of those tablets and watch YouTube videos. But not attend lessons. With people. That was never my thing, people. Not before all this happened, I suspected, and certainly not now. He could see my reticence.

'It's all set up,' he said. 'A new class starts this Thursday evening. You're all signed up, just turn up, seven-thirty, I think it is, but I'll double-check that.'

'Listen, doctor, thank you for this. I do appreciate it, really. But I'm not sure, about the lessons, I mean.'

But then he told me what I feared. That the art wasn't just a new hobby. That it was part of my rehabilitation, as he put it. 'So I have to do it?'

'I think it'll help with your family.'

'You mean, help me forget my family?'

He seemed taken aback and looked hurt that I would even suggest such a thing. He shook his head a number of times before he spoke. 'No, David. Absolutely not. The last thing I want is for you to forget them. I want you to *remember* them. These lessons will help you to remember them. This art will make sure they're never forgotten.'

His words hung heavily in the air, and I wanted to believe him. But it was clear that we weren't going to find my family, not like I'd wanted. We were going to find them in some pseudo-psychotherapy-game way. I was completely deflated.

'You've told me on several occasions how much you enjoy art but that you never had the chance to learn how to do it properly,' he said. 'This is your chance. Use it to…bring them to life.'

I turned to face him. He looked awkward, like he'd just realised how inappropriate his words were. 'Did you just say "bring them to life"?'

He squirmed a bit, but held resolute. 'Yes. Absolutely. Bring them to life.'

He wasn't convincing either of us. I asked again if I had a choice regarding the art lessons and he did his usual skit about there always being a choice. But then, in the same breath, the reality of the choice was once again revealed. 'It is, however, a requirement of your release.'

Ah. There it was. The rub. I go to these art classes, or I go…back. Back to that depressingly perfect place. Back to insanity. Backwards. I didn't know where my family were but I did know they weren't back there.

'That's not much of a choice,' I told him.

'I guess you're right, David. It's not much of a choice.' He smiled at me and I very nearly found myself returning the favour. 'All I'm asking is for you give it a shot. If it doesn't work out, we'll talk again.' With that, he stood up and put his coat back on.

'Okay,' I said. 'I'll give it a shot. As a thank you, for the equipment.'

As he walked past me, he put his hand on my shoulder and told me I was most welcome. He left the flat, closing the door gently behind him.

I crashed down into the armchair and stared at the blank canvas. I thought about making a mark. Something simple, like a tree or a bowl of fruit. Or…just jump right into it. Portraits of my wife, my children.

I went to the bathroom and splashed water over my face. In the mirror, I saw what my first sketch should be. A self-portrait. Until I was worthy of them.

Back in the living room, now dominated by the canvases, I turned the radio on. It blasted out at me. I hated the way the volume reset when the power was switched off. Every time I turned it back on, it was so loud. The result was a crazy game I played against it whereby I frantically smashed the decrease volume button as it warmed up. Now and then, I thought it helped, but usually it did nothing to temper the noise. Including this time.

'…Sykes has very much become the favourite for the win since his impressive media appearances….'

What else but the Winnies and that strange Damo bloke. Big budget, no class. It seemed to me that the Winnies belonged on one of the other stations, not the BBC. A sign of the times.

I'd managed to get the sound down to a sensible level. It wasn't muted, but it was close. That's how I liked it, a quiet background hum to hide the silence.

'…I remember how difficult it was for me when I first realised my special powers…'

A kid who could breathe underwater. A superfast middle-aged guy with a gut. A human X-ray machine! Forget the self-portrait, I could draw these freaks. I turned the volume down further, closed my eyes and pictured them in my mind's eye. But the only faces I saw were those of my family.

I opened my eyes. The blank canvas stared back at me. I could see their faces emerging. All I needed to do was trust my visions. I picked up the pencil.

Yes, I had a plan to see my family again. But it was a very different plan to the one that Doctor Richards had.

11

DOCTOR

Michael rested on the family veranda. He sat in a rocking chair for two, although he sat alone and, having never really enjoyed the swaying sensation it provided, especially when reading, had cranked the lever that locked it into a stationary position.

He looked out on a middle-aged suburb. His life was, on paper at least, all he had ever wanted. He had the house, not a massive one, but with more space than they needed. It was in a good part of town, with almost no crime, and streets that the girls could walk along safely. He had time to play golf, probably enough time to get really good at it, although he never took it seriously – 'The better you get, the less fun you have' being a personal mantra. But more than anything, it was the house that his wife had dreamed of.

Susanna was a smart, strong, driven woman, but she was still young when she met Michael. That, along with his practice, meant that despite her superior intellect she'd had to play the traditional role of homemaker as early as her mid-twenties. Only since his heart attack had she started making noises about returning to work; how much of that was to allow Michael to slow down and how much of it was for herself, he wasn't sure. What was certain was what a fantastic mother she'd been to the girls. She'd always put her family before herself, and he wondered if he could say the same thing.

She appeared with a glass of Châteauneuf-du-Pape in hand. 'This'll help,' she said.

'Isn't that against doctor's orders?'

'I won't tell if you don't.'

She had a deal. Michael brought the glass to his mouth and, as he'd done so much more now that wine wasn't part of his daily routine, took in its aroma before really tasting it.

'Ah, I see,' Susanna said, nodding towards the newspaper article on Michael's lap.

'See what?'

'Why you're so tense.'

Michael looked down to remind himself what he'd been reading. 'Blade Runner 2049 is a gargantuan spectacle of pure hallucinatory madness…'

He'd first read *Do Androids Dream of Electric Sheep?* as a pupil, at the suggestion of Mr Curry. A passionate, controversial, borderline-insane English teacher, Curry had been as much a fan of science fiction as he was of the classics.

Like all who met Curry, his pupils fell into one of two camps: they either saw him as a dangerously eccentric educator or as a true inspiration. Michael was very much in the latter camp. He saw Curry as a mentor, although, looking back over the years, Michael thought the relationship had probably not been as close as he'd thought at the time. Back then, Michael would hang on his teacher's every word and actively seek out recommended texts to read. *Androids* was the second or third novel of Philip K. Dick's that Curry had passed his way, and, if Michael was honest with himself, he liked it the least. He remembered not really understanding it, but of course he didn't share that with his idol. Instead, he focused on the parts of the book he did like and did understand. When Curry spoke of the mood organs and Mercer, Michael just nodded and made concurring noises, or said he'd like to read it one more time before being certain about what this meant, what that meant, what was real, what was fake. Looking back now, he knew that Curry had seen through his act, and that embarrassed him a little even to this day. Only a few years ago, he wrote a long-winded letter to Curry containing a whole new appreciation of various texts his mentor had passed his way. But he never posted it. Now, in a way that could have been part of the *Android's* post-apocalyptic world, Michael was connected to Curry via social media 'friendship'. It would be easy to message him, too easy, perhaps. It felt too impersonal. Anyway, Michael would probably have to ask Rachael to help him send it, and that sealed the deal not to bother.

'So, it's happened, then?' Susanna's words brought him back to the present. 'They've finally got around to the sequel?'

'I knew it would. It was inevitable,' said Michael. 'I'm amazed it's taken this long, to be honest. Issues with the rights, I believe. I was starting to think – well, hope – it wouldn't happen, in my lifetime, anyway.'

'Well, it very nearly didn't,' she said, pointing to his chest.

'Ah, so close,' he said, taking her hand and winking to ensure she knew he was joking.

'What's the verdict?'

Michael held up the newspaper for her to see.

'Wow. Five stars.'

'I know. They're saying it's a masterpiece. Everyone is.'

'Well then, I guess you'll have to go see it.'

'Maybe.'

'*Maybe*?'

Michael sighed.

'Oh not all this again, Michael. Really?'

'I know it seems daft, but…'

'May I?' asked Susanna, taking the paper. She started to read the article.

Ridley Scott's *Blade Runner* had become one of Michael's favourite cinematic experiences. The first time he'd seen it, he'd headed to its screening not actually realising it was an adaptation of the novel he'd been recommended a few years earlier. Having purposely read nothing about the movie he was attending, something he always enjoyed doing (and was easily able to do in those pre-internet days) he assumed it was going to be a rip-off of *Star Wars*, which had changed the cinematic landscape a few years before. He'd hoped, however, that it was closer to *2001: A Space Odyssey*, partly because Curry had liked that film better, but also because Michael couldn't imagine anything beating *Star Wars* (and its recent sequel) at its own game.

To his annoyance, Michael and his friends entered the cinema late from the pub, missing the trailers, and the main event had just started too. It was only as they stumbled into the theatre, searching for seats in the dark, that Michael had looked up to see the word 'replicant' in red on the screen. And then he saw 'Nexus 6'. *Oh no.* Michael felt dread. His treasured book, Dick's visionary novel, Curry's beloved text, had been given the full Hollywood treatment. He expected nothing but complete and utter disappointment.

Two hours later, he sat there a changed man. His friends filtered out as soon as the credits rolled but Michael stayed put. Not just through the credits, either; he sat there so long thinking about whether Deckard was a replicant or not that the cleaners came in.

'You're eager,' said one of them. 'It doesn't start for another twenty minutes yet.'

'I'm sorry?' said Michael.

'The picture, twenty minutes yet. They shouldn't have let you in this early.'

Michael didn't go anywhere. Instead, he sat through the film a second time. He needed to be sure.

Later, he caught up with his mates back at the pub.

'Where the fuck have you been?' asked Phil.

'I had to watch it again,' said Michael. 'Had to be *sure.*'

'Sure of what?'

'You know, whether Deckard is a replicant.'

'Wait, which one was Deckard again?' asked Phil.

'Are you joking? The main character. The cop. The *blade runner.*'

'Oh, right, Han Solo.'

Michael rolled his eyes. 'If you like, yes.'

'So, what about him?'

'Whether he's a replicant.'

'I'm not with you. Here, Johnny, what's Mike on about?'

'Johnny,' said Michael. 'Deckard's one of them, you got that, right?'

'One of who?'

'The replicants.'

'Hang on, I thought Deckard was the guy who *killed* the robots.'

'Replicants.'

'Yeah, replicants.'

'He was. But he was one too. He was a replicant too.'

'Was he?'

'Yes. Well, I think so. I mean, the clues were there, all the way through. Deckard, a replicant. Wow. Didn't you see the clues?'

'To be honest,' said Johnny, 'I thought the whole fucking thing was shit.'

Michael went back, by himself, and watched *Blade Runner* three more times over the following weeks. Each time, he became more and more convinced that Rick Deckard was indeed a Nexus 6 himself. He revisited *Do Androids Dream of Electric Sheep?* to see if it was there too. He feared it was, and that he'd missed it. Maybe Mr Curry had mentioned it and Michael had responded in a similar way to Johnny and Phil, completely oblivious. But if it was in the book, it wasn't obvious. That was a relief. Perhaps Mr Curry hadn't seen him for the complete fool he was.

The explosion of home movies allowed Michael to become a true *Blade Runner* fanatic. VHS changed everything; he could watch Deckard again and again, each time convincing himself more and more that the man's memories were not his own. A little later, just around the time his third VHS tape had worn through, something amazing happened. It was called LaserDisc, and it was the future. Almost as sci-fi as the film it presented, the visuals were stunning, the audio amazing. It was the future. There was no doubt in Michael's mind. So he bought the most expensive player on the market with the honest intention of populating his film collection to justify the outlay. Of course, that didn't happen. By the time DVD arrived, Michael's LaserDisc collection remained at just one.

Despite owning the film in numerous formats, Michael still made a point of watching it whenever it was broadcast on TV. He accepted that the scenes with the strippers and prostitutes baring their breasts were cut, and that a couple of swearwords were dubbed over with little subtlety. Fair enough. But there was one time, one crisp February evening in 1986, when a US broadcast version was shown in the UK. It blew Michael's mind for all the wrong reasons. He was horrified. Not by the film itself, it hadn't even started yet. Instead, by the teaser shown before the film, which stated very clearly that Deckard was *not* a replicant.

Michael was astounded. Not that Deckard wasn't a replicant – that remained a fascinating conversation he was eager to have with anyone willing. No, rather that they, whoever *they* were, were willing to make that decision for the audience, before the film even started, no less, and to not let them decide for themselves. It was also around that time that he read about how unhappy Ridley Scott had been with the originally released picture. At first, this left him feeling cheated, as if he'd been wrong. But then details about a director's cut came to light. The film was becoming a saga all of its own. Rather than leaving it alone, he found himself watching it more and more. That opening night, Phil and Johnny and the others hadn't picked up on the subtext; they just watched the movie and took it at face value. Maybe they'd been right all along.

And then, like a love letter, the director's cut was released. The first time Michael saw the unicorn dream sequence he was so relieved he cried. Apparently Ridley Scott still wasn't completely happy, but Michael Richards was. At least, he was at first. Later on it would be more bittersweet, Michael pining for the days when his theory was based on subtler storytelling than a rather unambiguous dream sequence. But the liberation of knowing he was right all along, that Deckard's memories were not his own but those of someone else's, was worth the nostalgia.

The fancy DVD version that now superseded all previous home versions had five of the seven versions of the film on it. The two it didn't have, a San Diego sneak preview and that same US broadcast version with the now even more inexcusable *not a replicant* teaser had still evaded Michael. Knowing that they existed irked him whenever he thought about it. The US broadcast version, in particular. He'd wanted to be sure he hadn't imagined it. Internet research – with help from his own Rachael, whom Susanna had allowed him to name after the film's character – had confirmed it was a real memory of Michael's, unlike many of Deckard's. He still wanted to see it again though, with his own eyes, just to be sure.

'You are funny,' said Susanna. 'For an educated man, you don't half worry about silliness.'

'I know.'

'There's no mention of it in this review.'

'No, I know. I made sure before reading it. I had Carissa read it first, just in case.'

'You didn't?'

'Just in case. And she didn't mind.'

Susanna shook her head in disbelief.

'Anyway,' continued Michael, 'apparently all of the reviews are what they call "spoiler-free"'.

'Okay. So, let's say you go see it, and you find out he's not a robot after all–'

'Replicant.'

'Excuse me, *replicant.* We find out he's not a replicant. He's just a human being. Will it really be the end of the world?'

'Well, no, of course not.'

'That's what I thought.'

'I guess I'd be kind of... disappointed, if after all of this time, we find out that actually David's memories are in fact real. I don't know how that would affect me.'

'*David's* memories?'

'Huh?'

'You said "David"'.

'I did?' asked Michael. 'I meant *Deckard*, obviously.'

'Okay.'

'It's not important, is it?'

'I don't know, you tell me.'

Michael looked at his wife. 'It's not important. Silliness, as you say.'

'In that case, what's really bothering you?'

Michael had another drink of the wine. 'It *is* partly the replicant thing...'

Susanna rolled her eyes.

'...but mostly it's the new patient.'

'So we're back to David then?'

'He's agreed to give the art idea a try.'

'That's good,' said Susanna.

She obviously didn't understand the problem and he didn't blame her. It was hard to explain without mentioning Jennifer, which he really didn't want to do. 'I'm just concerned that he may regress while we're away.' He'd picked his words carefully, given the recent tension between them regarding not only this patient, but generally the amount of work he was doing since his heart attack.

'You're not changing your mind?' It was only a half question at most, and more an order to not even dare consider cancelling the family holiday they were about to embark on, the first for all four of them together in five years. Michael took a gulp of wine. 'Michael?'

'No, no. Absolutely not. We need this break. This family comes first,' he said.

She was back on side.

Michael picked up one of the two novels he was currently reading. He liked it that way. Sometimes he found interesting parallels between the lead characters, but usually he read this way just to keep things fresh. A chapter or two of one book here, then a chapter of the other.

For a long time after *Androids*, and reading purely to impress Mr Curry, Michael had been put off anything other than medical journals. New theories, new thoughts, new approaches. Arguments for and against. He had a study full of published works on his subject. Despite his best efforts, he read like his father.

He even had one he'd written himself, its title inspired, of course, by Deckard: *Wait, Did That Really Happen? How the Past Lies to Us*. He had been proud of the book, of finishing it, getting it published. When he read it now, years later, he cringed somewhat at both the naivety and the gusto of his ideas. But he knew it was a snapshot in time, and, although he was embarrassed, it had all come from a genuine place. Besides which, he was probably the only one still reading it. The book had sold only a few hundred copies in total, which meant, colleagues, friends and family members taken out of the equation, it was probably sitting on the shelf of fewer than fifty practitioners around the world, whom he didn't know. Still, it was an accomplishment, although not one he was looking to repeat. His time putting ideas into words for others to consider was long gone. He still had ideas, of course, but they were so patient-specific that to suggest them beyond the confines of his own work was at the least presumptuous and at worst irresponsible. In short, he'd learnt his lesson.

He chose to start with the psychological thriller that was getting five stars everywhere. Barely a page read, he put the novel down and reached for his laptop.

'My God, you're the slowest reader I've ever met,' said Susanna.

'What the hell is "Arafah"?' he asked, searching the internet.

'Muslim holiday. Holy day.'

'Ah, yes. Right…' said Michael as he returned to the novel.

Susanna rolled her eyes again. Typical Michael, he couldn't let anything go – be it a word he didn't know, a cultural reference that went over his head. Whatever it was, he had to stop and look in the dictionary or, more often now, on the web. Even the pronunciation of a word needed to be clear in his head for him to continue.

Susanna was the opposite. She would ignore the rare unknown word and blast through novels in barely more time than the film adaptation would take to watch. Especially when using her tablet, which was ironic because it had a built-in dictionary that she never used. Michael, on the other hand, liked to feel the paper pages in his hand, liked to pull the book from the shelf, fold the page when he was done and return it to its place.

The only time Michael had read more than now was in his mid-twenties, for around a year. The reason was a well-read woman, who was halfway through writing her first novel about a woman who thought she was a man, or thought she killed a man, or something. He couldn't quite remember. It was inspired by Polanski's *The Tenant* – he definitely remembered that, because she watched the film over and over until he heard the screams in his dreams. Once, he came home to find her all bandaged up and lying in bed. That freaked him out enough to end the relationship, and with it his appetite for reading had ended too.

Now, he read for himself. No more trying to impress or reading for others – Curry, girlfriends, anyone else. And it often had the bonus of time spent with the woman he loved and nothing beat *that*. Well, at least until his daughters came along, anyway. Then reading really filled him with joy. Reading to Carissa, and then Rachael, and then *with* them. Everyday, throw-away moments that actually meant everything. They were gone as soon as you experienced them, like tears in rain, Michael thought.

'So, who'll check in on David while we're gone?' asked Susanna.

She clearly wasn't done making her point. He couldn't remember if he'd told her already, or whether it should have been obvious that Doctor Reyes would look out for David. Either way, he knew why she'd asked.

'Olivia knows David,' he said, already on the back foot. 'It was she who first brought him to me, remember?'

Susanna made a 'hmm-hmm' sound.

Michael continued his justification. 'You know, them knowing each other in a professional context, it's the reason we can go on this holiday in the first place. It's thanks to Olivia, if you think about it. Without her, we, well, I, couldn't go and leave David.'

'I must be sure to thank her.'

Michael smiled.

'Well, let's hope she does a good job.'

'I'm sure she'll be fine,' said Michael. 'It's just, well, she's not...'

'It's just that she's not *you*.'

'I was going to say "a psychotherapist".'

'Well, that too.'

'This is what I do, right?'

'This *is* what you do,' she said, 'and you're the best at it, no doubt about that. But don't you ever worry that being the best could be part of the problem?'

He knew what she was getting at, but chose to argue anyway. 'How can being the best ever be a bad thing?'

Her response was more cutting than he expected. 'Because you have to make sacrifices to stay the best, that's why.'

Michael put his wine down and sighed. 'I've put you through so much,' he said. 'You and the girls. All in the name of my career.'

'In the name of helping others.'

'Maybe. Nonetheless, you've all been through so much. Too much.'

'This is true,' said Susanna.

Michael smiled and reached out for his wife. She put her wine down and sat on his knee, not fully submitting to his charms just yet.

'I love you, Susie. You're not just my wife, you're my soulmate and my best friend. I'm so lucky to have you.'

'That's the truth.'

'To have you, the girls, to have all this…' he continued, 'David, my other patients, they don't have this. All they have is…well, me.'

Susanna nodded.

'The balance has been wrong before, I know that. But it won't be again. There's room for them in my life too. Really. But I won't ever again let that threaten what we have here. I promise.'

Susanna picked up the bottle of wine, topped up both glasses and passed one to her husband. 'Thank you,' she said. 'That's what I needed to hear.'

They kissed like married people in love.

12

PATIENT

He watched over me as I sketched, which should have been annoying, intimidating even. I didn't mind it, though, because it was *him*. Anyone else, no, but Doctor Richards, okay. That didn't mean I was happy with my skills as an artist. Despite a few lessons, I was really quite embarrassed about my work. I'd taken full advantage of the offer of more canvases and had been drawing every day. No paints, though. For some reason my memories were always black and white, no colour, so shading sufficed. I had a few examples of my portraiture around the flat, especially here in the living room where the light was best, and I was damned happy to be drawing. But their lack of detail meant they were unrecognisable as my beautiful wife and children. I wasn't even close to doing them justice, and that frustrated me. I wondered if I would ever be able to capture their beauty. I wondered if that was even possible.

He sat, as was the routine, in the armchair that was always strewn with clothes, which he never removed. Once again, the radio was on for background hum, which I found even more welcoming when he was there. It meant we could talk, but didn't have to; there was no silence to fill. I even turned the volume up slightly when I heard him knock on the front door.

I'd given up trying to avoid the Winnies, such was its saturation of the media. But beyond that, if I was honest with myself, it was hard to resist. Even if you didn't fall for Damo's charms, and I didn't, there was something for everyone. The stories were incredible, the personalities astonishing.

'…Sykes versus the others, it seems. That's not my opinion, it's the bookies', people!'

Clearly they'd been well-drilled, well-rehearsed. It was easier to succumb than fight against it. It was all building up to the big awards show, which seemed to be on any day now, although it never quite came. For better or worse, they were the backdrop to my artwork.

'So, the art is working out then?' he asked.

It was, I guess, despite my frustrations. And I hated to admit it, but Richards had been right about the lessons. The woman who took them was annoying, but she had shown me things that had started to help. Her voice though, my God, her voice was so condescending. I felt like a schoolchild being taught his times tables and constantly getting them wrong, the way she talked to me. Not just me, the whole class. I saw them looking at each other, first with shock, then annoyance, and then, to everyone's pleasure, with rolling eyes and knowing smiles. There were about nine of us when everyone attended. Sometimes, people didn't come. I think they had that choice. I didn't. 'Go or go back,' he'd said. So I went. I could handle her patronising tone only because I had no choice. The others got annoyed and stayed away. I didn't blame them. I would have too.

Still, she *had* helped me, although I got the feeling she was there because she had to be as much as I was there because I had to be. Maybe she had her own deal going on; she would have to go back, wherever back was, if she didn't teach. Maybe Richards was orchestrating the entire thing. It wasn't the first time I'd entertained the thought that this guy, who seemed to be fighting in my corner, had his own agenda.

'It is working out, yes, thank you, doctor. I guess, I love…what it does…' I said, somewhat abashed. He stood up and walked around the room, looking at a number of the sketches I'd been working on. He made pleased sounds, probably because the sketches meant the strategy was working rather than because he was actually impressed by the work.

He took his time, touching the edges of the canvases as if he needed to connect physically to them. It was getting a little weird.

'And what does it do, David?' he asked, as if he didn't know. He knew. He was looking for confirmation of this master plan he had devised.

I touched my temple. 'It gets them out of *here*,' I said, playing along. Then I heard what I'd said and recoiled. 'Wait, no, I don't mean, I don't mean…'

I didn't ever want them out, but I did need something to change. They were eating me up. I thought back to the day I'd met Doctor Richards, and how when he'd thought and spoken of his own family he'd touched his head and then touched his heart.

I tried again. 'I don't mean "get them out" as in lose them, I mean…'

He took over. 'It's okay, David. I think I know what you mean. I get it, really, I do.'

I touched my head. 'I don't need to remember them in here any more, as long as they stay in here.' I slid my hand down to my chest.

He didn't answer, instead he just nodded and smiled.

A little embarrassed to have spoken so openly, I started drawing again.

'Well, you're getting good, David,' he said. 'You've clearly been practising.'

'Non-stop,' I said. 'It's all I do. But…' I trailed off and stopped drawing.

He asked me to continue both.

'You'll be ready for paint soon, eh?'

I shook my head. 'No colour…'

I felt I'd already shared a lot today, maybe too much. I tightened up, which only resulted in worse artwork. I always drew better when I was relaxed and distracted enough to not think too much. That was the zone I needed to be in. But even when I was at my best, the sketches were still pathetically basic.

'I'm not good enough,' I said before I realised. 'I'm not doing them justice. Look, it's rubbish, they're unrecognisable.'

'I can see a woman and two children.'

'Yeah, but come on, doctor, be honest. They could be anyone's wife and anyone's children. They *could* be mine, but they could just as easily be yours. I'm not good enough, that's the bottom line.' I put the pencil down. 'Maybe this is a waste of time.'

He put down the tea I'd made him and pulled out a pair of glasses from his jacket pocket. He looked over my artwork again and then gave me his assessment. 'You're wrong, David. This is good. You've hardly had any lessons. And I can see this is your wife you're drawing, not just some generic woman. Look at how her hair falls and curls at the ends, those details are the important ones. My wife's hair doesn't do that. Your wife's does and you've captured that.'

'That's meant to be her collarbone,' I said.

For perhaps the first time since we'd met, he seemed to be lost for words. 'Oh.'

'Like I said, this is a waste of time.'

He had about three seconds before I was done with the treatment all together, but I knew it was as important to him as it was to me; he'd invested time and ideas into my treatment, he'd told me about the resistance he'd come up against when it came to trying this therapy. He needed it to work out as much as I did, but for very different reasons. His reputation – which he'd never said anything about, but I could sense had taken a battering over the years – was at stake. But more than that, I got the feeling his personal life was also interlinked with the success of my treatment. He needed this to have not been a complete waste of time so that being away from his family to help me would turn out to be the right decision.

'No, I see it now. Yes, her neck, her collarbone. Her hair ends here on the shoulder. I was looking at it all wrong. The light in here creates a shadow, that's what it is. And these glasses are an old pair, I really should get them replaced. I see it now, though. I see her, your wife. This is good, David.'

He did a great job of convincing himself; me, not so much. Now, when I looked at the drawing, all I could see was her hair curling at the ends.

But before I could argue, he continued. 'You've barely had any lessons. Look at how far you've come in next to no time. More lessons are all you need. If you keep going to the classes, before you know it–'

'I'll be able to draw a collarbone,' I said.

He turned to me and laughed, and I couldn't help but smile too. He put his hand on my shoulder. 'I'm sorry, I didn't mean to laugh,' he said. 'It was very unprofessional of me.'

Actually, it had been exactly what I needed, and he could see that in my reaction.

'As you know, I'll be away for the next few weeks,' he said. 'I'm sure that, with the lessons between now and then, by the time I return you'll have come on in leaps and bounds.'

'Leaps and bounds, huh?'

'Absolutely.'

Every time he spoke of the lessons, my heart sank a little more. 'I was thinking, doctor…'

His expression changed, he must have known what I was going to say was important. It was rare that I would start a conversation. I had his full attention. His hand was still on my shoulder, which was becoming a bit awkward.

'I was thinking, perhaps I could leave the lessons now, maybe try another method? I found a YouTube channel on portraiture, it's really good. I've been finding that helps more than the lessons, if I'm honest. The videos haven't covered collarbones yet, clearly.'

My attempt at a joke was unsuccessful. Instead of smiling, Richards looked concerned.

'I don't understand,' he said. 'You just told me how desperate you are to get better and how you want to improve.'

I told him all I needed was time to practise, that I'd had all the teaching I needed.

He wasn't convinced. 'Is there something you're not telling me, David?'

There was plenty I wasn't telling him.

'Don't you enjoy the lessons?'

'The thing is…the woman there. The teacher, I mean. You know her, right? She's a friend of yours?'

'Leanne? Yes, well, sort of. A friend of a friend. More a colleague, really. Why?'

I was cautious, I didn't want to make trouble.

'It's okay,' he said. 'You can tell me.'

'Doctor-patient confidentiality and all that?'

He smiled. 'Well, yes. But I'd like to think we've gone slightly beyond that, David. You can tell me and it won't go any further.'

'Okay, well, it's probably me. You know how I like it quiet, to concentrate…' I said, as if there was any way he couldn't possibly know that. 'Well, how can I put this, she operates at a different volume to me.'

Now he smiled.

'And she likes the sound of her own voice,' I added, with some reservation.

He laughed as if he knew exactly what I meant.

'It's not that she doesn't mean well, and she knows what she's talking about. It's just that she gets in the way. Just when I'm getting into my zone, into my flow, she'll stop the class and talk some more. Or out of nowhere, her voice will boom from behind me and I'll lose track of what I'm doing.'

I could see he understood. 'You're talking about your visions,' he said, 'your memories.'

'They're so fragile, they disappear so easily…' I struggled for the words but Richards found them for me and finished my sentence perfectly.

'…like tears in rain?' he asked.

It was a surreal moment, as if he had reached into my mind and pulled out a beautiful phrase I didn't even know was there. Like tears in rain was exactly how it felt when their faces disappeared from my mind. He was a shrink, of course, so maybe it was something he had come across before. But, wow, he nailed it.

'Yes, doctor. Just like tears in rain. She means well, and, yes, she's helped me. But sometimes I wish she would just shut up and let me draw.' It had come out more abruptly than I'd meant it to. 'I mean, if she could just ease back a little. The memories, they come and go so easily. I remember something, a detail. The way my wife scrunched her nose. The way my youngest squeezed her eyes shut when cuddling. Details. Important details. Fragile details that get drowned out by her babbling.'

I looked up to see whether I'd perhaps laid it on a bit thick. I was about to backtrack so that Richards didn't feel completely unappreciated, but then he spoke.

‘I have to say, David, looking around, she’s doing and saying something right.’

I felt a little guilty. ‘You’re right. Sorry, doctor. I’m just eager to get better.’

‘I know, I know. And you will. Listen, let’s stick with the lessons for the moment, okay? If you feel the same way when I’m back from my trip, maybe we can work something else out.’

I couldn’t argue with that, and didn’t. Instead, I held out my hand for him to shake. It was a big gesture for me. It wasn’t the first time we’d shaken hands, but it was the first time I’d instigated it. ‘Thank you, doctor. For everything. Please enjoy your well-earned holiday.’

He shook my hand with extra might. He knew it was a big deal for me, and, although we could never be friends in the traditional sense, it did feel like we’d become something more than just doctor and patient. For the first time since this all happened, I didn’t feel completely alone. Then he turned and left me, to take his family on holiday.

13

DOCTOR

Michael and Susanna sat on a beautiful white-sand beach. It wasn't a private beach, but it was so quiet that it felt like one. Susanna was reading a trashy romance novel, the kind Michael would tease her about but had secretly read once or twice when she wasn't home. He, in turn, was reading a thriller recommended to him by a colleague because of the shocking twist it delivered in the third act, something he always enjoyed, providing it wasn't too far-fetched. So engrossed in the text was he that for once he decided to stick with it rather than flitting from one book to another. He was relaxed, perhaps for the first time in years. It was a world away from the troubles they'd been through recently.

He loved Susanna so much. He wondered whether she knew just how much. He'd threatened what they had with his dedication to his work and he regretted that, but from the moment he'd set eyes on Susanna he'd loved her with his whole heart.

It had been at a party that he wanted to avoid. The hosts were fleeing the country, flying away to a sun-soaked early retirement. She was a former partner of Michael's practice, with whom he'd once had a brief fling, which, to this day, her husband wasn't aware of. It wasn't a big deal, at least to Michael anyway. He'd been single at the time and she'd made it very clear that her marriage was over. And yet, there he was, many years later, wishing them a happy retirement together.

He'd had one last chance of avoiding the party. He'd found himself in a snug little pub where an all-female neo-punk band belted out tracks from his past. Unfortunately, his wingman at the time – Bob – had very clear orders to ensure that the party was their final destination. He also wasn't the punk fan that Michael was, and so there was no chance of persuading him to break with protocol. The punk was cut short and the farewell party was attended, much to Michael's disappointment.

It was at a semi-private yachting club complete with clichéd nautical artefacts adorning the walls and cheap alcohol behind the bar. Michael was quick to get the drinks in before he might have to address the happy couple. Stood at the bar, he daren't look around for fear of running into either of them, or, for that matter, any number of former colleagues who might want to catch up. When wingman Bob visited the men's room, Michael stared directly ahead at the various poisons on offer while the hired help did their best to keep up with demand. He could see his reflection in the bar mirror between the bottles of Scotch, and then, way behind him, *her* reflection. She was tucked up in a corner booth far across the room.

Even from that distance, he could tell that she had the most beautiful eyes he had ever seen. *That anyone has ever seen,* he thought. They shone. He spun around and looked straight at her. The rest of the room melted away. Everything became background noise. He had to meet her, but she was shy, he could see that. It was clear she wasn't going to leave the safety of that corner booth. And despite his best efforts, he was unable to catch her eye.

When wingman Bob returned from the gents, Michael wasted no time asking about her.

'Yeah, I know who you mean,' Bob said. 'Stunning, isn't she? Yep, she's single. Plenty of fans, as you can imagine, but nobody on her arm, or anywhere else.'

Michael was elated. Sure, she was out of his league. Years younger. Decades, maybe. Way too pretty. She was perfection. But, surely, he had no chance. *How can she be single?*

'Want to meet her?' Bob asked.

Michael stared at him, realising this could all end in huge embarrassment. But looking back to see her smiling and laughing, he realised it didn't matter. He had to try. It was worth the potential embarrassment. She was heaven.

'Stay here. I'll be back,' he said, with a half-decent Schwarzenegger impersonation.

Michael watched as his pal approached her. But then Bob suddenly stopped short. *What's he…? Oh no.* Michael had that sinking sensation. The wrong girl. He was asking the wrong girl. Michael couldn't believe what was happening. And then it just got worse. He was bringing her over, a grin plastered across his face. There was no time for Michael to do anything, even if he could think of something, which he couldn't. A thousand lines went through his mind, but none were right and now it was too late.

'Michael,' said Bob, 'this is Amber. Amber, Michael.'

'I hear you're a doctor?' said Amber.

Oh, this is awkward. Michael had two options. He chose the wrong one. 'Hi, Amber is it? I'm Michael, yes. Yes, I'm a doctor. Not of medicine though…' He stopped. He had to stop. The girl of his dreams was across the room and here he was speaking to…

'I'm her sister,' she said.

He literally did a double take. 'I'm sorry?'

Wingman Bob was confused.

'I saw you, Doctor Michael,' she said. 'I saw you staring at my baby sister. Let me ask you something, doctor…' She was a little drunk. 'Do you want to meet my baby sister?'

He looked at her, unsure if they were on the same wavelength. Yeah, he thought, they were. She knew he had been watching. She knew, thanks to years of men fancying both of them. They were both gorgeous. But there was a difference. When they wanted her, Amber, they went for it. She was approachable, and, with a drink in her, an extrovert. And if they didn't go for her, she probably went for them. Her little sister, on the other hand, was different, as were the men who seemed to want her. They didn't plough in. They looked from afar. They weren't welcomed with a flirt. They were met with a wall of shyness.

Michael wanted to meet her, yes, more than anything. He spoke like an embarrassed child asking for dessert after not eating his dinner. 'Yes,' he said, then cleared his throat. 'Yes, please.'

'She isn't like me,' she said, with a different, sterner tone. Now she seemed more like a bodyguard than a matchmaker. Perhaps she had experience at playing both roles, perhaps they were the same role. She was looking him dead in the eye. This was not a woman to mess with, that was clear. 'She isn't like any other girl.'

He was supposed to be put off by her words, but the opposite was happening.

'She's special, my sister, okay?'

He was sold. He looked at Amber and, as honestly as he could, he replied, 'I know. That's why I have to meet her.' He was worried that he was coming across as rude. Maybe he was. But maybe, looking back, that's what was required to get past this sisterly protector.

He got past.

Susanna was tipsy, but not drunk. Just the right amount of alcohol to keep the conversation flowing and fun. They spoke for hours. Then the party ended and she was leaving, but not before they played a cat and mouse game of guessing each other's middle names. Susanna guessed Michael's was Robert within just a few attempts, but he'd been trying without luck for nearly an hour now. They exchanged numbers and he kissed her on the cheek. Amber watched the whole time, ready to pounce.

Michael sat in the back of the cab. He entered Susanna's number into his phone. He wanted desperately to call her. When he had suggested a second date, all she said was that she didn't consider this evening to be a first date. She had smiled though, and that gave him hope. But then she was probably drunk by that stage, if he was honest with himself. And young. And way too beautiful for him. His confidence drained away in an instance.

'What middle name would you say goes with "Susanna"?' asked Michael.

'Jane,' came an abrupt reply from a barely conscious Bob.

No, Michael had tried that one.

'I dunno, then,' Bob said before he slumped against the cab window and passed out.

Michael unlocked his phone and started a text. He typed a long, gushing message, again and again rewording it to come across as interested but not desperate. The taxi drove them through the city centre. There were red and blue flashing lights up ahead. As they got closer, Michael saw that they weren't the silent sirens of the police but those of a fluorescent shop sign for a tattoo studio. They drove past and Michael instantly knew Susanna's secret.

He deleted the bloated message and instead typed a single word: 'Rose'.

Two minutes later, his phone buzzed and displayed a smile and a kiss. Against all his urges, he didn't reply. *Interested, but not desperate.* Instead, he edited the contact name in his phone from 'Susanna' to 'Susanna Rose'. Even to this day, many mobile phones later, it remained that way.

They sat on the beach reading, blissful, just the two of them in the entire world...except of course they weren't. And here came their babies running up the beach towards them. As usual, their exchanges were half best friend and half arch enemy.

'Oh my God, you have to come and try the water! It's so clear and so warm and so lovely,' said Carissa.

'It's heavenly!' Rachael agreed, and, of course, had to one-up her sister. 'I saw a dolphin swim right past me.'

Carissa, hand on hip, turned to her sister. 'You did *not* see a dolphin.'

'I did! I saw a dolphin! It was so close, it practically touched me.'

Their parents had by now saved their pages and put their novels down.

'Touched you? With what? Its hands?' mocked Carissa.

'Its nose, obviously!'

'Dolphins don't have noses, they have beaks.'

'Same thing, nose, beak, whatever.'

'You're such a liar, Rachael Anne Richards. No dolphin touched you with its nose or beak or snout or hand or anything!'

'I said *practically* touched me, Carissa Rose, not actual touched me.'

'The whole thing is a lie.'

'I did see a dolphin! You're just jealous because you didn't see it and–'

'Well, obviously I didn't see it. It *wasn't there.*'

'Girls, please, enough,' Susanna said.

But Rachael wanted the last word, of course. Under her breath she muttered, 'It was there. It came up to the surface and took one look at your ugly face and then swam away as quickly as it could.'

Carissa heard her just fine. 'Shut up!' she said.

Again, Susanna pleaded with the girls to let it go. Here they were, in the most idyllic setting, with the beach practically all to themselves and all they could do was fight.

'She started it by calling me a liar,' said Rachael.

'No, you started it by lying,' said Carissa.

'Enough!' said Michael. He wasn't the strict one, but the girls knew that he had a line. It was usually because their arguing got in the way of completing paperwork or reading newspapers on a Sunday morning. 'Your mum is right. This is a family holiday. Now, you have five seconds head start before I come after you. If I catch you, dolphin or no dolphin, you're going in that sea head first.'

The girls looked at each other. He had certainly shut them up.

'Five…'

They shrieked, turned and ran flat out.

'Four…'

Michael abandoned the count and chased after his giggling daughters. Susanna watched, laughed and then returned to her trashy romance.

The tide had retreated to its lowest ebb, meaning the beach in front of Michael and Susanna stretched out a hundred yards in front of them before the water's edge, where Carissa and Rachael were catching the waist-high waves on their brand-new boogie boards. The beach was busier now. Two young lifeguards were on duty and were busy topping up their tans. A couple walked along the shoreline hand in hand. An amateur photographer leant against the rocks and attempted to capture the serene setting on a smart phone.

'This was a wonderful idea,' said Susanna, her head on Michael's shoulder. The girls caught a wave together and crashed, each sliding off their boards. Michael and Susanna laughed. 'We need to do this more often.'

'We should have done this years ago,' he said.

Susanna lifted her head and pulled her husband's gaze away from the sea. 'Let's look forwards, not back, okay?'

He smiled. She squeezed his arm. 'God, I love you. You're amazing,' he said.

'And don't you forget it.'

She was the same girl from the corner booth all those years ago. Michael looked back towards the sea. The couple had stopped to hug and kiss. The photographer by the rocks had moved on. The lifeguards soaked up the rays. The girls, post-crash, were arguing over whose fault it was.

'Here we go again. More peace talks required.' Susanna put her book down and started towards the distant shoreline. After a few steps, she stopped and turned. 'Save my page for me?'

'Done,' he said.

Susanna returned from a dip in the lukewarm water. Michael saw her coming and took a moment to admire the physical beauty of his youthful wife. He knew he hadn't fulfilled his vows in recent years, that he hadn't always put her first. He'd been an idiot. He also knew he couldn't repeat that mistake or she'd be gone. The girls too. And rightly so. His life would be over, and it would be all his own doing. He wouldn't let it happen.

She was within earshot now. 'Nice?' he asked.

'Oh, they're right, it really is like a bathtub,' she said. 'You have to try it, honey.'

'Absolutely,' he said. 'Just give me time to finish this book. Apparently, it has a big twist at the end.'

'You and your twists!'

'Yeah, I know. Go and surf some more; show the girls how it's done.'

'I don't know, those waves are getting bigger. I nearly lost my bikini top on that last one.'

Michael changed his tone. 'Hmm…in that case, maybe I do fancy a dip after all.'

Susanna smiled. 'Well, you know where to find *us* if you change your mind.' She walked away flirtatiously. He was about to go after her, but then she reminded him, 'Hope you don't see the twist coming.'

At first, he looked up after every chapter. Susanna and the girls were surfing, splashing each other, jumping over the waves. As the tension built in his novel, he looked up less often.

Michael closed his book. 'Wow,' he said to himself. 'It was the father, all along. Never saw it coming.'

He looked up for the first time in a long while. The tide was moving fast now that it had pushed over the low-tide sandbank. Susanna and the girls were still enjoying the waves, although the water had become choppy from the onshore breeze. They waved to Michael from the sea and he returned the gesture. Then, hand in the air, he froze.

The same figure from before, the one taking photos, was back, taking more photos, but this time they were very obviously of the Richards family in the sea. Michael put his book down and began walking towards the rocks. He didn't call out, but the figure, who immediately jumped down off the rocks and walked away, must have known Michael was coming.

'Excuse me! You! Hello!' called Michael.

There was no response, and instead the photographer disappeared behind a bigger rock.

'Hey, wait a sec!' Michael sped up.

When he got to the rock, he found only boot prints in the sand. He followed them down the beach and towards a grotto. The tide was pushing fast now and the prints were being washed away with every swell that hit the shore. Michael arrived at the man-made cave to find no sign of the photographer. He looked back down at the boot prints and realised that the person had carefully walked back over them and hidden somewhere along the beach. *Susie. The girls.*

Michael felt a sudden thud of fear hit his stomach. He ran back towards his family. It was the hardest he had pushed his body in a long time, and his chest was aching. When he rounded the big rock to catch a glimpse of where Susie and the girls had been, he saw that they were still there, happily playing in the sea, just as he had left them. He calmed himself and slowed to a steady walk, holding his torso. He looked around but couldn't see any sign of the photographer.

When Susanna spotted her husband approaching, she left the water to meet him. 'So, are you shocked?' she asked him.

Michael assumed Susanna was referring to the photographer. 'You saw him?' he asked. 'Did he say anything?'

'What?'

'Did you recognise him?'

'Who? What are you talking about?'

'The man, of course,' said Michael. 'The one taking the photos. What are *you* talking about?'

'The big twist,' she said, 'in your novel.'

He told her to forget the novel. He told her about the figure, and how it was obvious the camera phone had been focused on her and the girls. He told her he had followed, chased, without success. 'Who knew we were coming here?'

She didn't answer. She was still processing what she'd been told.

'Susie,' he repeated, 'who knew?'

She called to the girls to come and join them before answering him. 'Just my parents, your mother, Doctor Reyes…'

'Anyone else?' he asked.

'No,' she said. 'Nobody else.'

Carissa joined them. 'Are you finally coming in, Dad?' She noticed her parents were holding each other. 'What's going on? Mum?'

Michael didn't hesitate. 'Nothing's wrong. Everything's fine.' He looked at Susanna while speaking to Carissa. 'Go get your sister, Carrie. We're leaving.'

14

PATIENT

My beautiful family.

I could see them like never before. My wife, my two daughters. These were more than the visions I'd had. Now, I was seeing them. I was watching them.

15

DOCTOR

Half an hour into the meal, the restaurant the Richards had chosen seemed to be ticking all the boxes. The appetisers – crab meat and celery sticks – were new ones, even for a family who felt they'd experimented with the more unusual Spanish tapas over the years, both when dining out and, more recently, when preparing at home in the Richards' family kitchen.

The decor was right up their street too; it was completely genuine in terms of its attention to detail. The lights were low but accentuating, with a red hue that reflected off each wall just enough to rose the sunburnt cheeks of the three companions Michael was lucky enough to be entertaining. Likewise, the background music was both authentic and modern in a perfect cocktail that reminded Michael of his time in and around Spain's most bohemian city. Even the curtains, although nothing in themselves to marvel at, had a fluorescent quality that seemed to absorb the dark night's neon promises and relay them in a subdued, inoffensive and safe manner for the refined, family-oriented observer inside the safe haven of the Spanish cove.

Perhaps the only downside was the inevitable popularity of the place, which meant it was bursting with diners, with more again waiting, hoping, for a table to become free. Four-people-deep crowds at the bar meant the noise level was way above what the girls were used to, especially for the Richards' Spanish evening, which was, of all evenings, a chance for the family to talk about their day – Carissa of how 'bitchy' the girls were at school; Rachael, of how bored she was at primary and how the new Year 6 supply teacher wasn't up to scratch; Susanna, who did everything she could to not mention Michael's work; and Michael, who did his best not mention his time in Barcelona, despite the menu.

Michael preferred the quietness of home life these days. And while he looked back fondly on those hot and noisy nights in Spain, the hustle and bustle was no match for a comfy armchair. The young drinkers were just starting their evening out, not concluding it like Michael was. *Those were the days*, he thought to himself. And then he looked at the three loves of his life around the table and realised that, no, *these* are the days.

Rose-tinted glasses, that's all it was. And the location, so key to his past, played its part. But he here was, and he couldn't be happier.

The background noise did little to get in the way of the girls' constant conversation. They spoke in silent code, whispers, knowing looks, hand gestures. Michael and Susanna looked at each other, with no idea of what was going on but happy that their girls were not just sisters but friends too.

'We're going to the loo,' said Rachael, and she and her sister jumped to their feet.

Michael did what he always did and over-reacted. 'Mum will go too,' he said, practically shouting.

Susanna put a hand on her husband's shoulder. 'Go ahead, girls' she said. 'We'll wait here.'

Michael sank back into his chair. He fired Susanna a look, but she nodded assurance and he knew not to argue. Just the latest in a long line of times when Michael was overly protective and tried to fix problems before they existed. Susanna knew better.

'They'll be fine,' she said as the girls disappeared into the crowd.

'Yeah,' he said, 'I know. They have each other.'

'They always will.'

'Yes, they will.'

'Now, what's the verdict on the stuffed celery?'

'Hmm…' he said, 'jury's still out on that one.'

It was about three years before that, at an aunt's house, Rachael, all grown up in her own mind, had visited the toilet alone. The crying started when she was unable to get the door unlocked. It was barely a minute, but that was long enough for Rachael to start hyperventilating. Carissa was the one who had talked her baby sister through it.

'Why are you crying?'

'The lock is stuck,' said Rachael through the door. 'I'm locked in, Carrie!'

'Okay, it's all right, I'm here.'

'I can't get out!'

'Okay, Rach, listen, would you feel better if I was in there with you?'

'What?'

'Would you feel better if I was in the bathroom with you?'

'In here?'

'Yes, in there. In there, with you, right now. Would you be okay if I was with you?'

'Yes. I wish you were in here with me.'

'Okay, then.'

'But it's locked.'

'Close your eyes.'

'What?'

'Close your eyes, Rach.'

'Why?'

'Just do it Rach. Trust me, and close your eyes.'

'Okay. They're closed.'

'Good. Keep them closed.'

'I'm scared.'

'*I'm* not.'

'*I* am. I'm really scared.'

'But you're not scared if I'm stood next to you, right?'

'I suppose so.'

'Okay, keep your eyes closed.'

'They are.'

'Right, then, I'm next to you now. I'm right next to you, Rach.'

'No, you're not.'

'Rachael, believe me, I am, I'm right next to you. And I'm going to unlock the door now.'

'Open it, please,' said Rachael.

'I will, Rach, right now. I just need you to help me with one little bit, okay?'

'Okay.'

'Open your eyes now, and look only at the lock.'

'Okay.'

'Push the door and then slide the lock. Right now.'

'I already tried–'

'Quickly, push the door and slide the lock.'

Carissa heard the efforts of her baby sister inches away. 'That's good, Rach.'

'It's not working, it's stuck.'

'No, you've done it. One more thing and then I'll open the door. Just one more thing. Quickly, now *push* the door and slide the lock. *Push*, this time, not *pull*.'

'Please, Carrie, just open it.'

'Push it, Rach. That's it, I can feel you pushing it. Now slide the lock while pushing and I'll open the door. On three. Ready?'

'It's stuck. I can't do it.'

'Yes, you can. On three. One…two…'

Carissa pulled at the door handle as the lock finally slid across. She turned the knob and gently pushed the door open. When Rachael saw her big sister, she started crying again.

'Come here…' said Carissa, holding her arms out.

Rachael buried her face into her big sister's neck. Carissa comforted her, before turning around to see her mother standing behind them, hand over her mouth, tears in her eyes.

The bathroom of the restaurant was the same red hue as the dining area, but the lack of natural light meant it appeared more like a crimson red. Carissa was on look out and was leaning up against the stall door, meaning Rachael, inside, didn't have to lock the door. That was the established routine since that day at their aunt's. Carissa was the lock.

'Is there anyone out there?' asked Rachael.

'Just me, Rach.'

'Nobody else?'

'Nope. Are you done yet?'

'Nearly.'

'Well, come on. I'm hungry.'

'Don't rush me, Carissa, you know I can't go under pressure.'

'For God's sake.'

'I heard that.'

'Yeah, well, I said it *out loud*.'

The roar of the bar area came bursting into the bathroom. Carissa smiled at the two twenty-something-year-old women who entered.

'*Hola*,' said one of them.

'*Hola*,' said Carissa sheepishly.

'Carrie?' asked Rachael.

'It's okay,' said Carissa sticking her head into the stall. 'It's just a couple of Spanish ladies.'

'Do you mind?' said Rachael.

Carissa returned to her post to find the two women giggling at her.

'*Somos hermanas*,' said one of them. 'We,' she said, pointing to herself and her friend, 'er...how you say, sisters.'

Carissa smiled. 'Sisters, yes.'

'Carrie,' came the voice from inside the stall.

'Yes, Rachael?'

'Who are you talking to?'

Carissa rolled her eyes and the Spanish sisters giggled again. 'Nobody. Just hurry up. I'm hungry.'

'Don't rush me.'

The sisters checked themselves in the mirror. They were just starting their night out, thought Carissa. They'd be dancing and partying into the early hours. Maybe on a double date. Sisters who did everything together. Best friends. Carissa wondered if she and Rachael would be that close when they were older. She hoped so.

'*Adios*,' said the women in unison.

Twins, Carissa thought. 'Bye,' she said, and the women left.

The bustling noise infiltrated the room again, drowning out whatever it was that Rachael had just asked.

'I can't hear you,' said Carissa. 'I'm coming in.' Carissa entered the stall to find Rachael zipping up.

'Lucky for you, I'm all done.'

'About time. I'm starving.'

'Well, let's go, then,' Rachael said, pushing past her sister. 'Oh, where have those ladies gone?'

'They left, that's how long you were in there.'

'I wanted to practise my Spanish.'

'Uh, Rach, aren't you forgetting something?'

'I know. I tried to flush it but it's not working. Can you try for me?'

Carissa wondered if the Spanish sisters would stoop so low for each other. Maybe they would, they were twins after all. But Carissa had to draw the line somewhere. 'Yuck. Do it yourself.'

'OMG, Carissa Rose, it's only a little wee.'

'*Your* wee.'

'You don't even have to touch anything. It's one of those fancy flushes, like these taps. Except *these* are working.'

'What do you mean?'

'I mean I tried the flush but it didn't work. You try.'

'No. I'm not your slave. Do it yourself.'

Rachael let out an exaggerated sigh. 'Fine,' she said, as she strode away from the basins and back into the stall, once again pushing past her sister.

'Hey, watch it!'

Rachael tried again to activate the flush. 'See? It's not working.'

Then the sudden noise of the flush working made them both jump out of their skins. It was over in a few seconds, but the noise continued. A different noise, coming from outside the stall. It was the electric hand dryer. The girls looked at each other.

'Who's out there?' mouthed Rachael.

Carissa shrugged. She peered out around the stall door.

The hand dryers, two of them, were on the far wall. There was one on either side of the mirrors. Nobody was using either. Nobody was there.

'I can't see anyone,' whispered Carissa.

'What?' whispered Rachael.

'I said,' Carissa raised her voice to normal levels to compete with the drone, 'I–' But then the noise ceased abruptly, making her words more public than she intended '–can't see anyone.'

They stood there in that stall waiting for another noise – the door opening, the sound of the bar area, other people entering the bathroom, anything to break the silence.

But nothing came. It was only seconds, but to Carissa it seemed like forever. And she could see the terror building in her sister's eyes. She held her hand out and Rachael took it.

More silence.

And then the same noise as before screamed out again: the hand dryer. Carissa felt the squeeze of her sister's hand but before she could return the act, the sound was amplified. The second dryer unit provided the additional volume and the stereo noise was all around the girls. Rachael grabbed hold of Carissa and hugged her.

Carissa reached behind her sister and slowly pulled the stall door closed. She couldn't quite lock it though, as every time she relaxed her hold in order to reach the lock, her little sister squeezed tighter.

'Rach,' she whispered. 'I need to lock it.'

'Don't let go.'

'I have to lock it.'

'No.'

'Okay, okay I won't. *You* lock it instead, then.'

Rachael looked up to see the lock. She looked at her sister.

'I'm here, right next to you,' said Carissa.

Rachael nodded. There were tears in her eyes now. She let go of Carissa with one hand momentarily to slide the lock across on the stall door.

They stood there, holding each other as the noise rained down around them. The echoes of the white noise bouncing off the bathroom tiles sounded like voices. Like someone talking. Calling their names. *Carrie. Rachael.* The man from the beach. The one who Mum and Dad had spoken about in the car. They thought they were speaking in code – fooling Rachael, maybe, but not Carissa. Probably not Rachael either, the way she was holding on to Carissa right now.

'Carissa?'

Carissa heard it that time for sure. She heard the voice calling her name. The drone of the dryers distorted it, but it was there.

'Rachael?'

Whoever it was, he or she knew their names.

'Girls?'

The voice was closer now, on the other side of the door. But the door was locked, because Rachael had locked it. *Rachael. Locked it.* Carissa panicked. She opened an eye. She looked at the lock. It wasn't locked. It was open. And the door was opening.

'I've got you,' whispered Carissa to her baby sister.

'No, *I've* got you,' said the voice.

The girls screamed out, and Carissa felt a hand grab her arm.

16

PATIENT

I'd come so far, and was so close now. So close to being with them. There they were, my beautiful girls. They were so real. After all this time, doubting myself, being doubted by others, here they were. Visions of perfection. I was so close, now. I called out to them. And if I reached out, I could touch them.

17

DOCTOR

'I'm sorry I scared you, girls. I didn't mean to.'

Michael was glad his family was back together and around the table. Carissa and Rachael had been in the bathroom so long that Susanna had gone to find them.

'You properly freaked us out, Mum,' said Carissa.

'I'm sorry.'

'I'm still shaking,' said Rachael.

'Well, you were gone ages,' said Susanna, 'so we had no choice. You're lucky it was me and not your father.'

'She's right,' said Michael. 'Where the hell were you?'

It wasn't like Michael to swear in front of the girls, even mildly. But he had been shaken by their extended absence, especially with thoughts of the beach photographer still swirling around his head.

The girls didn't answer, they just glanced at each other and picked at their main meals, which had now gone cold around the edges.

'What happened?' asked Susanna.

'Nothing,' said Carissa. 'Right, Rach?'

'Yep,' said Rachael, subdued.

The family started eating. A few minutes of silence passed.

'Mum,' said Rachael.

'Yes?'

'The hand dryers.'

'Sorry?'

'The hand dryers in the bathroom. Was that you?'

Michael saw Carissa look up from her food, eager for a response. He coughed to enter the conversation. 'What are you talking about, Rach?'

'The hand dryers were on when I walked in,' said Susanna. 'I assumed it was you two.'

The sisters looked at each other.

'There was nobody else in there?' Michael asked Susanna.

'I don't think so,' said Susanna. 'Girls?'

There was no reply from the girls.

'Carissa?' asked Susanna.

'It was probably the Spanish women. The twins.'

'Who?' asked Michael.

'Just some locals. Nobody.'

'But you said they left,' said Rachael.

Carissa looked at her sister. 'I thought they did, maybe I was wrong.'

'Something's not right,' said Michael, putting his cutlery down with a clatter.

'Michael,' said Susanna, reaching for his arm. 'Calm down.'

He signalled for the waiter. '*La cuenta, por favor.*'

'Michael.'

'It's okay, Susie,' said Michael. 'I'm fine. I'm calm. I'm sorry girls, but it's time to go.'

'Back to the hotel?' asked Rachael.

Michael looked at Susanna, but they said nothing.

18

PATIENT

I put my pencil down on my latest piece – a drawing of my family, faces beaming with sunburn, around a table, enjoying Spanish tapas.

19

DOCTOR

Departures and arrivals were on one half of the flat-screens, the Winnies were on the other half. Even here, in a foreign airport, there was no escape.

They had cut the holiday short. The relaxation Michael had felt back on that beach, before the photographer, seemed like a lifetime ago. If that hadn't been enough to spoil the break by itself, the restaurant bathroom had. They'd tried to enjoy a couple more days in Spain, but everyone had been on edge, Michael especially. It was far from the holiday they'd planned. Susanna had ultimately taken the decision that they should head back home early. Now, at the airport, she was sorting out new flights.

Michael watched from across the departure lounge. He couldn't quite hear what was being said, but he had a good idea of what was going on.

Michael saw his wife collect the replacement tickets and pay what he assumed was a hugely inflated price. He had let her take charge in an attempt to get the best deal; she would always do better than Michael in such situations. But the truth of the matter was they were either paying way over the odds or sleeping overnight at the airport.

'All sorted,' she said, as she approached her family.

'Great,' said Michael. 'Not too painful, I hope.' She shot him a look, and Michael knew not to ask for a figure.

'We still have a few hours,' said Susanna. 'I'm going to get a book. Want one?'

'Thanks,' said Michael, 'but I think I've had enough…drama, for one holiday.'

Susanna kissed his forehead. 'Girls?'

Neither girl showed much enthusiasm, so she made the long walk to the airport bookshop alone.

Susanna perused the psychological thriller section out of habit but ultimately ended up with another romance novel under her arm.

'Good choice,' said the cashier.

'Thanks,' said Susanna.

'Your husband will like, *sí*?'

'I, well, no, probably not… Wait, my *husband*?'

'Yes. Him, he's over there watching,' said the cashier. 'The man, there, watching.'

Susanna turned to look. There was a figure, not Michael, by the entrance and with his back to her, briskly walking out of the shop.

'Your husband, no?'

'No,' said Susanna, to herself as much as the cashier.

'No? Not your husband?'

'No.'

'But he was watching you. He watched you walk around the shop. I thought he was…must be…?'

Susanna quickly paid for the book and returned to her family.

'A fatal… fling,' said Michael, attempting to read his wife's new novel's title as she approached. Susanna was still looking around for the man from the shop. He realised she was flustered. 'What is it?'

'It's nothing,' she said. 'Something silly at the shop.'

Michael took her on his lap.

'What happened?'

'Nothing happened. I didn't even see anyone.'

'*What*? What do you mean? Who didn't you see?'

'Nobody.'

'That's it. I've had enough. Nobody leaves my sight until we're home. We'll be home soon enough. Once we're back, this nightmare is over.'

'I hope you're right,' said Susanna.

'I'm sure,' said Michael.

Michael and Olivia sat opposite each other on the Richards' veranda.

'You're sure?' asked Michael.

Olivia told him she was completely sure, that she hadn't told anybody about their holiday location.

'And you checked in on David, as planned?'

'Yes. He's been a model patient.'

Michael apologised profusely. Of course Olivia wouldn't tell anyone, but he was struggling to find another explanation for what had happened on holiday.

'Who else knew where you were?' she asked him.

Michael told her it was only their parents. That was it. He'd already spoken to them all and they swore they hadn't said anything to anyone.

'Well, neither did I, Michael.'

Michael again apologised.

'Look, there are a lot of nutjobs out there,' said Olivia. 'Maybe it was just a case of the wrong place and the wrong time.'

Michael wasn't entirely convinced, but it was irrefutable that there were mental health problems everywhere.

'Besides,' said Olivia, 'even if someone knew where you were staying, there are so many beaches and coves along that coast, right?'

That was also true. Rachael had picked it randomly on the day just because it looked empty and she was convinced there were dolphins there.

'Hell, I knew where you were going and I'm pretty sure I wouldn't have found you,' Olivia said.

Michael relaxed. 'Just so you know,' he replied, 'the term "nutjob" isn't one we tend to use in the profession these days.'

Olivia smirked. 'Yeah, well, political correctness never was my forte.'

She walked over to Michael and bent down towards him.

'May I?' she asked.

'I…'

She reached for the newspaper laid next to Michael on the rocking chair.

'Oh, of course, yes, go ahead,' Michael fumbled. 'It's not today's I'm afraid. In fact it's from before we went away.'

Olivia flipped the paper over and, to Michael's surprise, sat herself down next to him on the rocking chair.

He shuffled over to ensure she had enough room.

'Wow, five stars.'

'What's that?' he asked.

'Something called *Blade Runner*.'

He sat up and shuffled back toward the paper, and her.

'Hang on, you've never heard of *Blade Runner*?'

'I don't know, maybe.'

'Not even the original?'

'Original *what*?'

'The original film. From 1982.' Michael leaned over. 'This one is a sequel.'

'Ah, I see.'

'You really haven't seen the original?'

'Nope. But then, it was before my time.'

Michael looked at Olivia, and was reminded how young she was. Like his wife, Olivia had not even been born at the time of the original film's release. Michael felt old.

'You think I should see the original first?' she asked, looking into his eyes.

'I do,' he said. 'I'll lend you my copy. Stay here, I'll go get it.'

Olivia put her hand on Michael's arm to stop him. 'Later. There'll be plenty of time for that, later.'

Susanna peeked through the blinds to see her husband and his doctor swinging together in the rocking chair on the porch.

20

PATIENT

I peeked through the window. I was surprised by what I saw. It was Michael. I turned up the radio volume, just slightly.

'...Sykes hasn't been available for comment...'

I tentatively opened the door. He was back from his trip early. Or maybe time had gone faster than I realised, what with my obsessive drawing. I didn't need to say anything, he could see my surprise and beat me to it.

'Hi, David. Sorry to drop by unannounced. I know I said it would be longer...'

It was true I wasn't prepared. But of the two of us, I seemed to be the most together. I could see he was troubled. And that was, if I'm honest, nice to see. A vulnerable side. That was new. A man so measured, so together. A man who had it all. And yet. Here he was, unsure. Unsettled. Undone.

'It's quite all right,' I said, feeling empowered. 'Please, come on in.'

He nodded and shuffled in.

'I trust everything is okay?' I asked, knowing it wasn't, but also unsure of how much to pry. While there was a part of me that liked seeing this side of him, the last time we'd spoken the fabric of our relationship had changed. We weren't *friends*, I kept telling myself, but we were definitely *friendly*. That's what I hoped, anyway. Arriving here, now, unannounced, wasn't a professional thing for a doctor to do. But it was acceptable for a friend to drop by without notice, to chat about whatever. Something he's worried about. Stressed about. To vent. A chat with a mate. Girl problems, maybe, that sort of thing. I really wanted to call him 'Michael', but he'd never asked me to. Not yet, anyway.

'Yes, thank you, all's fine,' he said. 'We just had to come back early due to family issues. Nothing for you to worry about.'

He said it so quickly, not taking a beat, almost like he'd rehearsed it over and over in the car on the way over. The speedy delivery of the words also meant I couldn't get a handle on his tone, and the emotions beneath his words. Was he being dismissive because I was his patient? And therefore had no right to be concerned about his problems? Was it a one-way street, this relationship? Or was he concerned that I had my own issues, family issues, as he put it, to worry about and he genuinely wanted to put my mind at ease as quickly as possible?

'I see,' I said, offering nothing.

He gave a small smile, but nothing more. 'May I?' he asked, gesturing towards the living room. The *art* room.

I nodded, and walked him through.

'Have you been well?' he asked.

'I have, thank you, doctor. Hopefully you'll see that now in my art. I've been drawing a lot. Non-stop, you could say. You may be quite shocked.'

He *will* be shocked, I thought. He'll see that I can draw. He'll see me as an artist. But so much more than that, he'd be able to see that my wife and daughters were real people; my art would show them to be real.

'That's wonderful. And the lessons?'

'The lessons? Ah…'

'Oh, is that a good 'ah' or a bad 'ah'?'

'It's not great.'

'Go on, tell me.'

'The new teacher.'

'Yes?' he said apprehensively.

'Even worse than the first one,' I said. 'He goes on and on, non-stop. Does my head in.'

'Ah,' he said, echoing me. 'Oh dear.'

'I know,' I said. 'Nightmare. Don't get me started.'

'That bad?'

'I'm afraid so,' I said. 'But don't get me wrong. As bad as his constant drone is, I have to say, boy, can he draw. Which has helped me so, so much. As hopefully you'll see when you take a look at what I've done…'

I pushed open the living room door, like I was lifting the lid on Pandora's box. Richards gave me a little nod and smile before he walked through. At first, he didn't even notice my artwork, even though the canvases were everywhere.

'That armchair, is it new?'

'I'm sorry?'

'It's…I like it.'

It was a strange comment, not because it wasn't a nice chair, but because he'd seen it many times before. Perhaps it looked different without all the clothes strewn over it; I'd emptied the room to make more space for the vast amount of art. But, no, the main reason it was so strange was because he didn't see what was going on all around him. And then a heartbeat later, he did.

The canvases that greeted him were quite a sight. There were at least a hundred of them piled up, mostly portraiture pieces. Some were incomplete, but they were all detailed to a level that made my earlier efforts tragic in comparison.

'Wow, you've been…' he took another step before finishing his sentence, '…busy.'

Canvas upon canvas, with the same subjects every time. My beautiful wife. My gorgeous daughters. I was now a decent artist, decent enough to capture them. I'd been thinking about this moment for such a long time, and, despite the unexpected suddenness of Richards' return, I was ready for him to finally see my memories. This achievement was as much his as it was mine. He'd given me the tools and the self-belief. He'd done so very much for me, and now I'd share with him my most special moments.

'My God,' he said.

Had I known he was coming, I probably would have shown them to him in some sort of order. What order that would be, however, I wasn't sure about. At one time, I'd thought chronology made sense, but then, except for the girls' ages, it was hard for me to know which moments came when. Or perhaps, the order that I'd drawn them in. Or perhaps, I could show him my favourite first – but then, would that be my favourite sketch or my favourite memory? The decision had been taken away from me anyway, with his surprise visit. It would be a free-for-all and I couldn't wait for his reaction. I felt like it was Christmas morning, the first one when you realise how much better giving is than receiving.

'I don't understand,' he said. 'What is this?' He turned to me. 'David? What *is* this?'

It wasn't the reaction I'd expected, or hoped for, to say the least. He looked seriously shocked. I'd thought he'd be shocked, but this was different. This wasn't amazed-shocked. This was appalled-shocked. Like I'd done something wrong. Something very wrong.

I said a load of words, half sentences, none of which made much sense. But it didn't matter, anyway; he wasn't listening. I searched his eyes, but then he was gone, moving all over the room, interrogating my pieces one by one. He darted between them, and then finally turned to face me.

He asked the same question again, but more forcefully. 'What *is* this, David? Tell me what this *is*.'

He was scaring me now. I'd done exactly what he'd wanted. He didn't understand? *I* didn't understand. This was his idea all along. I'd brought my family into this world, just as he'd asked me to. And he was right all along. It had worked. It had worked better than I'd ever imagined it could.

He took a step up to me, invading my personal space in a way he'd never done before. He knew I needed my space, and, as a professional, as a friend, he'd always respected that. I was on edge. And then it came, the moment that changed both of our lives forever.

'Why have you drawn my family?'

Silence.

Completely confused, I looked back at my drawings. He did the same. He walked over to them, stood by them. I could see he was getting more and more worked up. But so was I. *What is he on about? What is he seeing?*

'What *is* this?' He approached a sketch of my children playing in the park. 'My daughters? My *daughters*, David! What the hell have you done?'

I couldn't move. I couldn't react. Had something happened to this man, this doctor, this man of science? He was seeing things. Something must have happened to him. On holiday. That's why he was back early. *What had happened on holiday?*

He spun around to see a sketch of my wife skiing. Next to that was one of our children playing in our garden. 'I can't believe you've done this.'

'Done what?' I said quietly. I couldn't tell if he heard.

He was now at the one of my wife smiling on top of the Eiffel Tower. And then another, of her picking out a book at some airport shop. One of the three of them building a snowman in front of our house. An almost finished one of my wife handing our newborn daughter to her big sister.

'Doctor?' I asked.

He didn't hear me. He was somewhere else entirely, lost in his own madness.

'Doctor, what are you talking about?'

He came to one of my most recent pieces, an incomplete sketch of my wife and daughters playing in the sea. He seemed to recognise the scene. 'Oh my God…' He shivered. His shoulders dropped. His eyes glazed over. 'It was *you*,' he said. 'It was you, David. It was you.' He used my name but he didn't look at me. He picked up the canvas to find another behind it – my beautiful wife in her bikini. His muttering became louder. 'It was you. At the beach. And the airport. The other times. Oh my God, the girls, the restaurant. That was you, too. How *could* you?'

What is he on about? 'Beach? Airport? Doctor, I don't…'

'You bastard,' he said.

And in that moment, any ideas of this man ever being my friend vanished.

I didn't know what was happening, what he was accusing me of, but, actually, I didn't care about any of that. I had, up until that point, really believed that Richards was on my side. But that all shattered in front of me as he called me a bastard. The hatred in his voice was something I'd never expected from him. I still didn't even know why he was talking to me in this way. *What could possibly bring him to this?* And then, he told me.

'I can't believe it… I can't believe you've been stalking my family.'

What? I had nothing.

'How could you? After everything. After *everything* I've done for you. How could you do this to me?'

I didn't even know where to start. I was so confused. His accusations made no sense. Stalking his family*?* Drawing his family*?* Something was very wrong here. I felt like the sanest person in the room. That was quite the new sensation for me.

'Doctor, you're not making any sense,' I said carefully.

My attempt to diffuse the situation did little. Beyond my futile words, I really had no idea what to do. He was clearly insane.

He fell back into the armchair that he had, just moments before, in what seemed like a lifetime ago, been admiring. He slapped his hands over his eyes and let out a growl that sounded like it had been pent up for years. I had to keep talking.

'These drawings, these are the memories I told you about. These are my memories, doctor.' No response. His hands were still covering his face. I continued. 'This is…*my* family.'

He pulled his hands down off his face and clenched hold of the chair arms on either side of him. For a brief moment, he was distracted as he rubbed the leather and fingered the stitching.

'This is my family,' I said again.

'*Your* memories?' he said. '*Your* family? How dare you?' He was livid. He dug his nails into the leather, jumped to his feet and grabbed the nearest canvas. In a single motion, he cracked it down against the chair. It twisted and smashed apart. It was of my girls.

I went for the canvas, which meant I went for him. 'No,' I yelled. 'No!'

I grabbed it from him but he was already on to another piece. He held it up above his head and threw it to the floor. I had to stop him. He started wildly tearing and ripping through all of these pieces that I'd spent so long remembering and perfecting. He had completely flipped.

'Wait! Please, Doctor Richards, stop. Stop!'

But he couldn't hear me.

I had no choice but to stop him, whatever it took. He was important to me, yes, but not like *them*. I hadn't come this far to have anyone, even him, take them away from me now. These were my pieces, these were my memories and they were my family. And nobody was about to take them away from me. Not again.

I grabbed hold of his shoulders and yanked him towards me. He pulled away, but his hands were still searching for sketches to destroy. I was stronger than him. He lost his footing and fell to the floor with a thud. He kicked out at the easel and it came crashing down. He was like a wild animal. He got up and thrashed through another portrait of my wife, and then tore up a piece that showed my daughters reading together.

I put my hands on him again and, like a wrestler, grappled him to the floor. His limbs went in every direction and he caught me on the side of the head. My loosened grip allowed him to writhe away from me and slip from my grasp. I launched forward and caught him from behind, harder than I'd planned. I knocked him down with force. As he fell, he cracked his head on the corner of the glass table. There was a huge thud, and then silence. He lay motionless.

And then, a few seconds later, the blood started oozing from his head. The situation had flipped. I was the bad guy again. I'd done this. I froze for a moment before grabbing the phone and calling 999.

There was a delay while I searched for the right words. 'Please, please… There's a man here who needs help. His head is bleeding. He did it himself. He hurt himself…' The operative told me that someone was on the way.

I looked around the flat, trying to work out what I was guilty of.

21

DOCTOR

Michael didn't like to make a big deal out of his own issues. Other people's problems, yes, but his own, not so much. His head bandaged up, he sat in his leather armchair, in his living room, flanked somewhat awkwardly by his wife Susanna to his left and his doctor Olivia to his right. They'd met each other before, of course, but this occasion was far more intimate. Michael, who should have been focused on the issue at hand, could think only about the differences and similarities between these two young women on either side of him. Just the idea that they were both there for *him* stirred something deep within.

A police officer sat opposite them. Officer Allen had just talked through the entire judiciary process. The bizarre backstory of this case aside, the incident was otherwise nothing he hadn't likely seen a hundred times before. Therefore, he seemed to have all the information on hand and was prepared for just about any questions.

'What does "maximum" actually mean, officer?' asked Susanna.

'It means there's zero chance of him getting anywhere near you or your family,' he replied.

When he spoke, the officer directed his eyes and answers towards all three of them, which Michael could sense irked Susanna. He wasn't sure it was a good idea for both her and Olivia to be here for this, but he wasn't sure about a lot of things any more. Besides, he wanted to make sure Olivia was safe too.

'Thank God,' said Susanna.

She held on to Michael's arm more demonstratively than she usually did. Just when they had got over Michael's heart attack, this had happened. *What is happening to this family?*

The officer continued. 'The only question I don't have an answer to is how long. That will be decided at the hearing.'

'But we're talking years, right?' Susanna asked. Michael put his hand over his wife's.

'Almost certainly, Mrs Richards,' said the officer. 'Although the fact that he called the ambulance is in his favour. That makes it more credible that his story checks out, that it was all an accident.'

'Accident?' said Michael. He pointed to his bandaged head. 'This may have been an accident, officer…' He moved his hand down from his head and was reminded of the head and heart gestures that he and David had made to one another. '…but, but,' he struggled to get back on track, 'but stalking my family was *no* accident. That was very deliberate, indeed.'

The officer clearly didn't want to get into an argument or make any promises he couldn't keep. 'What's important right now is that your family is safe and you can concentrate on recovering,' he said.

'I'm fine,' said Michael. 'The bandage is over the top. I'm ready to return to work.'

'The hell you are,' said Olivia, cutting in before Susanna could. 'No rushing back. I'll take care of you. I mean, I'll take care of everything *for* you. You need to rest.' Before Michael could argue Olivia added, 'Doctor's orders.'

Susanna looked over and forced a smiled at Olivia.

Michael sat at the dining table. In front of him was a healthy, nutritious and completely bland breakfast. It had been a long time since a full English was on the menu at home, and so he'd had to go elsewhere for that fix. At least once a week, he'd visit the greasy spoon across town and order the gut buster – 'Free if you can finish it'. He never finished it, but he wasn't there for that. It was worth every penny of £6.99. Here at home, he faced sugar-free cereal, juice, brown toast with low-fat spread and tea. Since the heart attack, Susanna had banned his staple morning breakfast routine of white bread and coffee. But now she had gone further. This wasn't doctor's orders, this was Susanna being overprotective. Gone was his usual cereal, the one with the cartoon dinosaur on the box, and in its place was a boring bran-based brown one. No dinosaur, no cartoon characters at all and no spot-the-difference game, at which he loved to race Rachael.

Now that all that was gone, he looked around for what could be his treat. He had no option but to settle for kombucha tea. From the start, he'd liked it a little more than he'd let on, but lately he really had acquired a taste for it. There were four or five different flavours and although he couldn't tell which this one was or remember what the flavours were, the unknown factor provided the only excitement in his new breakfast routine; one that he knew would be with him for years to come. Perhaps forever. Joe's greasy spoon seemed like a world away. He wondered if Susanna knew about Joe's. She probably did; she seemed to know everything. If she did, that meant she'd allowed it and turned a blind eye all those times. Which meant she may still do so. But then, the cartoon dinosaurs were gone. Michael took a mouthful of the *Mint, maybe?* kombucha tea and tried to picture alternative cafes around the town he could frequent instead. They might have their own gut buster, or they might not. They'd have bacon, though, that was for sure.

Susanna appeared, as if she had entered his mind to stop any bacon-based ideas before their aroma took hold. He took another sip of the tea. 'Mint?' he asked.

She walked over, leant down and smelt the drink. 'Hey! I think you might be right,' she said, kissing him on the forehead. Carefully and purposely, she placed the post on the table next to his orange juice.

She began preparing the girls' breakfasts, which, Michael noticed, included dinosaur cereal for Rachael. He saw an official stamp on the topmost letter. It was the news they'd been waiting for.

They hadn't spoken about the incident so far this morning, and that had been nice. Last night, Susanna had suggested they have the whole day to themselves, today. There wasn't any more they could do until they heard some news, so they could try to forget it was even happening.

Michael had agreed, and, so far this morning, it had been working. But the letter would change that; he knew that and she knew that, assuming she'd seen the stamp too. Of course she had, she always sorted through the post and put the most important items on the top. *Why would today be any different?* Maybe they could ignore it for the day, as they'd planned. He finished his tea and turned to look at Susanna. She had her back to him, cutting lunch sandwiches now.

'It's okay,' she said. 'You weren't to know it would arrive today. It's early. But it's okay, we can ignore it tomorrow instead.'

He knew that wouldn't happen; once that letter was opened, all they would be thinking about would be the hearing. 'I love you, Susie.'

She turned around and told him with a smile to eat his breakfast, and then he heard the elephant stampede of his daughters heading down the stairs.

Michael stood at the French windows looking out over the lawn. The weather was 'unsettled', as the TV weatherman had put it, which actually meant it was windy and raining. Which, Michael thought, was actually not unsettled at all, quite the opposite, considering it had been like that for weeks now and would no doubt continue to be so. There were no birds around to land on the bird table Rachael had made at school. The bird food went uneaten.

Susanna entered the room behind him.

'Thursday,' Michael said, without turning around. 'The hearing is this Thursday.'

'That was quick,' said Susanna. 'Are you going?'

Michael didn't need to consider it, but he didn't answer. To his delight, a robin had found the bird table. He watched intently as it picked away at the food, which looked a lot like his own breakfast today.

'You're considering it?' Susanna asked.

'No. No, I'm not going. We've already decided.'

Susanna walked over and held her husband tightly from behind. 'I know. But I'll understand if you want to.'

'Look at that robin,' he said, 'not a care in the world except finding food. Which he has. What does he worry about? What a life.'

Susanna just held him. Their lives together had been full of joy, but they had also had plenty of woe. That was life. Complicated.

'I think Thursday would be just perfect for a fun family day out,' Michael said. 'Maybe we could try that adventure park with all the zip wires Rachael's always talking about. What do you think?'

'They have school,' Susanna said into his back.

He nodded. *Of course they do.*

'Carissa has exams at the end of the month. She can't miss any school.'

He was still nodding. 'Of course, yep. Bad idea,' he said.

'No, good idea, just bad timing.' She stretched around and squeezed him. 'Instead, I was thinking maybe cinema? I hear the new Harrison Ford movie is worth a look. You know, the one with the robots.'

Michael sniggered.

'How about it?'

'It's over two hours long, Susie. It's not your thing. You really don't have to…'

'Hey. *You're* my thing.'

Michael turned to his wife.

'Besides,' she continued, 'afterwards you can take me to the most expensive restaurant in town.'

Michael kissed her. 'No zip wires?'

'No zip wires.'

The restaurant was extravagant, not their usual sort of haunt. Not that they didn't eat out, and eat well, but they had their favourites – mostly Spanish – and tended to stick to them. Michael knew a few restaurant managers in the city and took advantage of this, usually in terms of getting the best tables or specials that weren't on the menu. On occasion, even eating out for free. But this place was on another level. The chef had two Michelin stars and a clientele of B-list celebs. Michael had once been taken there for a business lunch, but he wasn't paying that time. The place was booked up months in advance – in the evenings, that is. A Thursday late lunch slot meant Michael was just about able to get a table for two at a few days' notice.

'So she was his daughter, right?'

'Yep,' said Michael.

'And the new blade runner, he was his son?'

'No.'

'No?' asked Susanna.

'No. Well, I don't *think* so.'

'I thought they were twins or something.'

'Early on I thought that too. We were meant to think that. But later we found out that wasn't the case. The memories weren't…his.'

'I think maybe I rested my eyes during that bit.'

Michael was elsewhere.

'Or possibly, just briefly nodded off. Just briefly. Michael?'

Michael spoke, but to himself. 'The memories weren't *his*…'

'Okay I admit it, I fell asleep.'

'Yes,' Michael refocused, 'the snoring suggests that, yes, yes you did.'

'Oh god, did I really snore?'

'Yep. But a cute little snore.'

'I'm not sure any snore is cute,' she said.

'It doesn't matter, we were the only ones there. The perks of 10am viewings.'

'You enjoyed it though?'

'More than I could have ever hoped,' said Michael.

The meal, like the film, had lived up to his expectations, too. Susanna had picked apart a wild goats' cheese salad. Michael, as a special treat and with permission from both his wife and his doctor – who he had phoned to check with, much to Susanna's obvious annoyance – had ordered the *boeuf en croute* and polished off every mouthful in record time. Which was why he was struggling to finish his coffee *crème brûlée*. Susanna, known for having a sweet tooth, had already destroyed her bread and butter pudding and was eyeing up Michael's remaining desert.

'And we still actually don't know if Deckard's…?'

'Nope,' said Michael. 'They were smart, the filmmakers. They told this whole new story that builds perfectly on the original, and the really clever thing is that it works whether you believe he's a replicant or not. I mean, there were some clues, I think. But I'd need to see it again to be sure.'

'I might pass on another viewing if that's okay?'

'You've done your time,' said Michael. 'I won't put you through any more.'

'Thank you.'

'No, thank you, Susie.'

Michael, dressed in an awkward mix of his finest top and tails and a more standard lunchtime attire, was blown away by the spectacle that was his beautiful wife. Nothing awkward there. No half measures. She wore a black dress that both matched her elegance and the daytime date perfectly. Her hair was up, which was a rarity, and showed off the earrings that complemented the pearl necklace around her neck.

'You look...sensational,' he said, knowing no other word would suffice.

But just before Susanna could fully appreciate the sentiment, the moment was interrupted by Michael's mobile phone vibrating in his pocket. They'd agreed to leave it on, even in the cinema, knowing that news from the hearing was due at some point. Despite that, the timing of the call still irked them both.

'It's okay, take it,' Susanna said, although Michael sensed she spoke with as little annoyance as she could muster.

Michael smiled apologetically, picked up his almost untouched dessert and passed it to her. He walked around, kissed her forehead and left the restaurant.

The car park was full of expensive cars. It was like a show court. An employee of the restaurant was washing each of them, a perk of the service. Michael had been too slow to take the call, so he dialled the number back. It started raining again, so he opened up the umbrella he'd been handed by the *maître'd* as he'd left. The dialling tone rang and rang for what seemed like forever. The *crème brûlée* would be gone, he thought, trying to distract himself. Another Bentley pulled into the car park and parked right in front of Michael. He smiled under his umbrella, realising that these people don't stand in the rain, umbrella or no umbrella.

The phone finally connected and he spoke to Olivia.

'Okay. Yep. Got it. Thanks for letting me know. Appreciate it. Much obliged.' He hung up.

The *crème brûlée* was gone, long gone. Michael sat back down and waited for his wife to ask the question. He wasn't sure how she would react. It was years, yes, but only just.

'Forty months,' Susanna said very matter-of-factly. She'd done the maths quicker than Michael, who'd had to ask Olivia to confirm that in years. 'That's not even three and a half years.'

Michael went into reassurance mode, despite the fact that he himself was also feeling hard done by. 'That's minimum, for good behaviour. It could be longer than that.'

They both knew it wouldn't be longer than that. Although they hadn't discussed it in detail, and not at all during the fancy lunch, they'd both had a figure in mind. One that would see both girls through secondary school. This fell well short of that.

'Did she say anything else?' asked Susanna.

Michael considered not telling her. It wouldn't help after all. But, no. This was the end of one era and the start of a new one, one where the truth and complete honesty was needed.

'She's been to see him. Apparently, David is more certain than ever that you're his wife and the girls are his children.'

'It makes my skin crawl.' Susanna pushed the empty dessert pot away from her.

'He's clearly more ill than I realised,' said Michael. 'Than anyone realised. I'm sorry, Susie.' She ignored the apology, and Michael knew that the time for such words had come and gone. She'd moved on, and he needed to as well.

'It's over,' she said. 'That's the main thing. We can move on with our lives. We never have to hear the name David again, we never have to see him again, we can finally just–'

Michael squirmed in his seat.

'What is it?'

He went to take her hand but she withdrew, just enough to indicate 'Don't touch me, just tell me.'

'It's just one more thing. Olivia has been to visit him–'

'You already said that.'

'Well, apparently David has asked to apologise…to me…in person.'

Susanna withdrew her hands completely, reached up and touched her brand new necklace. She took her time in responding. 'If you're going, Michael, go now.'

He wasn't sure what she meant. '*Now*?'

'Yes, Michael, now,' she said, looking him dead in the eye. 'I want this over. This whole ordeal. I want it over today. Today, Michael. Do whatever it takes.'

He took a deep breath and nodded. 'I'll drop you–'

'No, you won't. I'll take a cab home.'

She glared at him. He gestured for the bill.

22

PATIENT

The guard was a big guy – as wide as he was tall, and he was plenty tall enough. He was young too, for a guard, I thought. Probably fresh out of training. He was on the phone, listening intently. His name badge said 'Jones'.

'Very good, sir,' he said, and replaced the receiver.

Waiting next to him was a man, and, although he was hidden from my view, I knew who it was. I'd expected his visit, although not quite so soon.

'Sorry,' said Jones. 'I have to check.'

'Of course,' came the unmistakable voice of Doctor Richards.

'People aren't always who they say they are,' said Jones.

'Yes, indeed.'

'I didn't mean, you know, that I thought you was lying or nothin'.'

'It's quite all right,' said Richards. 'Can't be too careful.'

They walked down the corridor towards my cell. Jones, apparently concerned about how long the visit might take, made it clear to Michael that his shift was over in a half an hour.

'Don't worry,' Richards said, 'this won't take long.'

He sounded driven, like he knew clear as day why he had come. *This will be interesting.*

It was a long walk to my cell. Long enough for the guard to do to Richards what he'd already done to me, and I suspect everyone else he'd ever met.

'Not like, in the same, like, way,' said Jones. 'But, you know, kind of the same.' Only the two sets of footsteps revealed he wasn't talking to himself. 'Like, he lifted a 4x4, you know, in one go. In one go. Impressive, you've got to admit.' He barely took a breath and certainly didn't wait for a response. 'It's not that *I* couldn't do that, it's more, like, well, I ain't had the chance, you know? But what I did do, can do, is pretty impressive too. If I told you, like, I reckon you'd be impressed, like. No doubt.'

It went on and on. He'd bored me with the same nonsense more than once. That was the worst part of this particular holding cell, Jones's idiocy in thinking he had superhuman powers.

When they finally arrived at my door, the guard knocked twice and then slid across the small window. 'Visitor!' he said.

He stepped aside to allow Richards a glimpse inside my cell. I saw him squinting to try to make sense of the darkness. *Just enough light to work by.*

'David?' he asked, as if uncertain it was me who was sat drawing in the middle of the room.

'Yes, doctor, it's me,' I said, but I didn't stop what I was doing. 'Thank you for coming.'

'Yes, well, I'm sure it will be worthwhile.'

I looked more closely at him. He was wearing a dinner jacket. He'd come from something important. That made *this* important. 'I do hope I haven't pulled you away…'

He looked down at his outfit and cleared his throat, but said nothing.

'How is your head?' I asked.

He reached up to gently touch the wound, as if needing a physical reminder of what had happened. I could tell he wasn't sure how genuine my concern was, but he seemed to treat it as sincere.

'Fine, thank you,' he said.

'I truly am sorry about that, doctor,' I said. 'I hope you know it was a complete accident, what happened that day at the flat.'

Again, he said nothing. My attempt at reconciliation clearly hadn't worked. When he did finally speak, his words baffled me. 'I came here for an apology, David.'

Didn't he just get that? Did he bang his head harder than I realised? Is he still insane?

I put my pencil down for the first time since he'd arrived. I slowly stood up and walked over towards the door. I got closer. There he was. Doctor Richards. I thought about how close to being friends we had once become. It was so ridiculously far from where we were now, that I could only smile at the sorrow of it all.

He was behind glass. That was probably a good thing. With our faces now mere inches apart, I could see the anger building beneath his skin. What I was going to say next was only ever going to make that worse.

'You came for an apology?'

'Yes, David.'

'I see.'

'Well?'

'And I can see that you came from somewhere important,' I said, '*for* your apology.'

'Okay,' he said, 'I see what you're doing. Enough games, David.'

'Doctor?'

'Look, I can see you aren't sorry. All right, yes, actually, I have come from somewhere important, much more important than you, so get on with it.' His words had venom in them.

'Get on with what?'

'The apology, of course,' he said. 'Sincere or not, I really don't care anymore. But seeing as you managed to get me here, I'd really quite like to hear you say the words.'

'You came here to hear me say sorry, right?'

'That's right.'

'So, then, you can leave now.'

'What?'

'You've had your apology, Doctor Richards. I said I was sorry, that it was an honest mistake, an accident.'

'What? No. Not my head. This isn't about my fucking head, David.' I'd had no idea he ever used such language. 'This is about my family, goddamn it.'

I narrowed my eyes, gave him a smirk and then turned my back on him.

'Apologise for my family, David!' he said, as I walked away.

I stopped, looked back at him and calmly delivered the truth he needed to know. 'You mean, *my* family, doctor.'

I sat down and once more started sketching.

'Are you ready to leave, then?' asked Jones, looking at his watch.

'No, I'm not,' said Richards. 'Not without my apology.'

I continued drawing. It was nearly complete, this, my latest piece.

'You hear me, David? I want my apology and I'm not leaving until I…' He stopped midsentence. His eyes must have adjusted to the dim light. I heard him push his face up against the opening to better see inside my cell, and then he blurted an instruction at the guard. 'Open this cell!'

I looked up. He repeated his order, this time looking Jones dead in the eye.

'Sir?' asked the guard.

'I need you to open this cell immediately.'

Jones stood his ground, chest puffed out, chin up. But there was uncertainty in his eyes. Maybe it was his youth, or his lack of intellect. Still, his body language was enough to tell Richards that it would take more than an empty order to get into my cell.

'There's evidence in there,' he said.

'Evidence?'

'Yes, evidence. Evidence that he's been stalking my family.'

'What evidence?'

Richards looked at me again, at my work, for confirmation. *You're right, doctor, you were right first time. You saw it.*

'This is most unusual, sir,' Jones said.

Richards was having none of it. He was convinced, and he was pretty convincing. He used the guard's youth against him, played the position-of-authority card. 'The person on the phone. She told you to do as I ask, no?'

'Yes, but–'

'Your job right now is to do as I say.'

'Yeah, but–'

'And I say, open this cell door immediately.'

'I need to make a call–'

'Do not make me ask again or your job will become someone else's.'

I'd never heard Richards speak like that to anyone. I didn't know he had it in him. I guess I was bringing it out. I suddenly felt a little guilty, for what I'd done to this man who'd helped me so much. But it was time for him to learn the truth.

Jones still wasn't on board.

'You like your job?' asked Richards, somewhat rhetorically.

'Yes, sir. Yes, I do.'

'You have a family to support?'

'I-I have a family. Yes.' Jones looked down at the ground.

'This is not an empty threat. If you do not open this door, I will do everything in my power to…' and then he seemed to stop himself. He changed tact, lowered his voice. 'Listen.' He put his hand on the guard's muscle-bound shoulder. 'Listen, this is bigger than you or me. You can trust me, okay? This is possibly the most important decision you will ever make. You could be…a hero.'

Jones looked around, at us both, gave a huge exaggerated sigh and then gestured for me to step to the back of the cell, something I'd become accustomed to doing since being incarcerated. I complied.

Of course I complied. After all, this was the moment I'd been waiting for.

The second the door was unlocked, Richards pushed past Jones and straight up to my latest piece. 'My God.'

There she was, my wife, sat in a restaurant in a little black dress. Her hair was up. In her hand was a black box. That's what I'd drawn. But I saw more than that. I saw that he'd see it. That he would be freaked out by it. He would claim this was *his* wife. But it wasn't. He was delusional. This was *my* wife. I'd even remembered her name: Susie. And our girls, Carrie and Rach. With every sketch I drew, they came back to me a little more, and soon it would be time to be reunited.

This recent vision had come to me only in the last hour or so, but it had been the most vivid one so far. It was beyond memories, beyond visions. It was something else. A sixth sense. It was *known*.

And so, because this latest moment, Susanna in the restaurant, was so very real to me, it took no time whatsoever to replicate on paper. But the picture wasn't quite complete. For the life of me, I couldn't see, couldn't remember, whatever it was in the black box that she held. It was a gift from me, I remembered that much. I'd put her through so much, and yet she'd stood by me. But what the gift was, that still escaped me.

'Sir?' said Jones.

When Richards finally spoke, it was only to himself. 'This was today. This was just now, an hour ago. What the fuck is this?' He spun around. 'Has he been out?' Jones looked baffled.

I stood back and let the moment unfold.

'Err…no, sir. He hasn't been out of his cell,' Jones finally said. 'That's not how it works.'

When Richards asked if he was sure, the guard reminded him of how his shift had started nearly twelve hours ago and was about to end.

Richards clutched at straws. 'Phone calls? Has he spoken to anyone?'

'He's *under arrest,* sir.'

'Nobody at all?'

'Just you and Doctor Reyes.'

Enough. I interrupted with some breaking news. 'It's a pearl necklace, isn't it?' I had Richards' attention. 'In the black box?'

'No, it can't–'

'No?'

'No, I mean, how can you–'

'Am I right?'

'Who told you that?'

Doesn't he get it yet? I spelt it out for him. 'I just remembered, right now. Not all the details came to me right away. But I remember now; I gave my wife a pearl necklace.'

Richards just stared at me. I returned the favour. But then I realised that he wasn't looking at me, he was looking *past* me. Beyond me. Behind me. He was looking at my other pieces. I had maybe ten or twelve drawings, mostly unfinished, in the cell. It had been Doctor Reyes who'd allowed me the equipment and the privilege to continue with my pieces. It should have been up to Richards, but she didn't want to trouble him with the decision. Instead, she took it upon herself, claiming I was more dangerous if I wasn't allowed to draw. I'm not sure I would have been more dangerous, but I don't know what would have happened if the visions had kept coming and I wasn't able to get them out of my head, especially now that I was technically able to. It would have been too much.

Richards was looking at one of the sketches I'd completed that morning. 'That one…what is that?'

It was of the girls playing video games in the living room. Carrie was sprawled out over the sofa, losing interest in playing every time her mobile buzzed. Rachael and her dog had swapped roles – Rach sat on the floor with her flexible legs curled up below her and Ginga was curled up snugly in the armchair. My armchair, with its worn light brown leather and dark brown stitching. I could see it and feel it as clearly as anything else. He walked over to the sketch and touched the girls' faces, then the stitching of the chair.

'Is that…'

He recognised his house. But before he could even communicate his newfound understanding, something else grabbed his attention. 'What the–' This was it. The beginning of the end. 'What is that? What are these drawings? Is that…my dining room?'

Well-spotted, doctor. Well-drawn, me. It was another one that I'd finished that morning and it was, technically, one of my best. 'That's the real reason I asked you to come, Michael.'

It was the first time I'd ever addressed him by his forename. He didn't notice. His attention was elsewhere, on the sketch of a shadowy figure hovering over Susie and the girls while they were seated at the dining table. There was something in the figure's hand.

'That person,' he said. 'I've seen him before. The way he's looking at them. It was at the beach. That's the person I saw at the beach. Was that you?'

'No.'

'David, that *was* you.'

'It wasn't and it isn't. I promise you.' I let it soak in just for a moment, before hitting him with what he needed to hear. 'But I believe they *are* in danger. Right now, they're at the mercy of…'

He stared at me. 'Who?'

'I can't be sure about details, but…' I stopped talking again and closed my eyes as tightly as I could. It helped. I shook a little.

He asked what I was doing. I told him to be quiet.

'There's something…holding something…what is that?' I asked myself.

'What?'

Ssh. 'It's…' I opened my eyes. 'Shit. It's gone. Damn it. But whoever it is, Michael, they mean Susie and the girls harm.'

'My God.'

'You need to go.' I used his name again. 'Michael, you need to go now.'

He was a statue. He didn't understand what was happening.

'Michael, look at me.' He looked through me, trying to find sense. 'Look at me.' He blinked, and tears rolled down his cheeks. 'You know I'm not making this up. They're going to be hurt. You have to go. Now.'

I'd convinced him. He knew it to be true, finally. He nodded. He turned and headed towards the cell door and a very confused young guard.

I had one more vision. 'Reyes,' I whispered. He stopped dead in his tracks. I made sure my eyes were shut when he turned.

'What did you say? Say it again.'

'Reyes,' I said. 'Michael, it's Doctor Reyes.' My eyes were still shut. 'It's always been Reyes, the whole time.' I opened my eyes, and met his gaze. 'Take me with you.'

23

DOCTOR

Rachael and Carissa, still dressed in their school uniforms, were playing Rachael's favourite card game, Uno, at the dining room table.

The radio was on in the background. It was tuned to the Ken Squires show, the official broadcast programme for the Winnies. The volume was loud enough for the girls to hear the big news of the day but not loud enough to get in the way of their game.

It had been the talk of the playground and it had been excruciating for many of the pupils, including Rachael, to have to wait until after school before they heard confirmation of the rumours – that there would be a replacement for the debunked contestant Evan Sykes. Rachael wouldn't believe it until she heard it straight from Damo himself, who was due on the radio any moment now.

As always, Ginga hung about underneath her boss, not understanding that it wasn't dinner time and that no scraps were going to fall his way. And, as was also always the case, it was only a matter of time before an argument broke out between the girls.

'Maybe if you were paying attention rather than looking at your mobile every five seconds, you'd stand half a chance against me,' Rachael said.

'Shut up. You're only jealous because…' the mobile buzzed again and Carissa trailed off mid-sentence.

Rachael muttered something under her breath.

'What was that?'

'Nothing.'

'No, Rachael, what *was* it?'

'I said, *nothing*.'

'Are you scared?'

'Nope.'

'Aww, are you going to cry?'

'Shut up.'

'You suck.'

'*You* suck.'

'Oh, nice come back, Rach.'

'Yeah? Are you going to reply to your text? "Ooh, I love you," ' Rachael said in a high-pitched, whiny voice. ' "I love you, text me back, please, please, please, kiss, kiss, kiss." '

'Shut up!'

'You shut up!'

'God, you're annoying.'

'God, you're vain.'

'Yeah, well, you'll be a teenager soon. You'll realise how hard it is.'

'Whatever.' Rachael attempted to shuffle the cards. 'How is Pete, anyway?'

'None of your business.'

'Do you *love* him?'

'I said, it's none of your business.'

' "Oh, Pete, Petey, Pete, Pete…" ' Rachael said, before picking up Ginga and cuddling him as if he were Pete and she were Carissa, much to Ginga's confusion and irritation.

The dog had learnt over the years to just let it happen. Now, approaching his more senior years, he was too docile to care and too tired to fight back. Carissa looked at her little sister slow dancing with the poor pooch and tried desperately not to laugh. But she failed, as she always did.

'If you must know,' Carissa said, 'it's not Pete, okay? Pete is old news. It's Kevin.'

'Kevin? Kevin! Ha ha! "All right, Kev?" ' Rachael said to Ginga. ' "How's it going, Kev?" '

Carissa laughed again. 'Oi, you, nothing wrong with the name Kevin. I think it's sweet.'

Rachael put Ginga down and returned to shuffling her cards. 'You don't half get through them, Carrie. Who's it going to be next week? Ronnie?'

'Who the hell is Ronnie?'

'I don't know, I just like the name. Think it's sweet.'

Carissa rolled her eyes, Rachael sniggered to herself and Ginga recovered on the floor.

It was unusual for them to be home alone, but they knew that the folks' meal together was a big deal.

'Shouldn't they be home by now?' asked Rachael, without looking up from her cards.

'I guess.'

'Do you think they'll be okay?'

It wasn't the first time she'd worried about them, nor the first time she'd asked Carissa for reassurance. When their dad had had his heart attack, they'd witnessed first-hand how hard it had hit their mum.

'They'll be fine, Rach. Don't worry.'

Her words were less than convincing. Still, Rachael liked to hear her big sister say them. Once, when they were younger and Rachael really had no idea what was going on, Carissa held her all night. They shared a room back then, not because of a lack of space in the house but rather through choice and circumstance. Problems between Michael and Susanna, arguments in the night, meant Rachael would slip into her parents' room. At first, her presence had helped diffuse the situation. Then, less and less so. And so, instead, she'd started going to Carissa for comfort. When her parents realised she was spending more nights with her sister than in her own room, they gave in and made the situation a semi-permanent fixture. It wasn't necessary now that she was older, but she still felt she needed the comfort Carissa brought her, and, on those occasions, all the silly arguments between them meant nothing. Carrie was there for her little sister when it mattered.

Everything was fine with the Uno game for the best part of half an hour. Rachael shuffled, Rachael dealt, Rachael kept score.

Carissa texted on her phone and occasionally showed interest in the game Rachael was playing against her. But then Carissa showed a little more interest, and that's when the trouble started.

'Wait a sec,' she said. 'What're you doing? You can't do that.'

'Yes, I can,' said Rachael.

'Oh my God, you always do this. You can't just put down when I've already made you pick up two!'

Carissa's logical approach to things had never held much weight with Rachael's wild imagination. 'Who says I can't?'

'The rules say you can't. That's who.'

Rachael didn't hesitate to defend herself. 'We're not playing normal rules. We're playing the Richards' family rules. Maybe if you weren't glued to that phone you would've known that. Let me remind you that in the Richards' family rules, you can put down this card, without first picking up. So now you need to pick up four. Ha!'

Olivia Reyes stood before the family home she was ready to destroy.

It had been a long time coming, and she'd prepared for this moment like a master tactician, like a chess grand master. All the pieces were in place now, and she'd deliver the killer blow tonight. When she woke up tomorrow morning, her world would be a very different place. As would Michael's.

But first, a little fun. Time to remove the shackles she'd worn her whole life. Before her was the castle she was owed, and now it was time to claim it. She knew Michael wasn't home and would be held up at the cell across town for a while. Susanna, however, would be home soon enough. For now, it was just the girls. She couldn't wait for it to start. *But calm yourself. You've worked too hard, waited too long and have sacrificed too much to get carried away and enjoy yourself too soon. It won't be long before Susanna's home. So play it cool. Don't blow it now.*

'So, what happened to Pete?' Rachael asked.

'Don't ask.'

'I liked Pete.'

'You've never met Pete.'

'I haven't?'

'Nope.'

'Not at netball? When we picked you up that time?'

'No, you're thinking of…I don't know who you're thinking of. Anyway, it definitely wasn't Pete.'

'Hmmm. So, what happened to him?'

'I said, don't ask.'

'Shame. I liked Pete.'

'For God's sake, Rachael, you've never met him, okay? And you wouldn't want to. He's not a nice person. You would *not* like him if I told you what he did.'

'Ooh, now you have to tell me.'

'No, I don't.'

'Please.'

'No.'

'Pleeeease.'

'No!'

Carissa got up from the table and went looking through the cupboards. Then the larder. Back to the cupboards again, and then into the fridge. She stuck her head right in and searched around for any post-school, pre-dinner snack she could find.

'If you must know,' said Carissa, with her head still in the fridge, 'he was going out with Tracy Legowski behind my back.'

'No way!' said Rachael.

'Yes. Are you happy now?'

'What a scumbag.'

'See, told you.'

'And isn't Tracy your *friend*?'

'She was. Not any more. I'm never speaking to that slut again.'

'Wow. Drama!'

'That's one word for it.'

'My life is so boring,' said Rachael, stroking Ginga, who had perked up when he heard the fridge door open. 'So, she knew about you and Pete?'

'Who?'

'Tracy.'

'Oh. No, she didn't know.'

'Wait, what? She didn't know?'

Carissa returned to the table a few grapes fuller. 'No.'

She could see her baby sister's confusion, her moral compass spinning wildly, trying to find north. 'I don't get it.'

'What don't you get? It's not rocket science. She was my friend, now she's not. He's a scumbag and now I know. Aren't you meant to be the smart one?'

Rachael was smart, and academically curious. Always wanting to learn, from her earliest years. Asking questions. Inquisitive was an understatement. Carissa, on the other hand, was more street smart; anyway, now that she'd hit her teenage years, knowing stuff wasn't exactly cool any more.

'I get why you hate Pete,' Rachael said, 'but not why you're angry at Tracy. You just said she didn't know about you and him. I put it to you, Carissa Rose Richards, that Tracy is completely innocent of any crime here and was simply following her heart, much as you were. And, to conclude, anything that Tracy is guilty of, you, Carissa Rose Richards, are equally guilty of yourself.'

Carissa thought about it for a moment. 'God, I hate it when you use my full name…'

'I know,' said Rachael.

'But maybe you've got a point, except…I was with him *first.*'

'Are you sure?' asked Rachael. She continued her cross-examination. 'Maybe Tracy thinks she was with him first. Have you considered that?'

'Well, no, not really.'

'The bottom line is, it's not Tracy Lingwalski's fault–'

'Legowski.'

'It's not Tracy Legwalksi's fault–'

'Legowski!'

'Well, whatever her chuffin' name is,' said Rachael, 'it's not *her* fault, all right?'

'All right, you've made your point.'

'Okay, then.'

'Fine.'

'Good.'

'Good.'

'So, how are you going to do it?' Rachael asked.

Carissa was back on her phone now. 'Do what?'

'Get revenge, of course.'

'Revenge?'

'On Pete the Scumbag. Oooh, I know, you and Tracy whatshername should team up and get revenge like in those silly American comedies you love so much.'

Carissa didn't say anything. Usually she would bite at that, but she was too busy considering how right her annoyingly intelligent little sister was. 'I might message Tracy,' she said.

'Be nice,' Rachael said.

'…Okay, people, here we go, the one and only Damo…'

Rachael jumped out of her seat and turned the volume on the radio right up.

Olivia walked up to the huge mahogany door and lifted the brass knocker. In a few seconds, one of the girls would answer the door and at that point there was no going back. A deep breath. Knock, knock, knock. She took a step back. There was no need to scare them. Not immediately. There'd be plenty of time for that later. For the inevitable screaming.

'…Hi Ken, great to be here once again…'

'…Thank you for your presence, Damo. As always, it's a delight…'

'Oh my God!' Rachael skipped about. 'Here it is!'

'Not too loud!' said Carissa, without looking up from her phone.

'…Not at all, it's my pleasure, Ken. You do a wonderful job, my friend, keeping everyone up to date with the incredible roller coaster that is the Winnies. Especially this year, you're right. This year more than ever. And you know, in a world of so many online sources of information, let me remind you that it's only here with Ken that you can be sure of the truth. Ken knows it all, and he's been through the process himself, remember…'

Olivia would be nice to them. She'd get them on side. They'd invite her in, make her a drink, have a chat. There was no rush to take him away from them. They'd had years together playing happy families, they could have a few hours more before it all came crashing down. Before Olivia took Michael to be with *her*. He would be hers tonight, that was a certainty, providing Olivia kept to the plan she'd so carefully orchestrated over all these months.

Pawns, all of them: Susanna, David, the girls and Michael himself. She was almost as happy that the plan had worked as she was to get Michael. But that would be her downfall if she let it. *Don't get ahead of yourself.* One evening to go. A few hours from now, when she and Michael would leave this house together to start a new life, that's when she could congratulate herself. Not now, not just yet. Once they were on the run, in hiding, that's when she could lay next to him and tell him just how clever she was and how the whole thing had worked.

There had been no answer to her knocking, so she rang the doorbell. Instantly, she heard the eager footsteps of one of the Richards girls approaching.

And so it began.

Just as Carissa was about to compose her message to Tracy, an interruption: the doorbell. Rachael let out a huff, clearly annoyed that there'd be a disruption just as Damo was on the airwaves. But Carissa knew she loved to play hostess.

Rachael dropped her cards and rushed through the dining room to the front door. 'I'll get it!' she yelled.

'Wait, what about…' Carissa stopped as she remembered her sister's free spirit. Rachael was smart, too. She was *right.* Carissa composed a text to Tracy. 'Hi Trace. Listen I tink we should get together & talk things out. I've realised it's not u who betrayed me, it's Pete. He's d one we should b angry at, not each other. If u feel d same way txt bck.'

The door opened to reveal the younger Richards girl. She looked Olivia up and down with some recognition, but scrunched up her face. 'Good afternoon. How may I help you?'

'Well, hello there,' said Olivia. 'What a lovely greeting. I'm Doctor–'

'Doctor Reyes,' Rachael said. 'Yes, I remember. From the hospital. How do you do?'

'Very well, thank you.'

'I'm very sorry to tell you this, but Daddy's not home.'

'He's not?'

'No, sorry. Mum neither.'

'Really? What a shame. May I come in anyway?'

24

PATIENT

'Take me with you,' I said. 'If you want to save them, you need me. Think about everything you've seen and you'll know I must come with you.'

Whether Michael was convinced or not, one thing was for sure. The guard, Jones, was most definitely not buying it. No chance. He started to take command of the situation, telling Michael to step to the side of the cell, away from me, away from him, away from the artwork that Michael continued to stare at all around us.

'I know what you're going to say, officer,' Michael said, talking with his hands as much as his voice.

'Hands down, sir,' said Jones, his own hands slowly taking position.

'Yes, sorry, look, I know what you're going to say and I completely understand where you're coming from.' He spoke fast, as if not allowing Jones a chance to respond was the same as getting him to agree. 'You're going to say that there's no way the prisoner can leave with me a-and, a-and–'

His stammering left Jones a gap, and when he spoke it was in a much more commanding voice than Michael's. 'He ain't going nowhere, sir.'

I knew that if we were to be successful and get out of this cell, it wouldn't be down to Michael convincing the guard. It would be down to me. I'd been working out an escape plan since the vision of the girls at the dining table had come to me earlier that day. It was such a clear memory – or future memory, or whatever it was – that I could draw it without even thinking. That meant my mind could focus elsewhere and work out other problems such as how to get out of this cell.

Michael continued to argue that I had to leave with him. He wasn't as convincing as I'd been. No matter what officer Jones heard, he simply referred back to the obvious truth, that I was a prisoner and that I was going nowhere without an order from the court. I could sense Michael's imminent defeat. *We don't have time for this! They're in danger.*

'Michael,' I said. I pointed at the sketch. 'This isn't the future, it's right now. This is happening right now, at the house. If we don't move now, it'll be too late.'

Jones took a step back and placed a hand over the baton on his belt.

'We're leaving,' Michael said aggressively, 'and there's nothing you can do…'

He trailed off as Jones took his hand off the baton and reached down inside his sock. 'Sir,' said Jones, pulling out a small handgun, 'I must ask you to leave the holding cell, alone, immediately.'

A non-standard-issue firearm. Jones's own gun. *Shit.* A strange Mexican stand-off, considering only one man had a weapon.

Except that I was also armed.

25

DOCTOR

'They shouldn't be too long,' Rachael assured her guest as they made their way to the dining room. 'And, of course, you're very welcome to stay until they're back. Damo's on the radio.'

'Oh, how very kind.'

'It's no bother at all.'

'Your parents have clearly done a wonderful job bringing you up.' Olivia could see that Rachael loved receiving compliments.

'Why, thank you. I'm told that a lot, but I never tire of hearing it again. Although,' she said, as they approached the dining room, 'let's see if you feel the same way about their parenting when you meet my sister.'

Olivia laughed and they entered to find Carissa clearing away the playing cards.

It wasn't the first time Olivia had been in the Richards' house. She'd been there on official duty a few times, in the early days of Michael's recovery and then, of course, in the aftermath of the holiday from hell. Beyond that, she'd been invited over for dinner on more than one occasion, although she'd mostly declined. It was easy enough to find an excuse in her profession: being on call, working late, extra paperwork landing on her desk. Usually there was no need to make something up, simply to elaborate the truth was enough. The real reason she spurned the invitations, however, was just how awkward she felt around the family. Around Susanna, in particular.

The first time she was asked, Olivia had actually accepted the invitation to dinner. She sat at one end of the dining table directly opposite Michael. His wife sat to his right. The sizeable table was able to accommodate many more than just the three of them. The girls had already gone to bed. It was more of a supper, as Olivia had just finished a late shift. She had declined the offer of bringing a plus one, something that Susanna kept asking about.

'I guess it's the job that makes it hard to meet people,' she remarked. 'The hours and everything?'

Olivia nodded. 'Yes, your choices are somewhat restricted to other medical staff, and, well, I don't need to tell you the dangers of being in a relationship with a doctor.' Olivia looked at Michael, not Susanna, as she said it. No smile, just a look, and then she turned back to Susanna. Then came the smile. Susanna returned it, eventually.

There was no more talk for an excruciatingly long time and then Michael spoke up with a cough. 'Oh, how about John?' he said to Susanna, 'John…what's his name? Accountant John. Bailey, that's it. How about John Bailey?'

Olivia tried to argue, but Susanna latched on to the idea and sprang to life. 'That's a good shout, actually. John's a lovely chap, a widower, unfortunately.'

'Or *fortunately*, you could say,' Michael said. 'I mean for you, Olivia, perhaps… Sorry, that was in bad taste, wasn't it?'

Susanna rolled her eyes at her husband, a man who clearly *listened* for a living. 'Yes, honey. Awful taste.'

'Sorry.'

'But I think you're right. John would be a great match.' Susanna was speaking about Olivia's lack of a love life as if she wasn't even in the room.

'Thank you,' Olivia said. 'I'm sure John's a lovely chap, but, really, I wouldn't have the time, even if I met the right man.'

'For the right man, you find time,' Susanna said, as she placed her hand on her husband's arm.

'Maybe you're right, Susanna. I must admit I'm very jealous of you. What you have here. What you two have, I'd love that for myself.'

It was more uncomfortable than it should have been, probably because even when she was speaking to Susanna, Olivia had a habit of staring directly at Michael. It was so obvious this time that even he seemed to notice, and he visibly squirmed in his seat.

'Maybe I'll give John a call and we can all get together for–' started Susanna.

'If you're asking me who my perfect man is,' Olivia interrupted, 'I guess I'd have to say an older man. Someone who's seen the world, and knows his place in the world. Also, someone who helps people professionally, someone who's gentle but firm. Looks are a bonus, of course, but more important is that he's someone I can trust.'

Susanna's eyes were locked on Olivia.

'John!' Michael shouted. 'You just described John! He must be forty by now, yes, wasn't he forty last year, had that big birthday bash we couldn't make? At the harbour club. And he's so kind. He's an accountant. Wait, he's kind *and* he's an accountant, I mean. Loaded, absolutely loaded too! Not that that matters to you, I'm sure, but you know, the complete package, that's John.'

Susanna barely spoke again for the rest of the evening, not to Olivia nor to her husband, even when they wished their guest a good night.

As she walked down the path, Olivia looked back through the kitchen window. She saw Susanna walk through to the living room and dump a blanket on to the armchair. It told Olivia everything she needed to know about how innocent Susanna felt her husband was. She smiled to herself.

The second and final time Olivia attended dinner at the Richards', she only got as far as the garden. She was more than a little late. Through the same kitchen window as before, she could see that the others had already sat down to start, including the unknown man whom she could only assume was John the accountant. Also at the table were the two daughters, Carissa and Rachael. She watched them through the window for about ten minutes before she left to make a phone call. When Susanna picked up the receiver, Olivia asked for Michael without even introducing herself. After the call, Olivia watched Michael making excuses for her. Then she watched Susanna, who looked both unimpressed and embarrassed, apologising to John.

Now, here she was, back in that dining room.

The radio was blasting out.

'…So, we can't ignore it, the elephant in the room: Sykes. Are you as disgusted as we all are, Damo?'

'Oh, where do I start? I feel terrible, like I've personally let down everyone.'

'Nobody blames you Damo.'

'I blame me, Ken, I do. I talked up this chap like he was the next, well, you know, the next Great Briton. He fooled me, and he made a fool of me. Yeah, I'm disgusted and I'm sorry, and I'm, I'm, angry, Ken, really angry. And, as you know, anger is not an emotion I'm familiar with, not one I like. But this guy, God, I can barely say his name, he makes me so angry at what he's done…'

This time Olivia was going nowhere. This time it was her rules, her guests, her house…and *her* Michael.

26

PATIENT

I knew Jones was a believer. He was a follower. He was one of the masses. He wanted to believe in all that supernatural stuff. He had gone on and on about his own super-strength. The fact that I was a prisoner and he my captor seemed to make no difference. The fact that I hadn't mentioned the Winnies at all also made no difference. He'd told me, he'd told Michael. It was a certainty that he told every person he met for more than five minutes about his incredible feats of power. Unlike Damo, who was of a relatively slight physique, Jones was built like a mountain and so feats of strength wouldn't be completely unexpected. But what he claimed to be able to do went beyond bulging biceps.

His claim wasn't the most outlandish or ridiculous one flying around (after all, *he* wasn't supposedly flying around). Not by a long shot. Not with the craziness on the TV, be it the Winnies or the succession of freaks on daytime chat shows and reality TV shows all claiming they had superpowers too. Some of them were beyond consideration, like the time-travelling guy who claimed to have won the Second World War for us, and that he had the photographic evidence to prove it. The quality of the image manipulation was so amateurish it was laughable, as was the lack of detail in his story. Nor the woman who was married to a puppy.

A puppy that, she claimed, had been her (human) husband who she had, somewhat by accident, transformed into a dog. She said that although she'd meant to do it, she didn't realise she was actually *able* to until it was too late. Now she found she couldn't change him back, and so was searching for someone out there with the opposite abilities to her. And when she explained that she needed to impose a small charge on anyone claiming to be legitimate, it seemed perfectly reasonable. After all, she didn't want any time-wasters. All the time, I wondered where the real husband was – actually, no, what I wondered was how come nobody else was asking where the real husband was. Did she kill him and bury him? Was he on a beach somewhere counting out the income? No, there he was, the puppy, but of course.

Jones's claim was one you'd at least consider. Well, the first time he told it, anyway. After the fifth or sixth time, not so much. But still, listening to the story and all the minute details – plenty of which seemed to change with each telling, if you had the patience to listen closely enough – had given me what I needed to fool him. It was probably the third time he was telling me the story of him and his cousin that I realised just how useful it could be to me and my situation.

It was the ultimate irony, I thought to myself, that in order to convince this man of my powers I would need to fake them. Not only that, I'd have to fake them in order to convince him that his own, fake, powers were actually real.

'You're like me,' I said to him.

'What?'

'You're the same as me. Your powers…are real. I've seen it.'

Jones was unsure, but he was listening, which was more than he'd been doing with Michael.

'Your powers are real, just like mine are. We're the same. You, me, the others…Damo. You're one of us.'

They were the words he'd longed to hear, and although I was hardly the authority to diagnose him, I could see it was doing the trick.

'I drew what you did.'

Without saying another word, I pulled out a canvas from behind two others. It was the first one I'd ever drawn that didn't have my wife or girls in it. Which was really strange, and difficult, but it was necessary. I held it up for the dim florescent light to mildly illuminate. Even from the other side of the cell, Jones knew what it was. He'd been telling the story for so long and to so many people. It was his special power, his gift, his chance to be something beyond the uniform he was wearing right now. Here it was on paper, in the physical world, and so it had to have really happened, it had to be real. That's how it worked after all. *Draw it, bring it to life.*

The sketch depicted two people, Jones and his cousin, in some sort of basement. A makeshift gym. On the bar were the weights – *all* the weights, and also paint pots, as well as the cousin pushing down as hard as he could. Jones was lifting the bar above his head with ease, and his cousin right off his feet. It was essentially a scene from M. Night Shyamalan's *Unbreakable*. At the time of its release, the movie had more of a cult following, but it was just one of a slew of films, TV shows and, in particular, comic books that had a tremendous rebirth in mainstream popularity since the whole Winnies and Damo thing exploded last year. The story of normal people with superpowers, normal people like this guard, who had chosen a profession in which he could protect people, just like the film's hero, was in the zeitgeist. I couldn't even be sure he'd seen *Unbreakable*, but the fact that it was on TV what seemed like every night suggested that he had, along with the remarkable similarity between his story and the basement scene in the film.

But I knew my picture wasn't going to be enough to convince him. Appease him, maybe, but not convince him to let me leave my cell. No, for that to happen it would take the same thing that it had taken for Michael to believe. The only difference being that in this case, it was a lie. This next vision wouldn't really happen. But that didn't matter. As long as I chose something that Jones wanted to happen so badly that he'd have no choice but to believe in me and do what I say.

'There's more,' I said. 'I haven't just seen what you've already done. I've also seen what you're going to do. So I drew that too.' I was deliberately enigmatic but also very matter-of-fact so that there would be no disputing my legitimacy. 'How, you know…' I lowered my voice, '…how your ability will be used in the future.'

He cleared his throat, his head no doubt telling him one thing while his heart and ego told him the opposite. He wanted to tell me to go on, but he was struggling to find words that wouldn't make him look like a complete fool. But that's what he was, another fool brainwashed by all the Winnies propaganda. It was like the lottery: 'It could be you.'

My power wasn't just to be able to see the past, present and future of my wife and children, it was also to be able to convince others by using that power. First, Michael and now Jones. A misuse of my gift this time, maybe – great power comes with great responsibility and all that – but this was no time for moral dilemmas. This was the time to save my family. Now that Michael was on my side, the only people who stood in my way were this delusional guard and, of course, Doctor Reyes. I'd have to defeat her, and I still had no idea how I'd do that. I hadn't yet seen what would happen, and so I didn't yet know what to do. But for the moment, I just had to get past this six foot obstacle.

'How's that?' Jones asked, his voice cracking.

I held up a new sketch; it depicted the moments after extreme weather conditions had caused a train to derail. The passengers were escaping the wreckage, but only thanks to Jones, who held one of the carriages above his head.

It was so ridiculous that I felt embarrassed showing it, just as I had while drawing it. I'd tried to achieve a balance between what would be believable and yet still fantastic. Perhaps this would miss the mark. It's too much, I'd thought as I drew his bulging bicep bigger and bigger until it was like something out of a Hulk comic or Popeye. But then, as I was about to scale it down, I remembered the puppy-husband and the time-travelling war hero and also the man who flew up to an asteroid and smashed it away from Earth, literally saving the world. No, the bicep shouldn't be smaller, it should be bigger. It *all* needed to be bigger.

'That's me… Wait, that's me?'

'Yes, it's you.'

'I haven't…'

'It's you, just not yet. But it will be. It's your future, your…destiny.'

He asked me to hold the picture up closer, and he looked over it. The flames, the twisted steel, the children running, the bicep. Mostly, he looked at the bicep. 'When?' he asked. 'Where?'

'I can't say for sure, but it's not that far in the future, that much I know. Do you catch the train often?'

I knew that he didn't, but he didn't know that. I'd overheard him talking to his mother about Christmas, and he'd mentioned the train he'd take. It was a couple of days ago, a throwaway comment that he wouldn't remember making, a short conversation among many other calls and, he'd have thought, out of my earshot anyway. A personal call while on duty. He'd probably forgotten it the moment he hung up.

'No, I don't take the train. Hardly ever.'

I needed him to make the connection himself. If I offered too much information, or led him there, he'd maybe know he was being played. I was also worried that Michael would start to feel played himself, by my real visions.

'No train travel... It's weird that you don't have any train journeys coming up...' *Come on, make the link.* I could see he wanted it to be true, but for the life of him his muscle-bound brain struggled to make it work. I had one more trick up my sleeve. 'What about the other people? Do you recognise them?'

He stepped a little closer. He narrowed his eyes.

Of course he won't recognise them. How could he? I made them up. But he wanted to so badly. 'What about this boy, here?' I said, pointing to the figure of a lad running away. But it wasn't the boy I needed him to see. 'The one carrying a package...a Christmas present, I think it is.'

'*Christmas* present?' said Jones. He looked again, and now he saw the Christmas lights hanging around the town that could be seen behind the destruction, and the wrapped presents thrown from the carriages and strewn about. 'Christmas. That's it.'

Yes.

'I might be taking the train at Christmas,' he said.

Michael and I exchanged glances. I widened my eyes to bring attention to the fact that this was part of my plan. He didn't react so I wasn't sure if he understood.

'My God,' said Jones. 'I knew it. I always knew it.'

'I'm sorry I can't be of more help,' I said. 'It's a fuzzy vision. If I knew when and where, I'd tell you.'

'It's okay,' he said. 'I think I know.' He stepped closer again. *I have him.* 'I think I know both where and...when.'

I was now able to gesture to Michael behind the guard's back. I did so with exaggerated movements. *Ready?* I mimed. Michael looked confused and then worried. Jones had a gun, after all. *Follow my lead*, I mouthed. He was clearly scared, but he nodded quickly. He knew there was no other way. He'd come too far and seen too much to walk away now. At least, I hoped that was the case.

'Yep, I know exactly when and where,' said Jones.

The guard was, for all intents and purposes, talking to himself now. Not that he realised it. He thought he was still engaged in an incredibly revelatory conversation. Now it was just a matter of how far he was willing to go, or how far he was willing to let me go, more to the point. We were about to find out.

'These visions always come true, without fail, that much I know. This *will* happen, I can promise you that,' I said. 'But it was hazy, which is why not all the details are there. Unlike my others…' I brought it back to the subject at hand. I brought him back, now that he was a believer. '…my others, like this one, where…' This was the moment I had dreaded. I knew the words would hurt as I said them. '…the one where his family, Doctor Richards' family, are in danger.'

I knew it was better if I lied, if I went along with the accepted story that they were *his* family. I knew it gave us the best chance of convincing Jones, which was all that mattered. I don't know what Michael's reaction to my words was, I didn't look to see. I don't know if he realised it was all a ploy or whether he thought that I'd come around to his thinking after all. It didn't matter, not yet. His family, my family. Whatever. *Just get out of there*. I looked at Jones's handgun. It was close enough to grab. I looked at Michael. He was shaking his head. It was tempting. But it was better if the guard let us walk. *Stick to Plan A*.

'They're in danger,' I said, 'and that's happening *right now*.'

'Please,' said Michael. 'We have to save them.'

'We?' the guard asked, as if we wanted him to come along. He probably thought we could do with his help. Why wouldn't we, if we thought he was a superhero?

'Yes, Doctor Richards and me,' I said. 'This is our destiny. *Ours*, not yours.' I gestured toward the train wreck sketch. 'We all have our destinies.'

He started nodding slowly and I had a feeling of elation. But then he spoke. 'Wait. Wait a minute. I need to think.'

Shit.

'I need to think about what's happening here.'

And in that moment, I knew that any chance we'd had of him letting us go was gone. The initial thrill of my fake vision was rapidly fading. Yes, it was everything he yearned for, but he wasn't relating it to our predicament. Whatever happened now, we were moving to Plan B. Maybe it's how it was always going to play out. I'd suspected as much, but the immediate future was unclear, even to me.

'I need a moment,' Jones said. 'I have to–'

'The boy,' I said, not letting him take that moment. 'The one with the present…' I pointed to the lad in the sketch. 'He's important to you, isn't he? He's…is he your son?'

This wasn't based on anything, no overheard phone conversation and certainly no vision. At best, he had a long-lost son who he was desperate to be reunited with, or perhaps he could be convinced this vision was from a future Christmas when he'd be a dad.

It was merely a distraction. He leant in again to take a look at the deliberately obscurely drawn face of the boy. He was inches from the canvas, and at his most vulnerable. His gun poked out at me and I knew it was time. I didn't look at Michael for his agreement, I just did it.

I grabbed the gun and spun it round in his direction before he could even react, blagging that I knew what to do with it. Wide-eyed, he redirected his gaze to me. His mouth formed words but I didn't hear them.

'Hands where I can see them,' I said.

He raised himself up from his hunched position and towered over me. I shook the gun at him and he slowly brought his hands up above his head.

'That's it, nice and slow.' My tone was commanding even if my words were a little textbook eighties cop show. It was the best I had. I backed into a corner so I could see Michael but still keep an eye and the gun on the guard. 'Michael, let's go.'

'No,' said Jones.

'Please don't make me hurt you,' I said.

'You wouldn't.'

'My family are in danger. Trust me, I would.'

'*Your* family? Thought it was *his* family?'

I looked at Michael. 'Yeah, well, it's complicated.'

'Yeah? Well, what about my destiny?'

'What about it?'

'Is it, you know, is it going to happen? Is it real?'

I looked at his searching eyes. He wanted it so badly. And then I saw Michael, whose eyes were also searching me for answers. I held a gun and yet I felt more vulnerable than ever. 'It's as real as you want it to be.'

'What the fuck does that mean?'

'It means we're leaving.'

It was time to find out whether Michael was as committed as I was. I gestured for him to swap places with me. He was hesitant, of course, but he came. He awkwardly took the pistol into both his hands while Jones protested.

'You need to hand that back, sir, right now,' he said.

Michael was so fixated on the gun itself that he didn't see Jones unclip the baton on his hip.

'Michael, watch him!' I said.

He saw the baton and quickly pointed the gun at the guard. I looked through the tiny window and then out into the corridor, checking that the coast was clear. Jones continued to slowly raise his baton.

'I don't want to hurt you, officer,' said Michael, repeating my words.

'Sir, listen to me, he's my prisoner.'

'No, not any more he's not. He's my patient.' He held the pistol steady now and told the guard to stand in the corner with a little more weight in his voice.

'The radio, too,' I told him.

Michael signalled for Jones to slide his radio to him, which he did.

'Sir, you're making a huge mistake. There's CCTV everywhere. They'll get you. Huge fuckin' mistake.'

Michael picked up the radio. 'I know it looks that way,' he said. For some reason, he must have felt he had to explain his actions.

'But I have to do this. I have to take him. You've seen what I've seen and you're not convinced?'

Jones told him that, yeah, maybe he was, but that there was no way he could just let us leave. 'There's a correct procedure, sir. You need to speak with the judge first thing tomorrow morning.'

'We don't have time for that.'

'Sir, you need to–'

'Leave!' I said, having had enough. 'We need to leave.'

'That's right,' Michael said. 'My family are in danger. I'm leaving and he's coming with me.'

Jones wasn't beaten just yet. 'Sir, this is your final warning. Hand me the gun.'

Michael looked down at the handgun.

'Doctor, we're running out of time,' I said.

'I'm sorry,' Michael said to the guard, as he backed away towards the door. Once we were out, I slammed the cell door shut and locked Jones inside. He ran up to the window but it was too late. We were free. The keys, which had been in the door, were now in my pocket. I knocked the radio out of Michael's hand and smashed it under my foot.

He looked at me and then at the gun in his hand. 'What the hell am I doing?' he asked.

He'd come this far; I knew he'd go all the way now. 'We have to save them. Together, we can do it. This is what it's all been about, Michael.' I held out my hand, requesting the gun. 'Trust me. We can save them.'

He reluctantly handed it over. 'How?'

'On the way,' I said. 'We don't have much time. She's already there.'

27

DOCTOR

'I'm sorry, you have *what*?' asked Olivia.

'Kombucha tea. It's all anyone at the gym talks about.'

Rachael was a natural entertainer. She enjoyed an audience and had the confidence to speak her mind together with the eloquence to be listened to.

'You go to the gym?' asked Olivia, playing along with the charade.

'When my busy schedule allows it,' replied Rachael.

Olivia saw Carissa roll her eyes at her sister, and she was reminded of the way Susanna did the same at Michael.

'Here she is,' said Rachael. 'Don't say I didn't warn you, doctor.'

'Ah, Carissa. How are you?' Carissa was not as welcoming as her sister. Teenagitis was taking hold, but it was more than that. She had a streak of her mother in her. Rachael was all Michael, a people person and perhaps easier to take advantage of because of that. Friendly, too friendly sometimes, which is exactly what Olivia had counted on. Carissa, like Susanna, would take more convincing.

'O…kay,' said Carissa. 'Who are *you*?'

Rachael took offence. 'She's a guest and you shouldn't speak to guests like that.'

Before an argument could break out Olivia intervened. 'No, no, it's quite all right. I'm Doctor Reyes. I'm sorry, I've seen so many photos of you that I feel like we've already met.'

'Oh, okay,' said Carissa. 'Yeah, I've heard Mum and Dad talking about you.'

'All good things, I hope?'

Her question went unanswered. There was a beat as Rachael stared at her sister. Instead of apologising for her coldness, Carissa continued her challenge. 'Do you have identification?'

Rachael looked ready to explode. 'Carissa, you're embarrassing me.'

'ID?' said Olivia. 'I…'

'Forget her, doctor,' said Rachael. 'She's having one of those days.'

'What does Mum always say?' asked Carissa, rhetorically. 'When they aren't here, *I'm* in charge. I'm three years older than you–'

'Two and a half, actually.'

'I'm *older* than you and I'm in charge,' said Carissa. 'You can't just let anyone into the house.'

Carissa made no apology for speaking about Olivia as if she wasn't there, and Olivia was transported back to that dinner in the very same room when Susanna did the very same thing. Her dislike for Susanna was rubbing off on to Carissa. Rachael, on the other hand, she liked. She saw herself in her, and, of course, Michael.

'Doctor Reyes isn't just *anyone*. She's Daddy's doctor.'

'It doesn't matter who she is to *Dad*,' said Carissa. 'It's who she is to *us* that matters, and to us she's a stranger. She could be anyone, a murderer for all we know. She could be a complete psycho.' Carissa turned to Olivia and said, 'No offence,' with a slightly acidic tongue.

Olivia had become quite the actress in the last few months, and a teenage girl's attitude wasn't going to be enough to spoil the party at this late stage. 'None taken, poppet,' she said.

'She's not a psycho,' said Rachael. 'Or a murderer. Are you, doctor?'

Olivia smiled. 'Of course not. But your sister is right. You need to be careful, Rachael. Not everybody is who they say they are.'

Rachael nodded, smiling at Olivia, and invited her to join them at the table. Carissa started using her phone again.

Rachael poured tea and changed the subject. 'So, do you have a favourite for the Winnies, doctor? I mean, can you believe the X-ray guy has been found out? OMG, I was not expecting that. Oh no, sorry, maybe you didn't see last night's show – have I just ruined it for you? I'm so sorry if I have!'

The radio filled the room. '…You considered Sykes a friend, right?'

'Oh, man, don't, you're getting me even more riled up! Yes, it's true I'd come to consider him as more than just a contestant. I made sure I never let that influence my work, of course, but, yes, we hung out, played golf, you know.'

'He hung you out to dry, more like.'

'That he did. May I, Ken?'

'Go ahead.'

'Okay, here goes. Evan, if you're listening, you're a fake. You're a fake and a fraud and everybody knows it now. You fooled us all, me included, and that hurts, yeah, but we see through your lies now, and all that's left is disgust. Maybe we should have known before, maybe I should have known, maybe I got too close. Your claims were outlandish, remarkable, but we wanted to believe you. We needed to believe you. You made a fool out of me, the contest and the general public, especially those who voted for you, Sykes. You owe them one huge damned apology…'

Olivia hadn't seen the show, but she knew anyway. It was impossible to avoid. Every network, every radio station, every newspaper headline was dedicated to the fact that the contestant, the favourite, Evan Sykes, who'd claimed to be a human X-ray machine, was a phoney.

'No, it's okay, I've already heard,' said Olivia, 'although I can't believe anyone could mastermind something that huge.'

Rachael plonked a newspaper in front of Olivia. 'It's all in here. Check out pages two and three for just how Sykes did it.'

Olivia had no choice now but to read it.

'…I'm sorry, I'm sorry for my language. Look, Sykes, that's what it means to me, to us. You've got me using bad language. I never swear, goddamn it. You've made a mockery of the whole thing, the whole contest. And do you know what? You need help, man. Get some help while you're locked up. I'm sorry, I'm sorry, I get worked up every time I think about it. Please, can we talk about something else? Let's talk about the remaining contestants…'

Sykes had staged the whole thing using an intricate and elaborate plot with multiple stages. Stage one had been to make promises to certain hospital staff, that Sykes would put them on his pay roll should he win the whole contest and become the 'next Damo'. Once a radiologist and a few nurses were in place, stage two involved finding a patient who'd had an X-ray that had detected something. Stage three was to switch or forge the X-ray results to show no sign of a tumour. Stage four was simply for Sykes to be on public transport at the same time as the patient and to deliver the bad news: that he saw cancer. He'd be believable enough to convince the person to go back to hospital, either right then and there, or, somewhat less impressively, later on when they became unwell.

So close, Olivia thought. She had no time for the idiocy of supernatural rubbish, but this mastermind and his plan impressed her mightily. She felt, ironically, that he now deserved to be recognised. Olivia was impressed by the whole thing, except, crucially, that he'd been caught. She would have done it slightly differently, she thought. Probably ensure the patient went back to the hospital with him. How would she have made sure? Maybe pay for his ticket, maybe call an ambulance, maybe drug him. She wasn't sure but she felt that with a little time she would have come up with something.

'What a liar,' Rachael said. 'He lied to everyone. Even his own family didn't know the truth.'

'Like I said, Rachael,' said Olivia, 'not everyone is who they say they are. Right, Carissa?'

Carissa was glued to her phone.

'Sorry, doctor,' said Rachael, embarrassed. 'Wait, you didn't answer my question. Come on, tell me, do you have a favourite? Now that Sykes is out, a lot of people are jumping on the force-field bandwagon. But not me; I've always liked the languages girl.

I think it's because I'm really good at French at school. How about you?'

'Oh no, not me,' Olivia said, still engrossed in the newspaper article. 'Spanish is my preferred second language.'

'Spanish? What…' asked Rachael. She started giggling. 'Oh, doctor, when I said "How about you?" I meant the Winnies, your favourite for the Winnies, not whether you were good at French!'

'Oh, I'm sorry, Rachael,' said Olivia. 'I was just reading all this stuff. It's quite incredible the lengths this Sykes chap went to. A favourite for the show? Well, remind me who's left in, then.'

Rachael turned the page of the newspaper to reveal the latest bookies' odds for the remaining contestants.

'…Okay, we have some news coming up.'

'That we do Ken.'

'But first, look who's out in front now. It's Geraldine Adams – isn't that amazing?'

'That really is incredible. She was the rank outsider, what, a week ago? It just goes to show what an appearance on the Damo show can do! Nah, seriously, she's a lovely lady who, unlike Sykes, is completely genuine. I can see why the public are falling in love with her. She's like everybody's favourite granny, you know? Except she can stop explosions! An added bonus.'

'You can say that again.'

'But, she's favourite, yeah, but take a look at the odds. There's nothing in it really, you know? Nobody's getting rich betting on this even if they win! Only the bookies, of course, always the bookies.'

'There's nothing between them, but we all have our own favourite. I bet you have yours, don't you, Damo?'

'Not really. Well, okay, yeah, I kind of do. Yeah, I have my favourite, but it wouldn't be right for me to say who that was. I don't want to influence the public, it's their choice after all. And really, it doesn't matter who they go for 'cos they're all worthy winners, now that Sykes is gone, of course…'

'What's this replacement they keep talking about?' Olivia asked.

Rachael turned back the page and then went forward a couple more before she found what she was looking for. There was speculation that there may be a replacement contestant since Sykes was removed from the competition. Previous applicants, those who didn't get through the earlier rounds, were in the papers declaring their rightful place had been taken by a scam artist. Last year's losing finalists (not including the humble chap that Michael had voted for, of course) were also claiming they should be put in as a replacement for Sykes. The decision hadn't been made, but the speculation was immense. The other option being suggested was that a brand new person would come in, someone who had demonstrated something extraordinary but had missed the first deadline. The decision would be made after careful consideration of all of the options. After all, they didn't want to make a mockery of the process. *God forbid,* thought Olivia.

'So, who do you fancy?' asked Rachael.

'Tough call,' said Olivia. 'But, I think, maybe, the underwater boy. What's his name?'

'Oh, Richie Dance, good choice,' said Rachael. 'He's very popular.'

'Right. Richie. He saved his sister, and, just like for you guys, family is really important to me.'

The heavy front door slammed closed. 'Girls, it's me!' shouted Susanna from the hallway.

'Ah, perfect timing. They're home,' Rachael said.

'Hi, guys! How was your meal?' Carissa called out.

Susanna replied that it was just her and that their father would be home a bit later.

'Well, he has a visitor!' shouted Rachael.

'Olivia is here!' Carissa said, with meaning.

Again, Rachael took exception to her tone and choice of name. 'That's Doctor Reyes to you.'

'Oh, okay,' called out Susanna, sounding surprised. 'I'll be right in.'

Olivia joined the conversation. 'No hurry, Susanna. The girls are taking very good care of me.'

'Rachael is,' muttered Rachael to herself.

'Girls, could you come and help me with my bags?' asked Susanna.

'Hang on, just texting,' said Carissa.

'Now please,' called Susanna.

'Hurry up, Carissa,' said Rachael.

'Why don't *you* go?'

'Someone needs to entertain the doctor,' said Rachael. 'It's rude to leave a guest alone.'

Carissa rolled her eyes again before heading out to help her mother.

'So, doctor…' said Rachael, '…how are you enjoying the kombucha?'

28

PATIENT

Michael skipped across the tarmacked car park doing his utmost to avoid puddles, as if that was still important. It made me wonder whether he was up to what was to come.

As we got to his car he shouted, 'Wait!', although it seemed to be directed more to himself than me.

Does he think now is a good time to stop and chat? Yes, we had smashed Jones's radio, but it was likely he had plenty of other ways of contacting the authorities. The CCTV at every corner of the facility. A silent alarm, probably, although perhaps not from within the cell. But then, maybe even a mobile phone. *Shit.* We didn't take his mobile. We had to assume the police were already alerted and on their way. We had no time to wait.

'You've got to be kidding, Michael,' I said, as he stopped and pulled his phone from his pocket. 'Now? You're making a call, now?'

He didn't reply. Instead, he punched in the key code to unlock his phone, swearing at it – at himself – for getting it wrong. And again. 'Fuck! Fucking thing's locked me out! Fuck!'

He was losing it. He'd done well, better than I'd expected, back in the cell. But now the emotion of what was going on was catching up with him and he didn't know how to deal with it. A breakdown was inevitable. He couldn't see, like I could, that it was all happening just as it needed to.

'Calm down, Michael.' He couldn't hear me. He was waiting for his phone to let him try again. 'You need to calm down.'

The bottom line was that I needed him. I'd needed him to break me out of that cell – or, rather, to give me the chance to break myself out. And I couldn't just dump him now I was out, no matter how much I wanted to. I still needed him. He was crucial. He had no idea how important he was.

'Michael,' I said, 'listen to me.' My tone was calm, gentle, friendly. The same tone he'd so delicately used on me throughout our treatments. 'I need you.'

He was still bashing at his keypad. 'Give me your phone,' he said, as if I would have such a device on me. He was completely caught up in a single thought, I guessed, to speak to his wife, to warn her. It was understandable, but misguided.

'Michael,' I put my hand on his, over the phone, 'it's too late.'

'What?' I realised he probably thought the worst.

'No, it's okay,' I backtracked. 'I didn't mean…'

'What is it?'

'She's okay. But it's too late to stop her from being taken. Reyes will take her.'

'But…' He held his chest.

Uh-oh. Shit. If he had another attack now, it would all be over.

'You need to calm down. Just breathe, okay? It's not too late to save her. It's not too late to save them all, Michael.'

He took a few deep breaths. He looked down at the ground and asked me, 'When did you start calling me by my first name?'

It was time to lay my cards on the table. 'We're not doctor and patient any more. We've gone way beyond that. We're connected somehow. And while I can't explain it yet, I have a strong feeling that everything will be clear by the end of the day.'

'I don't understand what's going on.'

'I need you. We need each other. To save them. Let's go and save them. I need to know if you're up to this? Are you with me?' I held out my hand. He hesitated for a second and then reached out to grab it. I shook my head. 'No, the *phone*.'

He looked at me, puzzled, and then reached out with his other hand and passed me his mobile. I punched in the correct key code and passed it back to him.

'I…I…how did you…?'

I shook my head again. 'Call Susanna if you need to, but understand that it won't help.'

'I have to try,' he said. He made the call. I could hear ringing at the other end. He waited, I waited; he waited for her to answer, I waited for the sirens.

'Michael, in the car. Come on.'

He wasn't having it. I couldn't believe flashing lights weren't upon us already, but then I remembered that Jones had used the landline phone, not a mobile, when calling his mother. Not only that but he'd asked her to call him back and given her the landline number. 'No signal down here,' he'd told her. That meant he hadn't been able to make a call. That meant we had a chance. If I could get Michael in the car, we actually had a chance to stop Reyes.

But he was still stationary. The phone at the other end continued to ring.

I looked around the car park. There was a scattering of vehicles. A green car caught my eye, but then Michael spoke.

'You saw him do that?'

I turned, expecting to see Michael speaking into the phone, but he was talking to me. 'You saw the guard save those children? The train derailment, you saw that in one of your visions?'

I cocked my head to one side. 'I only remember my family, you know that, Michael.'

The rings continued, and still Susanna wasn't picking up.

'It was all a lie?' he said, not really asking. 'To convince the guard, right?'

'Yes. It was a complete lie. Both of the drawings of Officer Jones were total fantasy. Necessary lies.'

He looked straight at me. 'And what about the *other* drawings?'

I don't know why but I let him stew for a few seconds. 'Of course, *they're* real. How can you ask me that after everything we've been through?'

The ringing stopped and the voicemail kicked in. He refocused. 'Susie, Susie, it's me, it's Michael. Listen, oh my God, listen, this is going to sound crazy, okay, but please, *please* get the girls right now and leave the city…'

'Reyes already has the girls,' I said.

'What? Oh, Jesus. Are you sure?'

'She has them.'

'Oh God. Susie,' he said into the phone. 'I think Olivia Reyes is dangerous. I mean, I *know* she is. But she doesn't know that I know. Use that to your advantage. If you can, get out of there. She wants to harm you and the girls. I know that sounds insane, I can't explain what's going on but you have to get the girls and take them to your parents' place. Call me as soon as you get this. I'm on my way to the house.' He went to hang up, then put the phone back to his mouth to deliver a final message. 'I love you, Susie.' He hit the red button.

And then there they were, the inevitable sirens. Off in the distance, not close, not yet, but heading in our direction. I closed my eyes and something started coming to me. Michael started to say something, but I told him to be quiet. The sirens had evoked a memory in me. There was a blurry image, a dark blue shape coming to me. I couldn't make out what it was at first. Droplets of rain landed on my face, rolled down my closed eyelids and refocused the image. It wasn't blue, it was green, a beautiful fast green shape, and it was parked twenty feet away.

29

DOCTOR

'Mum's waiting for you, Carrie,' Rachael said to Carissa as her older sister finished her latest text to Tracy.

The advice that Rachael had given Carissa regarding Cheating Pete and Tracy had led to a lengthy back and forth during which Tracy and Carissa had gone from enemies to allies.

'I just need to reply to this,' said Carissa. 'It's important.' She wrote, 'I still hv all his messages 2 me. If u hv yours, we could show everyone wot a player he thinks he is.'

'Not as important as helping out around the house,' said Rachael. 'You can plot your revenge any time.'

'Revenge?' asked Olivia, looking up from the newspaper. 'Oh, my. Such a young girl should never need to seek revenge. Is it something your parents know about?'

'I can handle it, thanks,' Carissa said, with a smirk.

Olivia smiled and said, 'Well, if you're quite sure.'

'Come on girls,' called Susanna. 'I need some help. And now my phone is ringing.'

'Carrie's on her way!' shouted Rachael.

Carissa gave Rachael a stare, slipped her mobile phone into her jeans pocket and moved towards the hallway.

'Bye, Carrie,' she heard from behind her. The sort of little dig that little sisters give, just because big sisters had to help with the bags. Carissa turned around and stuck her tongue out, only to find Rachael preoccupied over by the cupboard. To her surprise, it had been Olivia who'd said the words.

Olivia sipped her tea with a strange little smile on her face. Her eyes stayed on Carissa. Carissa retracted her tongue and just stood there, frozen, unsettled. Rachael then returned to find Carrie doing nothing, just standing there.

She tut-tutted at her sister. 'Mum's waiting, Carissa!'

Olivia gave the slightest of chuckles.

Carissa left the room, but then looked back again. She watched her little sister sit down opposite Olivia.

'I don't know, big sisters,' said Rachael. 'Know what I mean, doctor? Do you have any older siblings, if you don't mind me asking?'

'I don't, actually, no. Have any older siblings, I mean. And of course not, no, I don't mind at all, you can ask me whatever you wish.'

'Well, let me tell you, you're lucky. If you did, you'd know exactly what I mean. Older sisters are a nightmare. Can't imagine older brothers would be much better either.'

Carissa was tempted to go back and set the record straight about big sisters and little sisters. Instead, she continued to watch.

Olivia took another sip. 'That's family for you, Rachael.'

'Do you have a large family, doctor?'

'Well, let's just say it's complicated.'

'…So, I think I need to ask you a very difficult question now, Damo. And please excuse me for doing so, but there are lots of people out there who're asking this question and, well, you know, I try to be the voice of the people.'

'It's okay, Ken. I know people are questioning everything now. They're right to, it's shaken everyone. Hit me with it.'

'Well, okay. A lot of people today are asking themselves whether, in light of everything that happened with Sykes, whether they can believe anything or anyone on the show. What's not to say all of these guys are phoneys, and it's only Sykes who got caught? After all, if that hospital worker hadn't come forward we'd still be believing him and rooting for him. Is there a hospital worker just waiting to come forward for each of these other contestants too?'

Carissa finally left the dining room doorway, muttering to herself about multiple different things. Multiple people, mostly. Rachael, being annoying as always. Tracy, Pete and that whole mess. Doctor Reyes and her strangeness, her over-familiarity. And then Rachael again, seeming to buy into the doctor a little too easily. There was something about the whole situation that felt completely wrong to Carissa. But Mum was home now, so it would all be fine.

She went out into the hallway. 'Rachael is such a…' Her mother was bent over with her hand over her ear. 'Mum? What're you doing?'

'Ssh…' said Susanna.

Carissa realised her mum was on her phone. But not talking, only listening. The shopping bags, full of fresh produce, were ready to be taken through, so Carissa took the initiative and started to collect them up. She loaded up on the fruit and veg and started to move towards the kitchen. But a hand grabbed her by the wrist. It stopped her in her tracks and a few apples rolled out on to the polished oak floorboards with gentle thuds. Susanna pulled her backwards, still listening intently to the message.

Now that she was closer, Carissa could hear that the voice on the other end was that of her father. But a hurried, emotional version of her father, a version she hadn't heard before. She could pick out a few words: '…crazy…can't explain…parents' place. Call me…I love you.' It wasn't enough for Carissa to make sense of it, but it was enough, along with his tone, to know something was seriously wrong. Her mum's face had gone from intrigue to horror in the space of ten seconds. The message ended.

'Mum? What's the matter? Is Dad okay?'

Susanna didn't speak for a moment.

'Is Dad hurt again?'

Susanna looked at her. 'No, no, your dad's fine. He's fine. Where's your sister?'

'Mum, what is it?'

Susanna repeated herself with much more urgency. 'Where's Rachael, Carrie?'

Carissa was confused and unsettled. 'She won't leave a guest alone, says it's rude. She's being really–'

Susanna cut her short. 'We have to leave.'

'What?'

'We have to get your sister and leave right now.'

'What about Doctor Reyes? She's sat in there drinking…' Carissa stopped talking. 'It's *her*, isn't it?'

'What? Why would you say that? Did she do something to you?'

'Yeah. I mean, no, no, she didn't do anything. It's just the way she looked at me…she kind of freaked me out. It was like she…'

'What?'

'…Mum…'

'What is it?'

'Rach is with her, Mum.'

'Okay, okay. Let me think…' Susanna took Carissa's hand. 'Rachael, could you come out here for a moment?' she called, with an unwanted tremble in her voice.

The response was predictable. 'I'm entertaining!'

'It'll just take a second!'

And then there was silence.

'Rachael?' More silence. Rachael was not known for her silences.

'Rach?' called Susanna again, this time with a terror that she couldn't conceal one iota.

Silence.

Susanna looked at Carissa, who had tears forming. Susanna swallowed hard. 'There's no time for that, Carrie. Pull yourself together.'

Carissa blinked and the tears rolled.

'Listen, I'm going to need you. And I'm going to need you to be strong. Remember when Dad was in hospital, how tough you were, to show Rachael that everything was going to be fine? And it was, wasn't it? And remember how amazing you were when Rachael was locked in Aunt Zoe's bathroom that time?'

'Aunt Zoe's?'

'That day, what you did. You were….'

Carissa hung on her mother's next word.

'…extraordinary.'

Carissa and Susanna looked at each other, and Susanna nodded.

'I saw,' said Susanna.

'You did?'

'I did. And I need that again. Your sister needs you again. Okay?' Susanna held Carissa around the shoulders. 'You can do this. *We* can do this.'

Carissa nodded.

'You ready?'

Carissa nodded again, this time less confidently.

'Okay, then. You stay right here. I'm going to go get your sister.'

Carissa's eyes went wide and her head shook from side to panicked side. 'No, no, no, no, I'm staying with you, I can help. I'm coming with you.'

'I need you to stay here. Just in case…'

'Just in case of what? No, no, please, Mum, I don't want to.'

'Carrie, listen to me. I need you to stay here with this phone. Your dad might call. It's on silent, on vibrate. Make sure your phone is too. If I'm not back with your sister in the next two minutes I want you to call 999. Call them and tell them that your family is being held hostage…' The tears started rolling again. Susanna quickly wiped them away without acknowledging their existence and kept talking. 'Tell them we're being *held hostage*, give them our address, and then, without looking back, run over to the Hendersons' house and tell them what's happening. Okay? That's how you be *extraordinary* this time. You understand? Carrie?'

She nodded. 'Yes.'

'Say it back to me. What are you going to do?

'I'm going to wait and then…'

'Wait how long?'

'Two minutes. I'm going to wait for two minutes and if you're not back I'm going to run over to the Hendersons' and call the police–'

'Call the police first, before you go, you have signal here. They may not be in. You understand? Call and *then* run to the Hendersons'.'

'Okay.'

Carissa pulled out her phone and switched it to silent. Then she loaded the timer app and punched in two minutes.

Susanna gave her a huge hug.

Susanna entered the dining room to see Rachael and Olivia sat at the family table. Everything looked normal and peaceful.

'Rachael?' asked Susanna.

Nobody moved, it was like Susanna was staring at waxwork dummies of her daughter and her husband's doctor. She took a few steps further into the room. Now she could see that rather than not breathing at all, her youngest daughter was actually hyperventilating and staring in complete fear at Olivia and the handgun that was being pointed at her across the table.

Carissa listened, ready to hear her mother's voice shouting, 'It's okay, Carrie, we're all right, it's all fine, nothing to worry about, she's gone, come on in…' She wanted to hear it so badly. But it didn't come. She looked down at the timer. Only twenty seconds had passed. Plenty of time yet. She waited. The seconds sped up.

Back in the dining room, Olivia spoke. 'Susanna, how lovely to see you again. Please, won't you join us?'

30

PATIENT

He beeped the electronic key to unlock his Range Rover. He was in such a hurry that he was practically belted up before he realised I wasn't with him. He stuck his head out of the driver's window and asked what was going on. I didn't answer. I was fixated with what I saw. The green goddess. It was the answer. It was our ride.

'David?'

It was his turn to rush me, the difference being that my delay was a worthwhile one that would ultimately save us time. I stood in the car park staring at her. She was beautiful. I had started to doubt the world held such man-made beauty.

'His keys,' I said. My words didn't register with Michael. I turned to him and repeated myself. 'His *keys*, Michael.'

He probed his pockets for Jones's keys as he jumped down from the comfy cab of his unnecessarily big car. 'But we have to get moving. You said it yourself. We've got to go now. She's already there. We need to move.'

My thoughts exactly.

The Jaguar F-Type coupé in British racing green stared right at me. It had to be the guard's car – a good few years past its prime, but well looked after. I wasn't sure if I'd seen it, as his, in a vision or whether it was obvious; no other vehicle in the car park was a young man's car. Jones had good taste. Without looking away from the beast, I held my hand up to catch the keys that Michael threw to me. Despite his dodgy throw, I caught them and hoped that when I flipped over the fob I'd see a big cat. And I did. I smiled at Michael. We were in business.

We pounced on the car.

'You'd better drive,' I said.

He was hesitant. 'I should navigate.'

I shook my head.

'I know where I live,' he said.

'I get that,' I said. 'But I can't drive.'

'You can't drive?'

'I mean, I can't drive and do what's necessary. I need to concentrate on matters elsewhere. The visions are coming faster now, but I can't see them and drive at the same time. This isn't something I can do alone. I need you to take me there. That's your role in this. You busted me out, now you get me to the girls. Once we're there, I'll know what to do, how to save them.' I slid the keys across the roof of the car.

'Okay.'

With the doors unlocked, we slipped into the leather interior. Michael attempted to adjust his seat. I watched him searching for the bar. He was taking too long. Everything he did took too long. I could see he was a man who'd never had to rush for anything in his life. But the next hour wouldn't proceed at his usual leisurely pace.

'No bar,' I said. 'Electronic button down to your right. Down the bottom there.'

Finally, he found the button and moved the seat forwards and then back a little. *My God.* He fumbled the keys and they fell into the footwell.

'Damn it!' He couldn't reach them now that the seat was so far forward. 'Shit.' He searched for the bar again.

'*Button*,' I said.

Back went the seat again.

I closed my eyes. Not because of any vision, I just couldn't watch any more.

Finally, the Jaguar came to life with a purr and the next problem presented itself: the windscreen wipers had been left on at high speed and now they rasped against the dry glass.

'Come on, where *are* you?' he asked the car, while activating the indicators and turning on the radio in an attempt to stop the wipers.

Eyes still shut, I wondered how far up the road we would have been with me in the driving seat. But, no. This was the way it had to happen. *Keep faith.* In my visions and, what was much more difficult, in Michael.

'...We learnt a lot from Sykes. Yeah, he probably did us a favour, all things considered...'

Damo the Great, reminding us of the wonders we had to look forward to. I opened my eyes, grabbed the volume on the dashboard and turned the radio right down, but not off.

'...and the result is, I can one-hundred-per-cent guarantee that these four are the real deal. The absolute real deal...'

Michael found first gear. 'Okay, let's go,' he said, before immediately stalling the car. The radio fell dead too. 'Shit, third gear, sorry.'

Michael was panicking now, and the gearbox was feeling the brunt of his frustration. I closed my eyes again and told him to dip the clutch.

'I *know* how to drive.' He pushed down on the left pedal.

With my right hand, I guided the stick into first. 'Now, turn her over, and gently bring up the clutch–'

He misjudged the bite of the clutch. It jerked forward a couple times and stalled again.

'I said, *gently*, bring up the clutch *gently*.'

'Okay, okay.'

This time he listened, and we moved away, radio back on, and, agreeably, at the same low volume.

'...And what about the votes that went to Sykes? What's happening there?'

'How do you turn this off?' Michael asked, looking for the controls.

'No, no, leave it on.'

He asked why. I didn't really have an answer for him, I just knew it was important that we listened. 'Just concentrate on the road,' I told him.

I thought of Jones, locked up in his own cell, hearing the roar of his baby's engine and the crunching and grinding of the gears and the stalling. I saw him, heard him say 'Oh, you bastards,' when he realised it was his green goddess that we'd taken.

We were on our way, kind of. Michael had taken us out into the rush hour traffic and straight to a red light. Never had lights taken so long to change. We were at a pedestrian crossing with no pedestrians crossing.

'Come on, come on,' Michael pleaded with the god of traffic lights. And then, when they changed, he immediately stalled the car again. 'Shit!'

He fumbled with the controls, acting embarrassed like a learner driver holding up the traffic. Except that when the cars behind started honking their horns, he responded with anger not apologies.

'...Well,' continued the radio, 'I think we've kept people guessing for long enough don't you?'

Moving once more, we weaved through the other cars as best Michael could manage with his limited driving skills. He changed lanes again and again without ever really making any progress. The midlife crisis that manifests as a sports car had, unfortunately, not happened to him. That would have helped.

'Come on. Come on!' he shouted, at nobody or nothing in particular. We hit another red light. 'This is taking too long. I'm going, I'm just going.'

'No. We can't draw attention to ourselves.'

'What?'

'We have to stay under the radar.'

'But my family are in–'

'–danger. Yes, I know, Michael. I'm the one person who doesn't need reminding of that.'

He wasn't listening. 'I'm going!' He pulled the wheel to the left and floored it.

The car cranked around the corner before the other drivers realised what was happening, such was the torque. Unprepared, I was pinned back into my seat by the acceleration.

'…Okay, then, here goes. Beyond voting, there may be another reason to visit our website…'

Once the car was pointing back in a straight line, the conversation continued. 'That wasn't a wise move,' I said.

'We're away, aren't we?'

'You did all right, Michael, but the last thing we need is attention. Attention means the police. The police means we don't get to Reyes in time.'

'And you're certain it's Reyes?'

'Yes.'

'Doctor Reyes?' he asked again. 'Doctor Olivia Reyes?'

'It's her.'

'My God. Why? Why is she doing this?' The car changed lane again, and again.

'You tell me, Michael. She's your mate.'

'I honestly have no idea. She was–'

I told him to stop talking. I closed my eyes. Something was coming. *Oh, shit.* 'Michael.'

He looked at me.

'Drive faster. She has Susie.'

His foot hit the floor and the car took off. Once again, I was thrown back by the power under the bonnet.

31

DOCTOR

Carissa stood in the hallway, drenched in fear. She looked down at her phone again and again. A minute passed. One minute, not two. She told herself it was okay, her mum had said two minutes and she'd said two minutes for a very good reason. She wasn't sure why, but she didn't need to be. She knew her mum had a reason. It would take that long, two minutes. So it wasn't time to panic, not yet. Any second now she'd hear the shout, and the nightmare would be over.

She looked down again. Okay, so now it was a minute and a half, but still, there was plenty of time. How long did 'Carrie, everything's fine,' take to say, after all? Barely a second, so that was thirty, or twenty-five now, chances for that still to happen before she had to make a decision, before she had to make a call.

Olivia sat on one side of the dining table, Susanna and Rachael on the opposite. Between them was a handgun. Olivia's palms were laid down flat on the table on either side of the weapon.

She picked up her kombucha tea. 'I have to say, I was sceptical, Rachael, but you've won me over.' She took a big sip.

'…Say that again, Damo!'

Rachael huddled behind her mother, and then whispered in her ear. 'Where's Carrie?'

Olivia heard her. 'That's a good question, Rach, thank you for reminding me about Carissa. "Carrie" you call her? I like that. It suits her. Now, answer your daughter, Susanna. Where's Carrie? I do hope she's okay?'

'...Yes, it's true. Sykes's place on the show will be up for grabs...'

Carissa watched the digital numbers fold over, past forty, forty-five and fifty. She lifted her head and closed her eyes in the desperate hope that she might hear her mum or baby sister call out to her. She didn't count; she just listened. She knew that the moment she opened her eyes, the time would be up. She quickly peeked, hoping she could close them again and have an extension. She saw that it had already clocked over to two minutes and four seconds. She closed her eyes again and told herself to wait just a little longer, that she hadn't seen it yet and that she would kick herself if she called the police when everything was fine after all and she should have just waited a few, ten, twenty seconds, longer. What was twenty seconds? Thirty extra seconds? Nothing.

Except it was.

It was too long. It was far too long. Carrie was not going to escape this horror any more than her mother or sister would.

'...Someone out there, currently a complete nobody, will be in the final of this year's Winnies!'

'Answer your daughter, Susanna,' said Olivia. 'Excuse me, I mean, Susie. She's Carrie, you're Susie, right? Two peas in a pod, you two. Am I right? Like mother, like daughter?'

Susanna said nothing.

'Answer your daughter. Tell her where her sister is. Actually, better still, why don't you call out to Carrie? Call out, tell her it's all okay.'

Susanna didn't respond.

'I said, call her.'

'She's gone already.'

'Is that right?'

'Yep. She's a smart girl. She had her instructions. Two minutes without a word, then just go.'

'That's what you told her?'

'Yep.'

'And it's been two minutes, hasn't it?'

'Yes. It has.'

'So…'

'So, she's long gone, and that means the police are on their way.'

'The police?'

'She's called them. Told them everything.'

'Oh, my.'

'If you left now, you'd get away.'

'You think?'

'Please, just leave…'

'Okay,' said Olivia. 'Well, you're right, maybe I should leave. You know, before the police get here. Yes, that sounds like a good idea.'

'Yes.'

'Just before I go, though…'

'Yes?' Susanna swallowed hard.

'A favour. It's nothing, really. Silly. But, if you don't mind?'

Susanna nodded.

'Carissa's gone. Long gone, as you say. Which is a shame.' Olivia was talking to herself now. 'Such a shame.'

Rachael squeezed her mother harder.

Olivia came out of her daydream. 'Sorry, I was miles away. Anyway, call out to Carrie, Susie.'

Susanna's eyes flicked around, while Olivia sipped her tea.

'I know it's a silly thing to do, what with her being long gone, but please, indulge me.'

Susanna looked at Rachael.

'She's not there to hear you. She's long gone, we know that. So she can't possibly be tricked into coming in here and sitting with us, can she?'

Rachael's breathing became louder.

'So…call out to her, Susie. Say "Everything's okay, come on in".' Olivia picked up the gun and pointed it at Rachael. 'Now.'

'Okay, okay,' said Susanna. 'Please, just put the gun down.'

'…This is insane. Nothing like this has ever happened before on the Winnies, or, I doubt, will ever happen again…'

Olivia didn't put the gun down. She was the one giving the orders. She cocked her head slightly as if to say, 'You first.'

Susanna looked at Rachael and then turned towards the hallway. 'Carrie? Carrie…Carrie, if you can hear me…run, honey, run, run!'

A deafening blast from the handgun roared out. The sound of the gunshot gave way to screams.

Whose screams they were wasn't clear to Olivia. There were three Richards family members opposite her now, Carissa having run in following the blast. Susanna grabbed hold of Rachael and squeezed her, and then pushed her away at arm's length to check her for injuries. As if at this distance, there would be just an injury. If the shot hadn't been just a warning, there would have been only death, instant and messy death. No injury. But Rachael was fine, of course, apart from the shock of having just been shot at. Carissa cried and held her mother. Olivia sipped her tea.

'Do you think I want to kill you?' she asked. 'Don't you think if that's what I wanted, I'd have done it by now? And yet you goad me, you tempt me to kill you, Susie, and your daughters too. Why would you want that? Why would you want them dead? Is that what you want? I just don't get it. Why would you put me in a position where I had every right to kill them? Why not just do as I ask?'

There was no answer. It wasn't even clear if Susanna could hear what Olivia was saying.

'Welcome back, by the way, Carrie. We feared you were *long gone.*'

'Why are you doing this?' asked Carissa.

Olivia pondered the question as the radio barked on.

'…Wow. I'm almost speechless. Let's take a moment to gather our thoughts. Let's get our groove on. Damo will be back with us with all the details you need in three…'

What possible answer could Olivia give that would satisfy Carissa? In their eyes, they were the good guys and she was the evil one. It was that cut and dried, that straightforward. Nothing Olivia could say would change that, not even the truth about their family. Or would it? Perhaps now was the time.

She took another drink of the tea while considering her next move. 'This really is delicious. And good for my heart you say, Rachael? An added bonus. Thank you for sharing.'

No, she decided. It wasn't quite time. The plan was working and it had to be stuck to. This was the only threat to its success; not Susanna nor her daughters. Not the police. Not Michael storming in to save the day. None of those things were a real threat to the plan. The only threat was the same one it had been all along: Olivia's own enthusiasm to get it done and dusted. Over-eagerness would lead to failure. She had a plan and if she stuck to it nothing could stop her from taking Michael away from this fake family of his. If she showed her hand too soon, it wouldn't happen. She had worked too hard and planned too perfectly to let it slip away now. Don't be a Sykes, don't fall at the last hurdle. *You're here, you're here where you need to be. Take your time and let it play out.*

'Oh, before I forget,' she said, 'I must thank you, Carrie.'

Carissa recoiled in disgust. 'What for?'

'The constant flow of holiday photos you posted online. Tagged with the exact GPS location. Wow. Made finding you guys so much easier.' She finished the last of her tea. 'Isn't technology wonderful?'

And then, in a single motion, Olivia slammed down the empty mug with one hand and spun the handgun on the table with the other.

The girls screamed. They squeezed each other in anguish.

'Why are you doing this?' asked Susanna. 'Tell us.'

'All in good time, Susie.'

'We're not your enemy.'

'You're not?' Olivia asked. She looked down. The contrast between the spinning handgun and the beautiful mahogany table perfectly summed up what this was about. But Susanna couldn't see what Olivia could see.

Olivia deserved more.

It was *she* who deserved the mahogany table, not them.

It was *she* who deserved Michael, not them.

32

PATIENT

'…Time is of the essence, right, Damo?'

'That's right, Ken. You have two weeks, that's it, just two weeks. Two weeks from today. Four p.m., to be exact. So, two additional weeks to nominate yourself, a family member, a loved one, a neighbour, a stranger who did something special, anyone who you believe is on a par with our other potential Great British Heroes. This is insane!'

Michael's constant questions were becoming painful.

'How the hell can you know what's happening?' he asked.

After all he had seen and heard, was he still doubting me? 'I don't know how,' I said. 'I just do.'

We ran another red light. This time, other motorists noticed and horns blasted. Michael gestured apologies to them. We were taking too many risks.

'It's not that I doubt you, David. I just, I can't work out what, these visions, this, super-vision you seem to have…'

'*You* don't understand, *I* don't understand. It doesn't matter. Stay focused on what matters. The girls. The *girls*, Michael! They're at her mercy. We have to stop Reyes.'

There were a few seconds when he didn't ask anything. It was quiet. It was heaven. It was short-lived.

'Can you see what will happen next?'

For fuck's sake! 'I'm working on it, Michael.'

The Jaguar skidded around a corner, very nearly colliding with a parked car.

'*Working* on it?' He kept on. On and on.

'I told you before, it takes time.'

'We don't have time!'

What a twat.

We were on our way to save them because of *me*. We were in a fast car because of *me*. I closed my eyes, partly because another vision was coming and partly to block out what was about to happen. The top of a hill, going at high speed with a low-lying chassis. We flew and landed heavily, sparks flying, exhaust blowing.

'…So, there you have it, folks, straight from the mouth of Damo himself. There'll be a new contestant to replace the disgraced Evan Sykes. Could it be you? Could it be someone you know? Now, as always, terms and conditions are on the Great Briton Awards website but hang on now and listen carefully, because some things are not as you may expect…'

'Reyes has finished her tea,' I said.

'Tea?'

'Yeah, some herbal crap.'

Michael spoke to himself. 'Kombucha.'

I opened my eyes. The traffic was building. 'We need to get off this road.'

33

DOCTOR

Perfectly balanced, the handgun spun and spun.

'…Four new rules. Doesn't matter how amazing you are, the next Damo even, it doesn't mean anything if you don't follow these rules. Rule 1: oh, this is a biggie, this is going to upset an awful lot of you out there. Nobody who has previously entered will be considered. Wow. Let me say that again. No former entries. At all. Without exception. Don't bother reapplying, it's a waste of time. They're looking for something fresh, someone completely new, someone they haven't read about or heard about at all before, okay?'

The spinning gun wobbled slightly.

'…Now, I know that's going to mean a whole chunk of people listening are out of the running right away. Yeah, well, I'm sorry about that. There's nothing to stop you applying next year, but this time, for this special Sykes replacement, sorry, you're no good…'

Olivia took the time to meet the eyes of each of her captives. She showed no emotion. No guilt or sympathy. No remorse or regret.

'….Okay, time for Rule 2. This one's a direct result of everything that's happened. Now, I'm paraphrasing here, but basically, if you're full of bull, you're going to be found out. Listen,

Sykes was a wake-up call. We all know some of the people who've applied are full of it, but here's the thing: they get found out. They always do. Okay, Sykes got much further than anyone else, too far, but they're going to pick you apart even more since his situation unfolded. So, if you aren't one hundred per cent completely and utterly legit, forget it, okay? But not only that folks, they haven't got the patience for timewasters. So here's what they're doing: you waste their time with bull, they're going to sue. Let me say that again. They are going to take you to court. But no publicity like with Sykes, nope, no publicity at all, just pain, money and maybe even cell time. And don't think they won't, okay? This has always been in the rules, but they're making it crystal clear now; you make crap up, you pay all expenses. You can thank Sykes for that one, well, all of these rules I guess. That guy is going to be paying them back all his life. So, unless you've got super-deep pockets and fancy taking them on, forget about it…'

Olivia took an intake of breath and closed her eyes, wanting to savour every second. The radio continued to fill the silence.

'…Rule 3 is a simple one, okay? They're up against it time-wise, as Damo said, so entries need to be via online submission only. Online only, people. Right, the fourth and final rule for the Sykes replacement is coming up right now after these messages from our sponsors. And believe me, you're going to want to hear this final rule!'

Eyes still closed, Olivia heard whimpers through the darkness. *Yes*, she thought, *be scared. You're right to be scared.* She imagined their faces, like long-lost memories, in her mind. She had seen this before, in her visions, how it would go. This was a moment she'd envisaged ever since that first instant she'd seen them. Their smug little faces, *not so smug now.* She was taking Susie's husband and the girls' father from them, and they didn't even know it. They were too worried about staying alive. Olivia slowly opened her eyes to see the gun come to the most serene of halts.

'The moment of truth arrives,' she said.

Her hand reached down to lift up the gun and point it at her first victim, the mother of two.

Olivia didn't know if it was resignation, an admission of defeat or a challenge, but Susanna looked her dead in the eye. Unlike her daughters, Susanna didn't look as Olivia had always dreamed. She didn't look scared at all. She didn't have fear in her eyes. Instead, she had a steely stare that was directed straight back at Olivia. She looked ready to die, this woman who had prevented Michael from being with Olivia. Perhaps she thought that dying would save the lives of her daughters. It wouldn't. All three of them had the same destiny. It was irrelevant where the gun had stopped spinning.

Without hesitation, Olivia pulled the trigger.

34

PATIENT

'…Will you be the next Damo? The next sir? The next millionaire?'

It was the first time I'd heard about the monetary prize fund. I'd always thought money wouldn't be all that important, not when you had superpowers. But a million quid, that was a decent chunk of change no matter who you were, no matter what you could or couldn't do.

'…For those of you just hearing the news, it's time to get moving! The show will select a replacement for Sykes, and it could be you, okay? But there's only two weeks to get your submissions in. And there are extra rules because of the short turnaround. We've had three and here's the final one…'

'I can see her,' I said, eyes closed tightly. 'Michael…' I opened my eyes. 'Michael…she has a gun.'

For once he didn't say anything, and instead let his actions do the talking. He slammed his foot down and we raced across a busy crossroads. Cars crashed into each other. Carnage. But it was behind us, we were through. That was good, but there was no staying incognito now. It was barely a few seconds later when sirens screamed out and then a police car appeared behind us from a side road.

'Shit!' I said.

'What do I do?' he asked.

'...This is going to affect a lot of the people out there who are thinking, "Yes, *I'm* going to be the next Damo." Yeah, well, what I'm about to say may well throw a huge spanner in your works. And remember, I'm just the messenger, okay, so no shooting...'

The good news was that it was only a patrol car. A Ford Fiesta. It was no match under the bonnet, even with Michael at the wheel.

'Lose him,' I said.

'But could he help us?'

He still doesn't get it. 'No.'

'But he's a police officer.'

'That's right. He's a police officer. And I'm a convicted criminal, a criminal who you have broken out of prison.'

I could see him struggling with the logic. After all, the police service had always been the answer for people like him, upper middle class as he was. He had no idea he wasn't that person any more. Those services weren't available to him now. They were *after* him.

'But if he follows us to the house he can...'

I couldn't take any more. 'Michael. Listen to me. If he catches us, Susanna and the girls are dead. You hear me? *Dead.* He will not believe us. He will not understand. He will not care. He will stop us. He will stop us, and then, they will *die.*'

Michael refocused on the road. Maybe he finally got it. No police, no rules. Just family. He hung a left at high speed when I wasn't expecting it. My head smashed hard against the side window and then bounced against the dashboard.

'Shit,' I heard. 'You okay, David? David?'

'...I'll say that again. Unique. Now, you're probably thinking, every single one of you, that of course you're unique, whether you're applying or not. And I can't argue with that. But they can, and they most certainly will. What do I mean? Well, I have a Winnies spokesman coming up after the next two songs, who'll explain exactly what this means, and, guys and girls, it's not what you expect. So stay tuned and all will be revealed after these classic nineties tracks...'

I dropped the sun visor and checked myself in the mirror. My head was bloodied. My eyes were watering. I touched the wound; it hurt like hell. 'Goddamn it.'

Michael was doing his best to get through the city traffic. 'You okay?'

'Fine. I'm fine. Just concentrate on the road.' I was matter-of-fact. 'Take this left.'

'It's the wrong way, though.'

'I know. Trust me.'

He cut off an SUV to make the turn. He did well. Once we on the faster road, the patrol car disappeared into the distance as if it was in reverse gear. Within a few seconds, we were free of the pursuit.

'We're heading south…' he said.

And?

'…my house is north.'

I closed my eyes, pain still emitting from the wound on my head.

'Susie and the girls, they're the other way.'

What does he want from me?

'I'm going to turn around.'

'No, you're not.'

'We're heading the wrong way…'

'Michael, listen, I've been here before.'

'What?'

'I've been here,' I said. 'Before.'

'What do you mean?' he asked. 'You know this part of town?'

He doesn't get it. 'No. I mean, I've *done* this…before.'

'You what?'

'Although…' I opened my eyes, '…last time *I* was driving.'

35

DOCTOR

The pistol clicked. No bang this time.

They screamed out in horror. Slowly, the realisation that the gun wasn't loaded set in, and Susie and the girls held each other in confused relief.

Olivia, calm as you like, put the gun back down on the table. 'Just a trial run,' she said.

'...Thanks for joining us, Charles,' said the radio. 'You don't mind me calling you "Charlie", do you?'

'Actually, I do.'

'Sweet. So, Charlie, tell us more about this Rule 4...'

'Please,' said Susanna, steely gaze now *long gone*. 'We've done nothing. Please, Olivia...'

Olivia was having none of it. She opened her jacket pocket and pulled out a single bullet.

'Please, no,' pleaded Susanna.

Olivia picked up the gun and loaded it, while staring intently at Susanna.

'It doesn't have to be this way.'

Olivia cocked the gun. 'I'm afraid it does, Susie. I'm afraid it very much does.' She slammed the now-loaded gun down on to the table and once again spun it.

36

PATIENT

We were in trouble. There were now two more police cars on our tail. The problem was that they weren't simply patrol vehicles.

'It's okay, hang on,' said Michael, again not getting it.

'They're traffic cops. They're trained to do this.'

A BMW 530d and an Audi S3. But it wasn't just the firepower they had, it was the expertise behind the wheel. *Versus Michael? No contest.*

'So, what then?' he asked. 'What do I do?'

'I need to think.' I covered my eyes with my hand. My head hurt like hell. 'No talking.'

'But David–'

'No talking.'

'...Okay, okay, here we go. About ten minutes ago, I told the nation that they needed to be unique to be considered, and that this was a new rule. Charlie, baby, come on, how is that a new rule? Surely that's *the* rule, rule *numero uno*, and always has been? It's what the Winnies is all about, no? So, what are we talking about here? Spill the beans, because I have it in front of me here and I think there's going to be a lot of disappointed people out there. People who no longer qualify for the chance of being Sykes's replacement, am I right?'

'Well, yes and no, I would think. This rule is slightly trickier than the others so I hope everyone out there will listen carefully.'

'You have their undivided attention, Charlie, trust me.'

'Good. Okay. So, as a committee, when we make our decisions we like to pick the very best contestants for the show. Now that sounds obvious, I know, but what constitutes the "best contestants for the show" isn't perhaps quite as simple as one may think. While we'd like to simply pick the five people who most excite us with their heroism, their abilities, their amazing feats, it doesn't always make for the best show. Let me give you an example from last year. We had two or three people who all demonstrated incredibly brave feats of heroism that required incredible strength. Now, one could say that they all deserved a place in the latter stages of the competition. However, for the good of the show it was decided that only one of those contestants would go forward. You see, if the final was made up of people with the same stories, powers and abilities, it wouldn't be, well, the incredibly versatile show it is today, I'm sure you'd agree...'

'David, they're getting closer–'

'Ssh.'

'...We don't want to waste anyone's time, including our own, so here's what we've agreed. We're only looking for what we consider to be unique stories and unique people, compared to the four finalists we already have in place. In other words, if your story is similar to one of theirs, then, I'm sorry, for this year at least, we'd ask you not to apply as you will not be considered. If, however, your story is completely different, unique from that of our four finalists, well, you could be who we're looking for.'

'Well, there you have it, folks. "Unique" means even more than it used to. You must have something, be something, completely different to the current finalists to even be considered, let alone stand a chance of winning. And, as if you needed reminding, that means no force fields, no minibus racers, no linguistic geniuses and no underwater breathers! Thank you, Charlie boy, for coming in and clarifying.'

'It's Charles...'

'Okay, I know what to do,' I said.

'Thank God,' said Michael, 'because they're right behind us.'

'You need to do what I say, Michael. You need to do *exactly* what I say, and exactly when I say it,' I told him, knowing there was little real chance of that actually happening.

Slam.

Our Jaguar was shunted at high speed by the Audi cop car. Michael lost the steering wheel. I tried to grab it but was thrown back by a second jolt. I did my best to brace myself between the ceiling of the car and the dashboard. We slid wildly out of control, slamming into parked cars before coming to a stop against a brick wall.

He looked at me, dazed.

'Move,' I said.

Michael turned the key not realising the engine was already running. His head was all over the place. I reminded him of the urgency of the situation we were in, which was heightened by the sight of the BMW heading towards us in a controlled slide. It was merely feet away from blocking us in when Michael finally got the Jaguar into gear. Wheel spinning away, we left the BMW to slam into the brick wall behind us.

'Yes!' he shouted, happy with himself.

'Take this right,' I said.

He was too slow. 'Which right?' He realised, too late, that by 'this' I meant 'this'. 'Shit!'

Despite missing it, Michael spun the wheel and slammed the brakes on in an attempt to make the turn. The Jaguar slid across three lanes of traffic, narrowly missing oncoming cars and a bus.

I leant over to push the wheel and we made the turn. The Audi, trained driver behind the wheel, was back all over our tail. Then the BMW returned, swerving in front of us as we left the lane. We were the filling in a cop sandwich.

'What are they doing?' he asked me.

Their job.

'What do I do?'

I don't have all the answers.

Or do I?

The police were well rehearsed. They closed in from each end. We were being slowed down. We would be in handcuffs very soon.

'Slow down,' I said.

'What?'

'Let them slow us down. Gradually.'

'But–'

'Just do it.'

'Okay.'

He slammed on the brakes, causing the Audi to hit us from behind.

'For fuck's sake, Michael, I said, do it gradually!'

'Okay, shit, sorry.'

He eased off the brake pedal. The cops knew what they were doing and gently bumped us from each end, slowing us further. We were down to forty, then thirty miles an hour. Twenty, ten and, finally, we came to a halt.

'What now?'

'Stay calm. Wait for my cue.'

I reached over and pushed my foot down on to the clutch without Michael even noticing. He was too busy focusing on the officers who were getting out of their cars. I turned the steering wheel completely to the left. From my wing mirror, I could see the Audi driver pulling a Taser from his belt. The cop from the BMW was approaching from in front of us; he was speaking into a radio and his hand was unclipping a weapon.

Come on. Come on. Change. 'Change!' I said, not realising the word had slipped out.

Michael looked at me and realised I wasn't watching the approaching officers. I was watching the traffic lights at each end of the road. I watched and waited for what seemed like an eternity. Finally, I saw the lights change in my wing mirror.

Green. Go. 'Floor it.'

Michael, for once, didn't ask any questions. He slammed the pedal to the floor. But the car didn't move. It just screamed.

'Hang the fuck on.' I engaged second gear and released the clutch.

The back wheels spun and we were propelled forwards and to the left. We smashed into the back of the BMW as the wheels found traction. The brake lights smashed and the Jaguar's front bumper was destroyed, but we slid by anyway. We shot out across the lanes. Michael got hold of the wheel and we were away, just out in front of the next wave of released traffic. We were in fourth gear before the cops could even get back into their cars. In the mirror I could see that when they finally fired up and moved out, a wall of gridlocked traffic greeted them, while we squeezed through the next set of lights.

'Holy shit!' said Michael. 'That was amazing! How did we do that?'

We? We did it by you being completely unaware of what was going on so I could save the day – again.

I watched the road behind, but they were disappearing fast. We were in top gear now and flying with an open road ahead of us. We'd be at the house before they could catch us.

'We did it, we're only a few blocks away, I can't believe we did it.'

I closed my eyes and said, 'Not yet, we haven't.'

37

DOCTOR

The gun stopped spinning much more abruptly this time. It pointed not at Susanna, but instead halfway between her two daughters, who both immediately clamped on to their mother.

'Hmm…' Olivia said, as if trying to decide which flavour ice cream to try. 'Which to go for? I just can't decide.'

'Please don't do this, you don't have to do this,' begged Susanna.

'No, you're right, Susie. You're absolutely right. I *don't* have to do this. I *don't* have to decide. Tell you what, *you* decide for me.' Olivia looked at Susanna as if she was the ice cream seller and she was looking for a recommendation because she was so torn between two flavours. 'Choose for me.'

Susanna's lip quivered.

Reyes picked up the gun and waved it back and forth between the two girls.

'Choose, Susie, or…I'll kill them both.'

38

PATIENT

The cop cars were long gone. We'd made it to the house.

As we approached, Michael pressed a button on his key fob and the double doors of the garage opened. We disappeared inside.

I jumped out of the car and reached the front garden before the garage doors could close. A few steps in, I felt a sharp piercing pain resonate through my temple – the wound from the car window was now open to the elements and it stung like hell. I collapsed to the ground, holding my head. Michael said something, lots of things. 'What do I do?' probably.

I said what needed to be said. 'Her gun is loaded now. She's inside. Go and stop her. Do whatever it takes.' I held out the guard's pistol to him. He said something, I don't know what, I think I heard the word 'kombucha'. Jibberish. 'There's no time Michael. I've got you this far. Now it's down to you.'

He took the gun and left me.

The end was near.

39

DOCTOR

'Susanna,' said Olivia, 'you have precisely the time it takes me to walk over and turn that noise off to decide.'

She rose from the table and walked over to the radio, all the time holding the handgun in a casual manner as if who ultimately received the bullet was a matter of indifference to her. She turned off the obnoxious disc jockey and returned to her seat. There was still no decision from Susanna.

'I'm seriously running out of patience with you now, Susie. Choose, or I *will* kill them both, both of these girls, right now, in front of your eyes. Which would mean that not only would both your daughters be dead, but that you were directly responsible for one of their deaths.'

'No,' said Susanna.

'Yes. You would have killed them. You could have saved one and chose not to, just by not giving me a name. Not solely responsible, I give you that, and granted, I'll take complete blame for the first one, that's only fair, but the second one, the second murder, well, her blood will be on your hands, Susie. And, for that matter, on your face and pretty much everywhere else, I expect.'

'Please, please! There must be another way!' said Susanna, in desperation. 'We have money – it's yours, all of it.'

'Money?' asked Olivia. 'You think money can fix this? Money? Money might satisfy you, Susie, but not me. God, you're shallow. Is that all you care about? *Money*?'

'I care about my daughters.'

'Oh, you do? Then pick one.'

'I can't. How can I?'

'You really think this can be fixed with *money*?' asked Olivia again.

'I don't know,' said Susanna. 'I don't know what this is about. Tell me! Tell me what it's about so we can work something out. Whatever pain we've caused you, I'm sorry, I didn't know. Tell me. It's not too late.'

'Not *too late*?'

'You've given us a scare, yes, but that's all. If you stop now, that's all it will be, just a bit of a scare. We can deal with that, get you help…'

'Who's going to help me? Michael? You really have no idea what's going on here, do you? Look, Susie, it's quite simple. You can save the life of one of your daughters right now. All you need to do is choose. Just a name, that's all I need. Or you can say nothing and watch them both die right here in front of your eyes.'

'I beg you,' said Susanna. 'I'll do anything.'

'Last chance.' Olivia cocked the pistol.

'I'll do anything!'

'Time's up.' Olivia took a breath and then made her decision. 'Right, let's see. I…choose…Rachael. Yes, Rachael…'

'No, please!' begged Susanna again. Rachael squeezed her big sister like never before.

'Please, Susie, let me finish…Rachael, you've been kind to me today, very kind, indeed. The tea and everything. So, I've decided to reward you.' Olivia closed her eyes. 'Yes, oh, I'm so glad you didn't choose after all, Susie. This is definitely the way it should be.' She smiled. 'Yes, this feels right. Almost like it's the only possible way forward, almost like it's already happened and I'm just here to…make sure it stays…on course.' She opened her eyes to see her three hostages cradling each other. It was all so clear now. She'd seen this moment and the rest of the evening play out in her visions over and over again.

'Rachael…thank you again. So, I'm going to return the favour now and save you the horror of watching your sister die…by killing you first.'

With no more discussion Olivia pointed the gun directly at Rachael's face.

'Mum!' screamed Rachael.

A bang enveloped the room and all the screams within it.

40

PATIENT

I stumbled to a window, regaining my composure enough to see and hear Michael doing his best.

An almighty bang rang out as Michael burst into the dining room and the door slammed against the wall. Completely out of his comfort zone, he stumbled, his gun stuck in his jacket pocket. By the time he'd managed to wrestle it out and point it anywhere useful, Reyes had already redirected her gun at him. He came to an awkward stop halfway between the doorway and the table.

'Michael,' she said. 'Finally. Do you have any idea how long I've been waiting for you?'

41

DOCTOR

Olivia had an incredible assuredness about her. You'd think she'd just spotted a butterfly entering the room, the way she simply redirected her gaze and her gun. She behaved as though the scene was a play she was directing, with characters she'd created and dialogue she'd scripted, as though she had not only read the page ahead but had written it in the first place, and made notes in the margin, whimsical little thoughts and reminders of what to expect next.

Olivia closed her eyes. She could see it all unfolding and she barely had to do more than breathe, for it would take care of itself. This was everything she'd seen, this was everything she'd dreamt of. More than fate, this was truth.

She tried to think of a time before this truth had consumed her thoughts and dreams, but there was none. Especially so since she had seen Michael. Since that day, this was the only moment that had mattered in her life. And more than ever before, it was clear now, there was only one truth and one outcome: Michael Richards, a man who was currently pointing a gun at her, was going to leave this house and this life with her tonight.

She smiled. 'Welcome home. We've been waiting for you. And now you're here. Finally, the whole family is together. And I don't know about the others, but, personally, I couldn't be any happier.'

'Olivia…' said Michael.

'Yes?'

'…what are you doing?'

'I'm doing what's necessary. What are *you* doing?'

'I came to stop you.'

'Oh, I see. Well, go on, then.'

Michael said, and did, nothing.

It was clear to Olivia that Michael hadn't planned beyond this moment. 'Well done for making it this far. I mean it, you've exceeded my expectations. If I'm honest, I didn't think you had it in you.' Still nothing from Michael. He was a deer in the headlights. 'Someone helped you, didn't they?'

'What?'

'And now they're…gone?'

'Yes.'

'Just you?'

'Just me.'

'To stop me.'

'That's right,' Michael said, as though waking from a trance. 'To stop you. It's over, Olivia. Okay? It's over.'

As if he has a clue what's going on.

'Put the gun down,' he said, 'a-and, give it up.'

Olivia found this highly amusing. A giggle escaped her. She wasn't bothered by how strange that was, a giggle. She wasn't bothered by the bullet in Michael's gun. She wasn't bothered by anything outside this bubble of certainty she occupied.

'You're surrounded by armed police officers,' said Michael.

'Is that the best you can do? Surrounded by cops?'

'It's true.'

'No, it's not. You're full of shit. You're not convincing anyone. Not me, not your family, and not even yourself.' Olivia pitied him, but he'd brought all this on himself. It was necessary, all of this. There was no other way and now that he was here the long wait was almost over.

'You're wrong,' he said. 'We've been watching the whole thing, everything that's happened. We've surrounded the house. We've been watching you.'

More giggles from Olivia.

'I mean it.'

'Prove it.'

'Okay, okay… The gun…we knew it wasn't loaded before, that's why we didn't come in.'

His logic didn't hold up, although his knowledge of what had happened piqued her interest.

'We knew it wasn't loaded, but now, now, I've been sent in as your last chance. Listen to me. They're ready to finish this and shoot you from ten different angles, but I begged them to let me speak to you first. Please, Olivia.' He used her name; he was regaining his composure and his training was coming to the fore. 'Olivia, come on now, whatever this is about, you know you don't want to harm these people. Let's let them leave, okay? I'll stay, I'll take their place. You and me, we can sit down and sort this out. Nobody needs to get hurt here.'

'What makes you think this is about you, Michael?' Olivia asked.

'I don't know what it's about,' he said.

'Do you have a guilty conscience or something?'

Michael looked at his family, eyes pleading innocence. He returned to the same rhetoric as before. 'Come on, Olivia, let's you and me sit down and sort this mess out. Let the others go, eh?'

'Nah, I like them right here. But you're right, Michael, you're right that this is all about you. Me and you. Not so much *them*.'

'So, why not let them go?'

'Well, I think they need to be part of this. It's only fitting. They need to see it. I don't think they'd believe it, if they didn't witness it for themselves. I want them to see you…' she trailed off. *Not yet*, she told herself. *Not just yet*. 'I want them to see the real you, Michael,' she concluded.

'Olivia, I don't know what you're talking about. Listen to me, let them go and we can sort this out.'

'The real you. Who you really are.'

There was a moment in which everyone waited for something to happen.

'Let them go!' Michael raised his voice.

'Or what?'

'There are armed officers ready to…'

Olivia had had enough. 'You're lying, Michael.'

'I'm not. Give it up.'

'Yes, you are. You're lying.'

His family looked on in hope but Michael fluffed his lines. 'You put th-the gun down now or they, they w-will open fire.'

Olivia was getting annoyed. 'You're a terrible liar,' she said. 'Which surprises me. I expected more from you, what with all the practice you've had at lying to women. At lying to yourself.'

Michael started stammering again. He repeated himself about working it out, about the cops waiting outside. That's all he had and it wasn't working, but he kept trying anyway.

Olivia let out a huge exaggerated sigh. 'Enough. You're boring me now. You know, all these years, how hard I've worked, you're not actually worth it, are you?' And with that she redirected the gun back in the direction of Susie and the girls.

Michael jumped forward a step and pleaded. 'No, no, at me! Point it back at me!'

'I think it's time to start telling the truth.'

'Okay, okay, wait. Wait, all right. You're right. There aren't any police, I made all that up. It's just you, me and my family. It's just us, okay? That's the truth.'

Olivia closed her eyes. 'Is it the truth? Really? Are you sure you're alone? I think you might still be lying. How can I believe you? How can your wife and daughters believe you when they've been lied to for so very, very long?'

Michael stared at her.

Maybe he finally realises this is about something else. Not just the lies of the last few minutes.

Michael searched the eyes of his wife again and then of his children and then looked back at their captor. He stood there with nothing to offer.

'Come on, Michael, it's time to come clean.'

'I-I don't…' he said, stammering again.

'You've been lying for so long now you've even convinced yourself. That's how good you've become at it. I guess you've always been a liar. But now, here, tonight, it's time to stop. It's time for you to start telling the truth, Doctor Richards. Why don't you tell your lovely family the truth?'

Michael was a statue. He was either choosing to reveal nothing, or truly believed there was nothing to say.

'Come on. Don't make *me* tell them. This'll be hard enough for them as it is. It's better that it comes from you.'

Michael looked at Susanna again. Her face was full of a new kind of fear. He could see thoughts in her eyes, dark thoughts, sad thoughts. *Surely not, not Michael. He's devoted to me. What's Olivia implying? Not her. Not any other woman, surely. Especially not her.* It was written all over Susanna's face, more fear than of any bullet. Her eyes searched his and her head slowly shook from side to side, begging for it to be lies.

'What are you talking about?' asked Michael. He looked over at his wife. 'Susie…' he redirected his words from one woman to the other, '…I don't know what she's talking–'

Olivia snapped. 'Don't you dare!' she said. 'Don't you dare pretend it didn't happen!'

Susanna looked at Michael.

And then, much more quietly, and for the first time since all this started, with sorrow in her voice, Olivia followed up with the truth she'd held inside herself forever. 'Don't you dare pretend…that *I* didn't happen.'

Michael was slow on the uptake. He looked at Susanna, and then at Olivia, and then, finally, he *saw* who Olivia was. He saw her eyes, and, for the first time, recognised them not as belonging to his doctor, but to his lover.

42

PATIENT

I thought it was about time to intervene. I'd seen the action unfold in front of me through the kitchen window: Michael with the guard's gun, his family curled up in horror, Reyes in charge. It was like watching a bizarre, melodramatic soap opera. And now I would climb in through the TV screen and be the guest star. I was amazed it had got to this point. But, more than ever, now that I was here, now that we were *all* here, I knew exactly what I needed to do.

I was ready to blow their minds.

43

DOCTOR

Beautiful hazelnut eyes. He'd fallen in love with them the moment he'd seen them. No, not love. Lust. He'd seen them and gone after them.

It was hot in Barcelona, and the bar was packed as much for its air conditioning as for any other reason. He'd seen her hazel eyes from afar and, fuelled by scotch, went in for the kill. She was a local girl, he a tourist. He'd wooed her. It wasn't difficult; she was smart, but not worldly. He was a young doctor, not much older than she was, but well-travelled and well-spoken. His Spanish wasn't great but it was marginally better than her English, which meant a lot of non-verbal flirting. He'd leant over her to take his drink, and smelt her. He'd taken her hand and kissed it. Taken it away from the bar, to the street, to a cab and to his hotel.

'*Aún no*,' she'd said.

'It's okay,' he'd said. 'The bar, er, *solo el bar*.'

The hotel bar was quiet, unlike the busy and boisterous sports bar in which they'd met. This one was smoky, full of dark corners. Here, they could get to know each other; here, they were alone. They talked for hours, understanding little of each other's words, and only once did they kiss. A brief touch of the lips; it lasted for not even a second yet it lingered in the air for the whole evening.

Later, they'd made love, and then again in the morning. They'd held each other as the morning light shone through the window on to their bed.

Then, dressed in just his shirt, she'd nibbled at the room-service breakfast. He'd approached her from behind and kissed her neck.

'*No vayas*. Don't go.'

He'd made a call, one that would allow him to stay longer. A week became a month and then six weeks.

And then she'd told him she was late.

He was shocked. And hurt. She'd said she was taking precautions. She'd assured him.

Now, she had…trapped him.

His exams, just three months away, would determine his whole future. She knew this. His career was his life. She knew this too. She'd told him she was taking precautions. So she'd lied to him. *She's done this on purpose*, he'd decided, and it sickened him.

'Get rid of it,' he'd said, before he'd even considered his words, before he'd even thought what they might mean to her. When she hadn't replied, he'd realised his error and apologised. They'd held each other, and then he'd opened his wallet and given her all the notes in it. 'This should be enough.'

She hadn't needed to understand his words to understand his sentiment.

It was no less distasteful than his previous outburst, but he'd been too engrossed in counting the cash to notice her vacant stare. He'd told her he had to go away on business for a few days, maybe a week, maybe a little longer, which should give her time to sort it out. He'd kissed her on the forehead, gathered his things and left.

When he returned nearly three weeks later, he'd been relieved to hear the news he needed to hear. The time away had allowed Michael to clear his head, remind himself of what was important in his life, where he was going and what sacrifices it would take. He justified the decision he'd made, and the one he was likely to have to make next. There was no way he could have committed to being a father at that time, and so it was the best thing for everyone. They'd spent time together as before: in bars, at restaurants, walking through the city and in hotel rooms.

Except that something had changed. He'd felt it, and could tell she'd felt it too. At first, they did everything they could to ignore it. But it all felt forced.

He'd made the decision for them both. The second decision made by him. He'd told her it was over. She'd reacted badly, insanely, which told him just how right he was to end it. He decided it would be better to leave immediately. He'd tried to kiss her but she looked away. He'd walked out.

He was done with her, and with that phase of his life. Yes, maybe, he'd made promises to her, made her believe that she was more than just a fling. And he'd been convincing, to her and to himself. The truth was that he'd loved the idea of loving her more than he actually loved her. The pregnancy scare, the time away, the difference in her: it had been great while it lasted, but it had run its course. The idea of having a baby with her had proved that to him.

While he'd been there, she'd held it together. Then he'd walked out on her. And he'd walked out on the life inside of her. She'd held it together for the pregnancy too. But then the birth had happened, and she'd slowly spiralled out of control. She'd done her best as a mother, but she was never happy again.

She'd survived, though. She'd got by. But then, years later, while out walking in the square, she'd seen him. She saw Michael hand in hand with a young woman. They were so happy. Happiness that should have been *hers*. That night she'd gone to sleep, certain never to wake again.

Michael looked at his daughter. Not Carissa, and not Rachael. He looked at Olivia.

44

PATIENT

It's time.

45

DOCTOR

'Tell them, Michael,' said Olivia. 'Tell them who I am.' A lifetime of weight was lifting from her shoulders.

'Michael?' Susanna asked, perhaps realising already.

Michael was in a trance. He was reliving a time in his life that he'd done his best to forget. Before Susanna and the girls, long before this life he'd worked so hard to build for himself.

He spoke softly, not wanting to believe it yet. 'She...she told me she had...'

Olivia had envisaged this moment unfold in so many different ways over the years. The most satisfying fantasies were always those where she stood back and watched the family implode and tear themselves apart. But deep down she'd always known she wouldn't be able to resist the temptation to stick the knife in, to twist it.

'You wanted me dead before I even took a breath. Guess what? I survived.'

'Olivia, I–'

Olivia dropped a bombshell. 'She killed herself.'

'*What?*' Michael's face contorted in the same way it had when he'd heard about Jennifer's suicide.

'Oh God!' Susanna half-gasped, half-sobbed.

Olivia swallowed hard and composed herself. 'I knew I'd find you one day. I *knew* it. I never gave up, even when I realised it wasn't worth pursuing this. Even when I knew that the best thing for me to do was to go on with my life and pretend you didn't exist. You know, kind of like you did with me. But then, *that* day, I couldn't believe it. Not even in my wildest dreams did I believe karma would be so kind as to deliver you to me like that.'

'Mild cardiac arrest. Stable and comfortable. Doctor Michael Richards.' She'd scanned Michael's paperwork but it wasn't until she looked at the patient that she recognised the man as her father. *Surely not.* All she had to go on was an old photo of a man twenty-five years younger. Her mother had never even spoken his name. As different as he looked now, yes, she was certain, it was him. The photo was long gone, lost over time, and now replaced by a framed one of a woman, child and baby by his bedside. But it didn't matter; his face was burnt into her mind. It was him.

She stared at Michael, a thousand thoughts going through her mind. Her emotions threatened to take over. Something she was *not* known for.

'His family has just arrived,' said the nurse.

Family? She looked at the framed photo again. His family.

Michael's eyes opened and Olivia realised just how special this gift was. One not to be wasted. She had to be smart. A sudden emotional reaction wouldn't result in justice. A measured, calm, slow approach was needed. Professionalism. After all, he wouldn't know who she was. She was merely a doctor, his doctor, and he a patient, her patient.

'Good morning, Michael,' said Olivia. 'I hope you're up to visitors?'

She'd surprised herself with how well she'd swallowed her anger, her confusion, her excitement and everything else she was feeling. She saw her father nod at her. *He doesn't know. How could he? Why would he? He doesn't care.*

'Just a few minutes, mind.'

Stay in character. Don't give it away. Now's not the time. You have him now, so there's no hurry. Do it right.

'You still need plenty of rest.' He went to sit up but the pain must have been too much. *What a shame. Hope it doesn't hurt too much,*

Dad. 'Your lovely family is here.' Just saying the words made her feel sick to her stomach.

Olivia walked away but not quite out of sight. There they were, his wife and children. They were so happy to see him, and he them. She had to capture the moment to believe it was really happening. She whipped out her mobile and discreetly videoed them embracing until Michael's wife closed the privacy curtain.

Olivia left them to their domestic bliss, and headed for the lift.

'I'm sorry,' Michael said.

She let him look at her for a moment, while Susanna cried. 'I'm sure you are.'

He said he hadn't realised. That he hadn't known.

'You didn't care,' she said. Her gun was still pointed at his family. She cocked the chamber.

'Wait!' Michael shouted. 'Olivia, wait!' He looked beyond her, as if someone was behind her, and then looked down at the dinner table, at the empty mug. 'How was the tea, Olivia? How was the kombucha tea?'

She looked down at the mug.

'Kombucha! Kombucha!' shouted Michael, as if ordering a brigade into battle.

The kitchen window behind Olivia smashed. She didn't jump. She was composed. She dropped to the floor and slid under the table. She saw Michael rushing his family out of the house towards safety. Olivia fired her gun from beneath the table, but she missed. A second shot, and this time she hit her target. Michael fell to the floor holding his leg. One loud crash, two piercing bangs and then nothing, except a whimpering Michael.

Olivia emerged from under her makeshift bunker and walked over to her father. 'Lying till the end, doctor. Well, here's some truth for you.' She took a syringe and a bottle of fluid from the inside pocket of her jacket. She filled the syringe halfway. 'I'm going to kill you.' Michael writhed in agony. Olivia continued to fill the syringe to the top. 'Then I'm going to kill your wife.'

Michael managed a whisper. 'Wait…'

'And then I'm going to kill your daughters…'

Michael coughed and spluttered, and whispered again. 'They're your sisters…' he said, but Olivia didn't care.

The young girls, huddled in the corner, only now realised what was going on.

'…so you can play happy families together in the afterlife,' said Olivia.

46

PATIENT

I casually walked over to a half-empty bottle of red wine on the kitchen worktop. I poured myself a glass. Châteauneuf-du-Pape. Nobody noticed. I was invisible to them.

'Hello, doctor,' I said, as if greeting my GP to discuss an annoying rash.

Reyes spun around, syringe in hand, confusion all over her face. 'What the hell? Why are *you* here?'

'Now, that's a very good question.' I took another sip of the fine wine. It hit the spot.

'And?'

'And, until a few moments ago, I wouldn't have had an answer for you.'

'Okay. And now?'

'Well, now, you see,' I said, 'hmm, now, it all makes perfect sense. I'm here for the same reason as you, Doctor Reyes.' I took another drink. She looked back and forth between me and her four hostages. Michael was still holding his leg, but he was quiet now. 'I also have a really good idea of how this will end.'

'Is that so?'

I nodded. 'It's a talent I've developed.'

'Is that right? You're one of those amazing people I've been reading about, huh? One of the special ones? Your superpower is, what? That you can see the future?'

'If you like.'

'What a coincidence, that's something we share.' She shot me a look, and I kind of felt her in my thoughts. It didn't shake my confidence.

'Well, go on, then' she said, 'let's hear it.'

'Nah, you'll find out soon enough.'

'Oh, come on, do tell.'

'You're not going to like it.'

'Try me.'

'Okay,' I said. 'But I warned you. Basically, you're going to be shot dead.'

She smiled. I guess she saw things panning out differently. Or perhaps she didn't. I wasn't sure of the visions I'd had since the head wound and was filling in the gaps as I went along, with a mix of best guesses and best wishes.

'Shot dead?' she asked. 'Really? You're right, in that I don't particularly like that. Any more details for me, so, you know, I can see it coming, like *you* can?'

'Chest. Shot dead, through the chest.'

'Chest? Ouch. Sounds nasty.' She held her chest and mimed how painful it might be. 'How long do I have?'

'Not long.'

'How long?'

'Oh, I'd say–'

'I'd say you don't know,' she said. 'You're stalling. You're a fraud, aren't you, David? Your family, your visions, it was all a lie, wasn't it? And now you're here and you've failed in whatever sick, twisted plan you had.'

I smiled at her and took another drink. 'I'm past caring whether people believe me or not,' I said, 'least of all you. But it's irrelevant now. In a minute or so, this'll all be over.'

'A minute? That's all I have? Ah, you must mean all the armed cops surrounding the house, huh?'

'Is that what Michael told you? Nah, he lied about that.'

'Yeah, well,' Reyes looked at Michael on the floor, 'that's what he does best.' She turned to me again. 'So, I guess you're going to draw and shoot me gunslinger style, is that it?'

I poured the rest of the wine and downed it in one. 'Not exactly.'

Click, from behind Reyes. Michael had cocked the guard's handgun and was pointing it at her back. He'd also recovered his voice. 'Put the gun down, Olivia. The syringe too.'

Michael with a gun, Reyes with a gun and a syringe, and me with an empty wine glass.

Reyes didn't seem scared in the slightest. She didn't believe that Michael would fire. Or maybe she knew he'd miss or chicken out, or perhaps she knew something else. She remained in complete control. 'Or what, Michael? You'll shoot me in the chest?'

'I'll do whatever it takes to protect my family…' Michael's words tailed off as if he realised they were ill-chosen.

'I guess that's where I get it from,' Reyes said. She raised her gun and pointed it at Susie and the girls. 'Lower the pistol, doctor, or I'll put a bullet in each of your three…'

I saw the chamber of her gun. I'd seen her load and fire the only bullets she'd had. *That's why she has a syringe.* 'Go ahead,' I said, 'shoot them.'

Michael lost his head. 'No, wait!' he shouted.

'It's okay, Michael. Michael, Michael, listen to me, it's okay. She's out of bullets.' Reyes turned to look at me uneasily. I smiled before continuing. 'She only loaded two. One is lodged in the wall over there, a warning shot across Rachael's bow. The other, as I'm sure you're aware, is in your leg.' I smiled again. 'Hence the syringe.'

Although she was shocked, Reyes wasn't finished. 'Okay, that's impressive. Impressive, but completely academic. It doesn't matter in the slightest. He could have a machine gun pointed at me, but the truth is my father isn't going to shoot me.' Reyes turned to Michael. 'Are you, Dad?'

What? 'Father?' I asked. 'Did you just call him "Dad"?'

Reyes mocked me. 'Oh? You didn't see that one coming, huh? Not so impressive, after all.'

She laughed and slipped the gun into her pocket. She held the syringe out in front of her. She started striding towards Michael, who still had the guard's gun pointed at her. But I could see he was wavering. If it was true, that Reyes was his daughter – his daughter! – I knew he couldn't do it.

'C'mon, old man, do it,' she taunted. 'Do it! Finish the job you started twenty-five years ago!' She struck her father hard across the arm and the guard's gun took flight. Michael lunged towards it as it hit the floor, but not before she stabbed him in the neck with the syringe and injected him. He continued after the gun for a few more steps, and then he dropped to his knees and fell forwards in the doorway to the living room. Reyes pushed his slumped frame into the living room with her foot. His limp body lay on the floor.

And just like that, Michael was gone.

Reyes removed the syringe from her father's neck and walked back across the kitchen towards Susie and the girls, who were screaming in the opposite corner. 'One down. Three to go.' She checked the fluid level in the syringe.

It had happened so fast. I realised I needed a weapon. I couldn't just rely on my visions any more. I had to take control of everybody's future. I spotted the guard's gun on the floor and took advantage of Reyes's new focus.

I grabbed the gun and shoved it into her back. 'I don't think so, doctor.'

She still acted cool. I couldn't believe it. 'What happened to "shot in the chest"?' she asked, with no change in her tone.

No, I thought, *not in the chest.* I raised the barrel of the gun up her spine until it was at chest height. 'No, doctor. Not *in* the chest. Through. *Through* the chest.' I cocked the gun, and slowly shepherded Reyes away from Susanna, Carissa and Rachael.

She complied and held her hands up. One of them still held the syringe, which was more than half full of a0 purple liquid. We were nearing the door, but I realised I didn't know what to do with her. For the first time since all this began, there was no plan.

She spoke, which gave me time to think. 'Tell me, David, what are you doing here? Why do you even care?'

I'd been thinking about it since I came to, out on the lawn. Well, I'd been thinking about it ever since I woke up in hospital all that time ago, but specifically since arriving here at the house, with my head bloodied and splitting. I'd had a new vision while I was out there on the grass. Not about what was going to happen, though, rather about why all this was happening to *me*. A whole new thought about why I was here, with this gift. I'd realised, looking through the window at Susanna and her daughters, watching them fear for their lives, watching their relief when their husband and father arrived to save them. I'd realised, finally, that, no, they weren't my family. I was never married to Susanna. We never exchanged rings. We never went on holiday to Paris. We never bought this house. I realised I'd never taken Rachael to football practice, or bought her her first goalkeeping gloves. I'd never banned Carissa from her mobile for a week after she'd signed up to a social network before she was of age. I'd never handed baby Rachael to two-year-old Carissa for their first cuddles together while Susanna beamed. Those memories weren't memories. They were messages. I was a messenger. The visions were real, but they weren't intended for me. I was merely a conduit.

'Why, David?' Reyes asked again. 'Why do you care about these people?'

So, it was clear to me now that they weren't my family. Susanna was Michael's wife. Rachael and Carissa were Michael's children. I'd been wrong all along. But it was okay. It was bittersweet, but it was still sweet. I still loved them. Reyes wouldn't understand, none of them would understand, but it was time, now that Michael was gone, it was time to set things straight.

'I love these people,' I said quietly. 'They're all I have.' I looked across the room, over at Michael's body. 'Michael was my…friend. I'm here to stop you, Reyes. You've taken my friend from me, and you've taken their father from them and her husband from her. But this is where it ends. I won't allow you to take these people from me. I won't allow you to take his family from me.' I looked at Susanna and the girls. I spoke at Reyes, but I was really speaking to them. 'I don't know how I was sent here, but I know why. I finally know why. I was sent here to save these people. For a long time, I believed them to be mine, to be my family. But they aren't mine, of course they aren't. I know that now. They are my *friend's* family. At least, they were. You've taken him from us. I won't let you take them too. I was sent here for a reason. I thought it was to love them. It's not. It's to save them.'

'Oh, wow,' said Reyes. 'That's the most beautiful thing I've ever heard. I'm choking up.'

It didn't matter what she said. I knew what to do. With the gun still held tight up against her back, I fished the Jaguar keys from Michael's prone body and offered them to Susanna. 'It's in the garage. You have to go.' As the keys were passed, our fingers touched. Susanna, through her tears, mouthed 'Thank you.'

I watched through the broken window as she drove the Jaguar away down the street, with her children inside it. Once they were out of sight, I picked up the Richards' landline phone and made a call. 'Police and ambulance.'

'Davey,' said Olivia from behind me.

I spun around to see Reyes dragging a limp Michael towards the door, and like a method actor leaving behind a lifetime performance, I awoke.

'A little help?' she said.

47

DOCTOR

Olivia knocked on the worn blue door. No response. The corridor stank of urine. There was no heating, no carpets. The lift was out of action, but even if it hadn't been she wouldn't have risked it. The thought of being stuck there for longer than was absolutely necessary made her shudder. It wasn't the kind of place she chose to visit unless she could help it. There was no other option. Doctor Michael Richards had come into her life today, out of nowhere, like a gift.

She'd walked up four floors, so she knocked again. There was still no response, and if the visit hadn't been of such importance, she would have gladly taken that opportunity to carefully leave the premises and slip back into her comfy, warm, luxury sedan. But she had to try once more; it was too important.

A third, louder knock finally got the desired response. Three or four bolts were forcefully released before the door creaked and very nearly fell off its hinges as it opened to reveal a long-haired man, unshaven and dishevelled. Nothing was said. More than a few seconds passed before the man finally stepped aside to allow Olivia entry.

The flat was a mess. Clothes were strewn everywhere. Paint peeled off the walls. It was dark and dingy. There was a heavy stench of recreational drugs. The only redeeming feature in the place was a portrait above the decrepit fireplace.

'I like what you've done with the place,' Olivia said.

She removed dirty clothes from the armchair and sat down without invitation. The long-haired man had followed her into the living room. He picked up a dirty zip-up hoodie and slid it on.

'What is it you want, Livi?'

Without making eye contact, Olivia delivered her news. 'Well, I thought I'd come and inform you that I've…found him.' She had the man's attention. He stopped fiddling with his zip and looked at her, wanting to hear the words again. She obliged. 'I found him, Davey.'

David stroked the long greasy hair away from his face. A wry smile hijacked his expression. 'Are you sure?'

'It's him, Davey,' she said. 'Trust me. I wouldn't be here…' she looked around, '…if I wasn't sure.'

David leaned back against a wall that had once been adorned with wallpaper, the remnants of which were still present in patches. 'I assume you have a plan?'

Olivia smiled. 'I have some thoughts, yes.'

She stood up and walked over to the fireplace. It had been redundant for years and the mantelpiece barely held itself up. But it wasn't the fireplace or the mantelpiece she was interested in. She reached up and lifted the portrait from the wall. She admired it. She stood there with it in her hands for an unnaturally long period of time.

'You always were the talented one, Davey.' The portrait was of three figures. A woman stood over her children, a boy and a girl of the same age. Her arms were wrapped around them. 'He's married.'

'Yeah?'

'And he has children. They have two children.' There was a symmetry about the situation. 'Two girls, though,' she said with a smile, 'and not twins.'

'Happy families, huh?' he asked.

'At the moment.' Without looking away from the portrait, she pulled out her mobile phone, unlocked it and handed it to David.

'Hit play,' she said, unsure whether he had even used such a device before. He pressed the sideways triangle and the video started playing. At first, it showed just some movements and then some empty hospital beds. Then the footage panned across and zoomed in on to a scene of people around a single bed. Susanna and her two daughters were grabbing and kissing and hugging Doctor Michael Richards. The video wasn't long, but it was long enough.

David watched it again. And again.

'It doesn't change, it's the same every time,' Olivia said, still looking at, and now touching the faces in the painting.

'I'm trying to make out his face,' said David. 'Can you get in closer?'

'You mean, zoom in?'

'Whatever, so I can see his face.'

Olivia was getting annoyed. This was taking longer than she'd planned. 'Look, Davey, it's him, okay? I *know* it's him. I've been as close to him as we are now. Closer, and I'm telling you it's him.'

'But you don't have the photo for comparison.'

'It doesn't matter, I know it's him.'

'So, you don't even want to see it? The photo, I mean.'

Olivia was surprised. She'd thought the photograph of their father had been lost years ago. David didn't wait for a response. He disappeared into the kitchen and returned with a small faded photograph. He watched the video once again, trying to compare. 'I can't see…yeah, maybe, although he's a lot older…but if you say it's him…'

'For the final time, Davey, it's him, okay?'

'Okay, okay. So, now what?'

'Payback. Finally, payback.'

'Meaning what?'

'*Venganza por madre.*'

'You're going to kill him?'

Olivia turned to face her brother. '*Kill* him? You think the answer is to kill our father?'

'I wouldn't put it past you, Livi. You've always done whatever it takes.'

'I'm not going to kill him.'

David looked at his sister. 'You'd better not be asking me to.'

'No, of course not. After all, we're not *him*,' she said. 'We're better than him. In fact, that's the point.'

'So, what?' David asked.

Olivia took a breath. She'd been thinking about what she'd do if she ever came across her father for years, but those thoughts were just vengeful fantasies that she'd never had to worry about actually carrying out. Now, today, that had all changed. Now he was a real person, and any plans for revenge would need to be grounded in reality. Driving over to David's flat, she'd brought it all down to one single thought. 'He needs to feel…' Olivia paused, '…our pain.'

David nodded. 'His family?'

'Exactly, Davey.'

David looked startled. 'Now, I know you're not suggesting we kill his family.'

'No, Davey. You're not getting it. Listen to me. Besides the fact that we're not murderers, that wouldn't be true revenge. It's not enough to take his family from him. We need to hurt him. We need him to hurt in the same way we've been hurting all these years.'

'Speak for yourself. I'm not hurting.'

Olivia looked around the flat. 'This looks pretty painful to me.'

'Oh, right. Yeah. You're the famous surgeon, I'm the failed artist.'

'Let's not go over this again, Davey. I've apologised for what happened, despite it not being my fault.'

'So it was *my* fault?'

'It was nobody's fault. Things worked out for me quicker than expected, they were slower for you. I tried to help…'

'I'm not a charity case, Livi. I didn't want your money.'

'You made that perfectly clear.'

'I should've stayed home,' said David, 'not followed you and your ambitions. I mean, what the fuck was I thinking, the accent reduction courses and all that shit. It was all because you had to be the best. Better than *him.* As if that would bring her back.'

Olivia paused, then sighed.

'We dealt with things in our own way,' she said. 'I had to prove him wrong. I had to be the best. I haven't made many friends along the way. But I *am* the best. Don't kid yourself. We're both hurting.'

The twins looked at each other.

'Have you considered that he probably doesn't even know what happened?' asked David.

'I don't care if he knows or not. Before, when I said it's nobody's fault, I misspoke. It's *his* fault. If you want someone to blame, here he is. Whether he knows or doesn't know, he went on with his life and, listen, Davey, you should *see* his life. Their life together.' She held her hands up to make the comparison to David's rancid flat. 'If you saw his life, you'd want revenge.'

'Okay. So, how the hell do we get this revenge you, we, so badly want?'

Olivia composed her thoughts. She needed her brother to fully agree to this. 'He needs to wake up one day to find out that they're happy without him. That the woman he fell in love with actually loves someone else. That his children belong to another man. He needs to live the rest of his miserable existence questioning whether they were ever really his. That's what we need to do to him. Everything he took from us, from *madre*, we'll take from him.'

'Again, Livi, exactly how are we supposed to do that?'

Olivia looked back at the portrait in her hands. A woman and her two children. Olivia noted the space David had left when painting it. The space where a father would be. 'I do have an idea. It won't be easy, though. It'll mean sacrifice on both our parts.' She looked around the flat again. 'It'll mean the end of this life you have.'

David scoffed. 'Is that a joke?'

'Still off the grid after all these years, huh?'

'I don't even have a national insurance number.'

'That's good, that'll help.'

'Okay.'

'I'll have to hurt you.'

'What?'

'Just physical pain, run you over with a car or something.'

'You're kidding?'

Olivia didn't respond.

'What about you, your career and everything?' asked David. 'Being the best of the best?'

'It was all for this.'

David just shook his head.

'I don't expect you to understand, Davey.'

'Just tell me what to do.'

'Okay, that's more like it. Leave *Davey* behind.'

'Huh?'

'You're no longer Davey. It's *David.*'

'David? Not too much of a stretch, is it?'

'It's a start. So, you don't have anyone special, then?'

David shook his head, now looking embarrassed.

'Nobody at all? What about friends?'

'I never saw the point. So, nobody, okay?' he said, now with a little annoyance in his voice.

'I guess we're more similar than we admit. It's no problem, dear brother, I'll employ some friends. Better that way, anyway, to use actors.' Olivia said, knowing this wouldn't make any sense. 'There'll be a photo too, of the girls, by your bed. Beautiful moment.'

David just stared at her.

'Don't worry, d'Artagnan, you'll understand when the time comes.'

David nodded. Olivia's focus had already returned to the portrait, which she replaced on the wall. She took a step back and continued to admire it, especially that space, that blank space where Michael should have been. She took the old worn photo from her brother and held it up, blocking out the blank space and placing Michael among his true family.

'A hero', she said, under her breath. 'His family…they'll need a hero.'

Olivia walked into the kitchen, where the radio was playing softly. She turned the volume up.

'…We're looking for the next me, the next hero, the next Sir Damo…'

She turned back to David, who was in the doorway. 'They'll need a hero, David.'

48

PATIENT

'A hero,' said Damo. 'This next chap is the very essence of a hero.'

I was embarrassed and uncomfortable.

'Let's recap his story, shall we?' he said. 'Roll VT.'

I was watching from backstage. The others were there too, in the green room, anxiously waiting for their big moment.

Geraldine Adams was quiet, but confident. She wasn't frail, as the media portrayed her. A couple of hours ago, when we'd arrived, she hadn't even looked as though she was in her seventies. But with time in the make-up chair and a change of wardrobe, she now looked every day her age. Most people want to look younger, but not her. Or, perhaps, not the producers of the show. After all, her age was a key part of her story. As were her fingertips, which she kept rubbing together when she thought nobody was looking.

Richie Dance was a lad. A real charmer. He shook everybody's hand and had a smile that filled the room. He had an assurance about him, a coolness. Almost an arrogance, but, crucially, not quite. Everyone wanted to be his friend. He had a cute face, a face for TV. A natural successor to Damo if ever there was one.

Jack McCann, on the other hand, didn't give a shit what anyone thought about him. Or maybe that was the angle he was playing. He moved around the table of complimentary food at such a rate that I started to believe he did indeed catch that minibus after all. He filled his face, pausing occasionally to scoff at the footage on the screen.

Francesca Southern sat quietly by herself, reading a Chinese novel. She looked up only occasionally and smiled at Geraldine Adams, who watched her admiringly.

And then there was me, David. Just David. The man with no surname. The man with no past. The man with the super-vision. *How the hell did I get here?*

They didn't speak to me, and I did nothing to try to change that.

A videotape of my story was playing. The voiceover was dramatic, like the guy who does the film trailers.

'…The man who woke up with no memories other than his first name and the faces of his wife and daughters. At least, that's what he thought. Turned out they weren't *his* memories, at all. They were visions, visions that allowed him to save the lives of Susanna Richards and her two daughters, Carissa and Rachael…'

A reconstruction of my story, in particular my artwork and the final showdown at the Richards' house, played out on screen.

'…The body of Doctor Michael Richards, along with his murderer-daughter, Doctor Olivia Reyes, is still missing…'

Back in the studio, Damo continued with the glowing reference. 'Not only does all that make him a hero, but he didn't even want recognition.'

Michael would approve.

'And it was only because of our show,' said Damo, 'and, of course, the actions of Evan Sykes, whose exclusive interview is coming up soon by the way, that David even got his shot. And now, here we are, just a month later, and David has a one in five chance of being the next, well…me! We'd have to call him Davo, eh?'

That got an equal mixture of groans and cheers from the excited live audience. I was all groan. *Davo. That's what I've become.*

'But we're getting ahead of ourselves,' Damo said. 'The truth is, there's nothing in it, folks. The race for the title of the next Great Briton is the closest it's ever been and my sources tell me that every single vote will count. Your vote could be the one that makes the difference, so get on that app, get on that website, text in, call up, whatever works for you, but vote! It's going down to the wire. Here are all the details again…'

The phone numbers and other contact details flashed up for everyone to spend even more money.

'Okay, time to get this show back on track. In an exclusive first, we'll now have all five contestants live on stage to answer questions at the same time. Well, not quite answering at the same time, that wouldn't make great TV, but you know what I mean. This is really exciting, I've been looking forward to this since I heard it was going to happen. Now, the finalists aren't aware of what the questions will be and so haven't been able to prepare answers. This is live television at its best. But there's more…' Damo beckoned the camera towards him, and started whispering. '…they don't know the whole story. We've got a twist for them, but they're listening backstage so I won't say any more right now. All I'll say is get ready for something special. But, before all that, we have something equally special. It's now time for the big interview you've all been waiting for. Evan Sykes dominated headlines in this year's Winnies when he went from favourite to being exposed as a total fraud. Last week, I caught up with him for the first time since all this happened. Now, for those of you who aren't aware, this is a difficult subject for me. I really liked Evan Sykes. We actually became friends away from the show, as much as the producers would allow, of course. This interview was an emotional one for me, and I'd like to apologise for my, well, my unprofessionalism. Hold on to your hats. Roll the tape.'

The interview was brilliant, absolutely brilliant. Sykes was shameless. He had no regrets, apart from getting caught, that is. In fact, he was proud of how far his fraud had gone and just how many millions of people he had fooled.

'That includes me, Evan,' said Damo. 'You took me for a ride. Don't you care at all about the people who believed in you?'

Damo was trying to hold back the tears while Sykes was trying just as hard to hold back his laughter. It was so good I couldn't believe it was real. Maybe it wasn't. Maybe it was all part of the show. But then, that would mean I was part of it. *I am, aren't I?* I was lying, I had no powers, no super-vision. But the producers didn't know that. Damo didn't know that. The other contestants didn't know that. *Do they?* I looked around the green room. They weren't interested. They weren't even watching the Sykes interview. No interest at all; just handshakes and sausage rolls, Mandarin and finger rubbing. Was it all fake? I mean, I knew it was all fake, but was everyone in on it?

Well, not everyone, clearly, because the moans, gasps and yells of the live studio audience told me that *they* still believed.

'They're all idiots,' Sykes said, not holding back at all. 'Every single one of them, believing it, I mean. I planned it well, really well. But it was so much easier to convince people than I thought it would be. You're all so desperate for it to be real. For it to rescue you from your pathetic, mundane lives. You were happy to believe it. I just gave you what you wanted.' Damo looked livid. But he wasn't responding. So Sykes kept going. 'You know, while I have all you morons watching, I'm going to say this as simply as I can, okay? Superpowers are *not* real. Okay? Whether it's human X-ray machines or someone who claims to have the strength to lift a 4x4…'

Brilliant. Now *this* was TV.

'Don't you f-*beep* dare! Don't you f-*beep* dare!' Damo said. He was losing it. 'Don't you dare suggest that *I'm* like you.'

'I'm not suggesting anything, my friend.'

'Don't call me that, I'm no friend of yours.'

'Whatever,' said Sykes. 'I'm not suggesting you're a fake, I'm *saying* you're a fake. You're a fake just like all the others on the show. I'm the most honest one of you all because at least I've come clean.'

I turned around again, expecting the other finalists to shout and scream at the screen. No reaction. An important-looking person with a clipboard and headpiece appeared and suddenly the finalists woke up. It was time for us to take to the stage.

I took a deep breath and thought of my sister. She'd worked so hard, sacrificed so much, for me to be here. All I had to do was not fuck up.

49

DOCTOR

Olivia lay on the worn old sofa, watching the events unfold on a tiny 4:3 cathode ray tube television. The sound was muted and the subtitles were on.

It disgusted her, what she was watching, of course it did. Everything about the show disgusted her. At least, until it had become part of her grand plan. Damo and the show's producers were all puppets in her plan, like every other person involved.

So she was enjoying it, especially the Sykes interview. Her appreciation of and respect for him, and what he'd almost pulled off, was offset only by the disappointment she felt that he'd ultimately failed. But in the interview with Damo, Sykes acted like a man who was completely satisfied with the outcome.

Maybe it was enough for him, to fool millions of people for that long. Maybe the journey was more important than the outcome. Not for Olivia, though. For her, it wasn't enough that she'd taken Michael from his family. The job wasn't complete. She still had to take his family *from him*. And that wasn't the same thing. It was so much more. It was everything.

If Michael was watching, he would indeed see his family with David. Yes, that would be good. But he wouldn't see them *happy* with David. He wouldn't see them looking like they had always been David's family.

But, soon enough, he would.

50

PATIENT

As we walked up to the stage, I could still hear the reactions of the crowd to Sykes's words. This was already more entertaining than I'd expected. Maybe it would be fun after all. No, I realised just as quickly, because I couldn't be like Sykes. I had to toe the line. The job wasn't complete. I had to stay in character for a little while longer. If I let on tonight, then Olivia and I would have done all this for nothing.

We were in the wings when the interview with Sykes ended prematurely.

'I'm sorry, folks,' Damo said, live again. 'I had to cut it short there. The things he was saying, well, you know I'm not a violent person but he was really pushing my buttons.'

The audience roared for Damo.

'You know, I can handle being called a fraud; it happens, of course. People are jealous, scared of what they don't understand. It's human nature. But not from him, not after what he did, and not when he also accused our wonderful finalists.'

Another roar, and he let it keep going this time. It was deafening. Clearly nothing Sykes had said mattered to the believers. It took a minute or more for the cheering to settle down.

I wasn't nervous. All this time, I'd treated my part as a role. I was acting, being someone else, and tonight was no different. It's easy to be someone else, much harder to be yourself. *That's* when the nerves kick in, when you have to be *you*. I looked around at my competition. They weren't nervous either. That told me everything I needed to know about who they really were.

'So, here we go people,' said Damo. 'It's time to bring them out, to bring them *all* out.'

More cheers.

'This is the first time all five will have been on stage together.'

Even more cheers.

'Put your hands together, folks. I want an almighty roar as we bring out, in the order that they qualified for the final, Richie, Jack, Geraldine, Francesca and, finally, David.'

We took our seats on a stage that looked part chat show and part party political debate.

'We've prepared three questions,' said Damo. 'Just three, but believe me they are *great* questions, designed to help you decide just who to vote for, should you still be deciding. All three questions will be asked to each of the five finalists. Their responses will no doubt determine just who will walk away with the title, the knighthood and the million pounds in the bank. As I said earlier, there's a final twist. As you know, the first question will be asked by Donny Malone, the eleven-year-old superfan who won our nationwide school contest. The second question will be asked by yours truly. Here's the twist: so far, you've all thought that the third and final question would also be asked by me. Well, as nice as that would've been, I think we have something even better.'

The audience was full of whispers, oohs and ahhs. Staff appeared, carrying additional seating. They placed the chairs next to us. Three, next to me. The crowd started clapping and cheering as if they knew what was coming. I'd known they were at the show tonight, and I'd expected that our paths would cross. But not like this. Until they told us about question number three a few hours ago. Of course, we were also told to act like we'd found out at the same time as the viewers, so everyone planned to gasp and hold their mouths, including me.

'But before we get to that business…' said Damo, as the crowd groaned in playful spirit, '…I know, I know. I share your eagerness! But, hey, I need my time in the limelight first. Especially as I'm going to be the reigning Great Briton for only a little while longer.'

The crowd started booing, and then, as if someone up in the rafters had ordered it, broke into a chorus of 'Damo! Damo! Damo!' He lapped it up. Even the other finalists joined in. So I had to, too. He played them like a conductor, and, in the same way, brought the noise down to a perfect silence. Without missing a beat, he was straight back into his routine.

'Too kind, just too kind. Boy, I'm going to miss being your Great Briton.' The audience were about to start up again but he was being hurried along off-camera. 'So, it's time. Time for the Q&A. Hundreds of thousands of schoolchildren submitted their questions, but this was the winner. Please welcome to the show, Donny Malone.'

Donny shuffled on to the stage, nervous. The difference was stark; he wasn't pretending to be anyone else.

'Donny, welcome, welcome, little man. How old are you, Donny?'

'Eleven,' said Donny, missing the microphone.

'Just eleven? Well, you're looking so fly in that suit my friend. Tell us, without giving the question away, how and why did you choose this question?'

The kid was star-struck, despite having been hanging around backstage all day. Damo was doing his best to coax the scripted answer out of the lad, but it wasn't happening. Ever the professional, he retold that quip about never working with children or animals and prompted Donny to ask his question.

The kid nervously stepped up and peered down at his cue cards. 'Which of the other, the other, finals, finaltists…'

'*Finalists*,' said Damo.

'Yeah, that,' said Donny, and the crowd laughed. 'Which of their powers would you borrow, like, if you could?'

Damo urged the lad to continue. 'Is that the *whole* question, Donny?'

'Yep.'

'You're sure?'

'Yep.'

'Well, it wasn't in *rehearsal*,' said Damo, and the crowd laughed again. 'Let me see that card...' He read out the final part of the question. '*...for just an hour*, folks.'

'Oh, yeah,' said Donny, 'I forgot that bit.'

It was an okay question, except, of course, that none of these people, including me, had any powers. That's what I was going to say. That would be my answer. No, it wouldn't, of course, it couldn't. It was then that I realised, in my disinterest, I had little idea of who on that stage could supposedly do what. Why would I when I knew none of them could do anything and it was all bullshit? Still, I had four answers to hear first. I could piggyback one of them, probably. Or if not, say some crap about how the powers are personal to them, and we should all only have to be ourselves. Yeah, that might work. Unless someone else said it first.

'Nice question, Donny,' said Damo. 'I can see why it won you a place here tonight. Hundreds of thousands of young people applied, and *you* won. You clearly have a superpower when it comes to questions!'

The crowd groaned.

'So, to give our finalists a few moments to come up with a winning answer, we'd like to present you with this commemorative Winnie award.'

Applause for Donny, and then the audience settled down to hear our answers.

'So, what do you think, Richie?' Damo asked. 'What powers from up there on the stage would you like to have for just an hour?'

'Right. Ha ha, okay, let's see now,' said Richie. 'Good question, by the way. Donny, is it?' He was stalling. 'If I could borrow a power for just one hour, I think I would go with...gosh, it's so difficult. I would have to say, yep, okay, I have it. I'd go with Miss Adams's force field powers. I probably shouldn't say this, but I think it's just the coolest thing ever, and, well, she's, like, the coolest person ever. My gran died last year and I can't help but see a little of her when I look at Miss Adams.'

The audience applauded, tears in their eyes.

What a load of horseshit.

'Well, I certainly can't argue with that,' said Damo. 'Can you, Donny?'

Donny wasn't up to ad-libs. He looked down at his cards and shrugged, wide-eyed.

'Okay, then,' said Damo. 'Jack McCann, whose powers would you like to have?'

'Mine.'

'No, I don't think you quite understood the quest–'

'No, Damo,' said McCann, 'I understand just fine, man, and I'm sorry, Donny, little guy, but there's only one power I'd ever want, be it for an hour, a week or forever. And that's my own power, man. I'm sorry that's a boring answer, probably not what you wanted, or what any of you guys in the audience or out there at home wanted, but it's the truth. I go to bed every night praying for my speed to return, I wake up every morning and go running hoping for it to return. No disrespect to any of these guys, but, well, that's how I feel.'

'Fair enough, man, I completely hear you,' said Damo. 'And I reckon a whole lot of people out there are going to appreciate your honesty. But let's move on now. Miss Adams, what's your take on Donny's question?'

'This is a no-brainer for me, Damo, and Donny,' said Geraldine Adams. 'Thank you for your question, by the way. Yes, I would borrow this young lady to my left's powers. You see, I travelled the world in my youth and I'm somewhat ashamed to say I relied on English-speaking foreigners. I'd like to do it again, but do it right. So I'd choose Francesca's amazing linguistic abilities. Even if it's just for an hour!'

'Just an hour, yeah, I was going to say, not sure how far you'd get!' said Damo. 'But another great answer. Well, Francesca, are you going to return the favour? Would you choose Geraldine's powers?'

'Yeah, sure,' said Francesca. 'Well, actually I'd choose anyone's. I know that's cheating a bit but I'd be happy with any of the powers you guys have.' She looked only to the right, not left to me. 'Really,' she said, 'give me any of them, even *yours*, Damo!'

'Ha ha, leave me out of this!' said Damo. 'Okay, that just leaves David.'

'None,' I said, without hesitation. I knew the answer I'd give. It had come to me in a flash. 'None of them. Not even *mine*.'

I didn't make eye contact with the other finalists, even though I could feel them staring at me. Instead, I focused on Damo and the crowd. A few seconds passed and I thought I may have gone too far. 'Look, the truth is, I just want to be a normal guy with a normal life. I'm not someone who's looking to do anything amazing. I still don't remember who I am, and so I'd just like to live a normal, quiet life. No superpowers. I know that's dull, but I feel like my moment has come and gone now. My purpose, if that's what it was, is done. I was able to save those amazing people, but that's over now. I just want to be like everyone else.'

There was a spattering of claps but mostly silence.

'Well, that's very honest of you, David,' said Damo. 'But actually, I think you're wrong. About the moment being over for you, I mean. And I don't think I'm alone in thinking that.'

I knew what he was referring to. They'd be out soon enough.

'But before we get to that, thank you, Donny, for a fabulous question. Congratulations on your award, let's give it up for Donny…'

The audience perked up, but Donny went nowhere.

'And that's your cue to leave, buddy,' said Damo.

Donny was escorted off stage.

'Okay, now it's my turn,' Damo said. 'Firstly, I'd like to say that I'm honoured to have been chosen to come up with a question. I think all of you are wonderful people, amazing people, all worthy winners. And, I'll be honest, this was hard for me. I had so many questions whirling around in my head. Now, some of them I've been able to ask you over the weeks and months on my show, but, to tell you the truth, those are mostly written for me. By people much smarter than me, I might add. So it was a challenge, as well as an honour.' He was taking too long and being hurried again from off-camera. 'Okay, yep, "get on with it", they're saying. Okay. Here's my question: if you win tonight, as I did twelve months ago, will you give me a job?'

The crowd fell over themselves with laughter.

'I'm kidding, I'm kidding.'

The audience settled down.

'No, really, I'll work for nothing, it's the limelight I need.'

Again the crowd laughed, although it felt a little forced now.

'Okay, no more messing around. Here's my real question.' He cleared his throat. 'If Evan Sykes was here in front of you tonight, what would you say to him?'

The audience booed.

'And people, keep it clean!'

The finalists looked at each other, raised eyebrows all around. Except for me, of course. I was here thanks to Sykes. I was coming at him from a completely different place. Besides, I actually liked him much more than I did these jokers on stage.

'The reason I chose this question is that, well, it's something I've had to answer recently, and who knows what may be required of you in the next twelve months should you win. Richie Dance, you're up first.'

'Well, I was hurt,' said Richie. 'When I heard the news, just as everybody did, on Ken's radio show, my first thought was disbelief. And then, very quickly, once I realised there hadn't been some mistake, there was just hurt. And that hurt remains to this day. I'm not sure it'll ever truly go away.'

This from the kid who was all smiles and high fives backstage, when Sykes was attacking him onscreen.

'So,' said Richie, 'what would I say to Mr Sykes if he was here tonight? I'd say "Ouch, Evan, ouch. Your words and your betrayal have caused me, and us all, great pain." ' That's all.'

The audience clapped.

'Thank you, Richie,' said Damo. 'Hurt is certainly the word. Jack McCann, same question.'

'Hurt? A little, maybe,' said McCann. 'Angry? Hell, yeah. If Sykes was here tonight, I wouldn't say a goddamn thing to him. I'd walk straight up to him and knock him on his arse, that's what I'd do. Are you with me?' he called out to the people, and they roared with approval.

I wondered how they'd react if they'd seen him more concerned with stuffing his face with pastries during the Sykes interview.

'Okay, well, I know that's how a lot of us feel,' said Damo. 'Lucky for Sykes, he's not here! Geraldine Adams, what would you say, or indeed do, to him if he were here?'

'I, I would, hmm, you see, yes, he hurt me,' said Geraldine. 'We were friends. We shared time. I was hurt, but that pain is nothing compared to the torment that must be in Evan's soul for him to have done what he did. So, if Evan was here I'd just tell him that I hoped he could find peace one day because he's clearly a very disturbed, sad person.' She hadn't rubbed her fingers once since we walked out.

'Very compassionate, Miss Adams,' said Damo. 'So typical of you. A much bigger person than I am. Okay, Francesca Southern, would you be as understanding as Geraldine?'

'I wouldn't even give him the time of day,' said Francesca. 'I'd ignore him. He doesn't deserve my time, our time, your time, and, no disrespect, Damo, but if it was up to me we wouldn't even be talking about him tonight.'

'Fair enough,' said Damo, 'fair enough. I know exactly what you mean. And so, we come to David. As I'm sure you don't need reminding, David is here literally because of Evan Sykes's diabolical actions. This should be interesting. David?'

I knew exactly what I wanted to say, and there was a moment when I thought it might escape my best efforts to subdue it. But I was so used to slipping back into the role whenever the truth threatened to raise its head that I simply smiled and told them what they wanted to hear.

'Thanks, Damo,' I said. 'Yes, it's very strange for me. I'm here thanks to the vileness of that man. That doesn't sit well with me, I don't mind telling you. But that's not what you asked. You asked what I would say to Mr Sykes. I'd simply say this: you're wrong. You are wrong. Superpowers *are* real. They really are. And not just up here on this stage. I know there are many people out there who have these powers, most of whom have no idea of how special they are. Just because *you're* a sham, Mr Sykes, that doesn't mean everyone else is.'

The audience cheered for me. *For Davo.*

I'd never used the word 'whom' before. I was someone else.

'Wow, thank you, David, and all the finalists, for your answers,' said Damo. 'You're all, in your own way, much better prepared for such challenges than I was. But it doesn't get any easier, I assure you. After these short messages from our sponsors, we'll be back with the big reveal. Don't go anywhere – as if you would!'

A commercial break, and I was receiving some nasty looks from the other finalists. Up until now, they'd been ignoring me, as though I was a gatecrasher at their members-only party. Now they'd realised they couldn't ignore me, I was here and I was out to win. *Is that necessary for the plan?* No, not necessary, but it wouldn't hurt, Livi had said, and she was – of course – right.

'Nice, David, my boy, nice,' said Damo as he walked towards me. 'You know what you're doing, man. You nailed that last question. Both, in fact. I'm impressed.'

The others looked down their noses at me.

And then we were back on air, and Damo was gone, welcoming everyone back into the madness.

'Before the break, we had superfan Donny come out and ask our finalists his question, followed by my own. Great answers all round, but now it gets serious. Not only do we have the third and final time that you'll hear from each of them before the vote count, but we also have a massive reveal. You know what, enough talk, let's bring them out…'

The music and lights cranked up a few notches. Figures walked out on to the stage from behind us. Children, friends, families. Susanna and the girls. All together. The audience went nuts.

Susanna, Rachael and Carissa sat down in the seats next to me. I smiled at them and my new family smiled back.

51

DOCTOR

Michael needed to see that his family was actually David's family. And he would. But not just yet. Yes, she could turn his docile head to the left, and his comatose eyes would see his wife and two daughters with David on the TV screen. Or she could un-mute the audio so he could hear them talking about him, their late husband and father. She could, but that wouldn't be enough. They would, after all, be talking about Michael, and while that would certainly hurt him, it wouldn't kill him inside. That's what Olivia needed.

And in order for that to happen, the girls would need to have moved on, forgotten him, removed Michael from their lives and from their hearts. They would need to be happy, blissful, loved, in love – all without him. He would need to see his wife and his girls loving another man, as a lover and as a father. That's what it would take to kill Michael inside. That would really kill him, unlike the paralysing fluid that was still working its magic inside him.

He would witness everything, experience it all, and be able to do nothing. For now, he lay limp on the tatty sofa next to his daughter; it was all still to come.

52

PATIENT

We all smiled, but it was awkward, because of the cameras – I hoped.

Susanna, in particular, hadn't really welcomed the media exposure that the past month had brought. Thankfully, Damo was being rushed along, meaning any unease was short-lived.

'Yes, indeed, you're right to cheer!' he said. 'Here they are, the people who experienced the amazing feats first-hand, the people who were *there*, and, in some cases, are only here today, still with us, I mean, because of the incredible acts of our finalists. So, what are they doing here? Well, they've each prepared a question for their respective heroes. That's right, the third and final question has been prepared and will be delivered by our most special of guests.'

The crowd kept cheering.

'So, let's start, of course, with Richie,' said Damo, 'and his special person, who – well, who else, it has to be Richie's little sister. Welcome, Emily.'

More cheering.

'Thank you, people, thank you, settle down. Emily, thank you so much for joining us this evening. I believe you have a question for your brother?'

Emily didn't have the natural charisma of her big brother, but, boy, did she know the gig. She'd been on the talk shows during the campaign trail. She was the best of supporting actresses. 'Richie, you saved my life,' she said, 'and while I still don't know how you did it, I just want to thank you, from the bottom of my heart, one more time.' She reached over and hugged her brother. The audience lapped it up, whooping and cheering.

'Go ahead with your question when you're ready, Emily,' said Damo.

She milked the moment for as long as she could. And why not? That's why they were here, after all. I watched her; she wasn't just prepped, she was primed. She was playing her role perfectly. I was entranced by her performance, and then, I saw Rachael watching her. I missed the question and Richie's answer. It must have worked, though. Everyone made the right noises at the right times. He would be the next Damo, odds on before tonight, no more bets now.

Next up, it was Jack McCann's turn. Sitting next to him was the minibus driver who he had caught up to on that fateful day. The crowd needed a bit more encouragement for these two. Her question was somewhat sterile; they certainly weren't going for the sympathy vote. But that was probably a wise move, being up against Richie and the others. So, they went down the 'It's true, people, honest,' route.

'Jack,' said the minibus driver, 'the image of you appearing at my door and banging for me to open it will never leave me. I remember looking down at the speedometer. It was in the thirties, that's for sure.'

Damo could see what they were doing and hurried her on to the question, which was something about taking on Usain Bolt for a charity event, something that Jack was very eager to do.

Susanna and the girls were looking back at me more often now. They knew we were getting close to our moment. It hadn't been the first time we'd met since the day their father and husband had died, but those occasions had been brief media appearances. No talk, not really. Mostly looks. Like now.

Geraldine Adams had as many people with her as I did – the family she had supposedly saved from a gas explosion. They got a cheer too, especially when Geraldine held her hands up in thanks, accidently-on-purpose showing her scorched fingertips to the voters at home for one final time. The eldest of the children was meant to ask the question of Miss Adams but at the last moment became too shy. Instead, the young mother asked it. It was something about how they could ever repay her, to which her reply was something so magnolia and predictable that I instantly forgot it. The crowd clapped anyway.

Rachael cupped her hand and whispered something to Susanna. Carissa looked at me. I smiled, and she mostly returned the favour. It would be our turn soon.

I didn't recognise the woman sat with Francesca Southern until she was introduced as the weather forecaster who had given the snowstorm warning on TV.

'Zěnme yàng?' She spoke in her native tongue, and Francesca replied, also in Mandarin. Nobody knew what they were saying, but this was Francesca's whole approach. They did the whole thing in Mandarin and while it meant almost nobody who could vote would understand what they were talking about, she kept playing that one card that the rest of us couldn't; she demonstrated her skill again and again. For that, I thought, *Yeah, maybe she deserves it.* Maybe her power was actually real. Who else on this stage could really say the same? And demonstrate it? But the crowd was underwhelmed. Which meant it wasn't a tough act to follow, no matter how impressive I found her to be.

And so Damo looked to us. This was it. The whole plan came down to these next couple of minutes. I knew Livi would be watching, wherever she was, with our father's limp body.

And that was the pressure I felt. She'd orchestrated this whole thing, and I'd promised her that I had the nerve to go through with it. It wasn't about winning the contest, it was about winning the family. It had always been about that.

'Susanna Richards, is it you who'll ask the big question or will it be one of your lovely daughters?' asked Damo.

Susanna said it would Rachael. Of course it would.

'Thank you, Damo,' said Rachael, 'it's a pleasure to be here tonight.' She took a deep breath, and I realised I needed one too. 'Our question to David…' she said, not looking directly at me and instead addressing the camera with the red light, '…is a bit different to everybody else's.' Then she turned to look right at me.

'Because, I'm sure you'd agree, Damo, everyone, that our situation is somewhat unique, even from the other, wonderful people up here tonight.' Damo smiled, which made Rachael blush. But she didn't lose her momentum. 'You spent a lot of time with our dad, Michael, in his final moments. We just wanted to be sure he knew how much we all loved him. That's all we want to know.'

I knew the answer even before she'd asked the question, not that it was a question. But I took my time anyway. Livi was watching. This was it, now. *Nail it.*

'He *knew*, Rachael,' I said. 'He knew all right. And I'll tell you what, after seeing how much love he had for you three, that's all I ever want for myself. No superpowers, no fame or fortune. I just want what he had.'

The crowd gave a collective 'Aww.'

'Wow, emotional stuff,' said Damo. 'I'm drained. I think we all need a break now. We'll be back after these messages, when we'll be crowning the new Great Briton. Don't. Go. Anywhere.'

The lights went down and Rachael asked us, 'Did I do okay?'

'You did great,' said Susanna.

'A natural,' said Carissa. 'You're destined for fame.'

'You both are,' said their mum. 'Greatness, I mean, destined for greatness.'

'I agree,' I said, and I looked away shyly.

Susanna smiled at me. And then they were gone, ushered backstage.

The results were in. The five of us, the finalists, stood in a line on the stage. The firing line. The lights went down and we were each illuminated by a spotlight. The music built in volume and tension. One way or another, it would be over soon enough.

'In no particular order,' said Damo, 'the first finalist who will *not* be crowned this year's Great Briton is…Francesca Southern.'

Francesca's light went out. The crowd moaned a little but not too much. Their sounds quickly became cheering. Francesca stepped up and thanked everyone in Mandarin and English, and then, just like that, she was gone and forgotten. I was disappointed. I wanted her to win.

'The second person who'll be leaving us now is…Jack McCann.'

McCann wasn't happy and he didn't attempt to hide it. He shook his head and made hand gestures. It was amusing, if juvenile.

Damo rushed through to the next runner-up, and it still wasn't me.

'Thank you so much to everyone who voted for me, supported me, believed in me…' said Geraldine Adams.

And so, we were down to two. Richie, the clear favourite, and me.

'We're going to announce the winner now, okay, chaps?' said Damo.

We nodded, and I stepped out of my spotlight to shake the little guy's hand. I'm not sure why I did it but, boy, did the crowd like it.

'Here we go,' Damo said. 'Millions of you voted, and here is the result. This year's Great Briton is…'

Richie, surely. It had to be Richie, he was born to be the next Damo. Except…

'David!'

The audience went crazy. Crazy for me. Richie grabbed his head in despair before being brought to Damo's microphone.

'Wow, wow. Hard luck, Richie,' said Damo. Richie had no words. He was gutted. And then he was gone, too. Damo asked for quiet. He was with me now, but not asking me any questions. We were just stood there in absolute silence, his finger in the air. And then he started chanting, very quietly, just the one word.

'Davo, Davo, Davo,' again and again, louder each time. The audience joined in. Within seconds, the whole place was chanting my name. Well, my new name.

And then the live music began. It took me by surprise, as it had completely slipped my mind. Each finalist had chosen a song to be performed live if they won. I had chosen – well, Livi had chosen – the hit Jennifer song, 'Unconditional'. But the chanting just got louder and louder and the live band was completely drowned out.

Susanna and the girls reappeared on stage to present me with the trophy. What a surreal moment. It had never been part of the plan – the show, and then winning – but it went hand in hand with convincing Susanna, Carissa and Rachael. The win, the money, was a bonus.

Until they find me out, anyway. But by that time, the real plan would be complete. As long as I came through tonight and convinced them. *And the million pounds should help*. And then Livi would put in place the final revenge.

I just had to pretend for a little longer. I'd lied to myself for so long, perhaps I could keep lying forever. Livi had been right. She'd said I would have to believe my own lie, and believe it absolutely. That had been the answer. Believe it *absolutely*. Not acting. A new personality, all encompassing. She helped me find him – David. *Leave Davey behind. You're David now. From this moment on, until once again you're my brother Davey, you're* David, *and you will act accordingly.* It wasn't hypnosis, but it was close. My twin sister was so clever it scared me sometimes.

Susanna ushered her daughters towards me. Damo asked for quiet, and the chanting died down. The live band was still playing, and the music could finally be heard.

Ooooh…Hours old, I dressed

This person, whom I knew not

Yet loved foreveeeeeer…

A sombre Carissa, her long dark hair covering her face, came forward and shook my hand. I dropped to one knee, reached out and tucked a strand of hair behind her ear to reveal tearful eyes and reddened cheeks. The crowd went crazy, drowning the music again. The cameras of the press flashed wildly, illuminating us.

'It'll be okay, Carissa,' I said. 'I promise.'

Carissa nodded and offered me her trademark half-smile.

In stark contrast, Rachael wrapped herself around me and squeezed with all her might. The cameras went into overdrive. The audience was in hysterics.

Susanna's turn. She stepped forward, and I did too, to meet her. Almost simultaneously, we held out our arms in awkward invitation. That helped break any tension and we shared a chuckle and embraced. The cameras lit us up. More cheers. The band had stopped. There was no point playing on, nobody could hear them over the noise. More than a few seconds passed, and when we did eventually break, Susanna repeated what she had once before whispered to me. 'Thank you.'

Our moment was interrupted by a photographer. 'Can we get one of the family?' he asked.

Susanna put her arms around her daughters and faced the cameras for photos.

'No…' said the snapper, '…with Davo too!'

I looked at Susanna sheepishly, but she gave me a smile and a nod. I stepped in to join the family.

'Closer, Davo!' another photographer said. 'Closer!'

I shuffled closer and tentatively put my arms around the two girls. When my hand accidently met that of Susanna's, she didn't pull away. Our fingers gently intertwined behind the girls' backs as the photographers and the whole world got their winning photograph, and Livi and I took one more step towards our revenge.

53

DOCTOR

'Superpowers aren't real.'

For a moment, Michael thought he'd said it himself. It was the sort of thing he would say, though, and had said, had needed to say, many times. But this time, it was someone else speaking, somewhere off in the distance.

Whoever they were, he could hear them chattering. Even without specific words, it was clear what the subject matter was. They were educated, their vocabulary suggested, but their subject matter was surprising low-brow: the Winnies, of course. They were talking about Damo, although sometimes it sounded to Michael more like *Davo.*

'That's it, that's the last straw,' the voice said. 'Surely now that he's admitted that even *he*, the almighty Damo, is a fraud, surely that's enough for everyone to discount every one of these phoneys? Am I sad that he's dead? Am I sad that he took his own life? Not really, no, not after the lie he told and kept telling. The world is a better place without Damo.'

Through the gaps in the bandage that almost completely covered his face and head, Michael could see a tiled ceiling and hear monotonous electronic beeps that pierced the somnolent atmosphere. But he couldn't move.

'Good morning.' It wasn't immediately apparent where the woman's voice was coming from. 'I hope you're up to visitors?'

The voice remained out of sight, off to Michael's left. He could only look straight up at the ceiling and the blinking fluorescent light.

'Just five minutes, though. You need to rest.'

Michael tried to move each limb. Then he tried to move his head. Then he tried to speak. Nothing. He was completely paralysed.

'Your beautiful family are here to see you.'

Michael strained his eyes. Anything to see Susanna, Carissa and Rachael alive and well. And then he just about saw them, through the gap in his half-closed privacy curtains. Twenty feet away, with huge smiles on their faces and coming rapidly towards him.

'Hang on, girls, take it steady,' said his wife.

They appeared so grown up, so much older than before all this had happened.

'Me, first!' said Rachael.

'Hey, don't push!' Carissa said.

Susanna did her best to rein in their enthusiasm. 'Girls, slow down.'

It was a familiar sight, a familiar fight.

As they approached, his eyes caught those of Susanna's. She smiled at him, and they locked eyes for the briefest, purest of moments. But he couldn't return the smile and he couldn't call out to her.

Susanna and the girls disappeared out of Michael's field of vision.

'I was so scared,' said Rachael. 'Are you okay?'

And then, feeling nothing, Michael realised his head was being turned to the right by a hand he couldn't see. His point of view now showed him his curtain, hiding the bed next to him.

'We were *all* worried, not just her,' Carissa said.

He could hear his daughters arguing, but not see them.

The same hand appeared again, this time to pull back the curtain slightly. Michael could now see his family seated on the bed next to him.

'Hey, stop it, girls,' said Susanna. 'I'm sorry. How are you, honey?'

The curtain opened further. There was a patient in the bed. Rachael squeezed the patient tightly. Carissa had her arms around his neck. Susanna held his hand. Michael, fixated, recognised the patient.

'Fine. I'm fine,' said David. 'Just a little shaken. I was on my way home from the studio when it happened. It was so fast, I couldn't do anything.'

'The doctor said it wasn't your fault.'

'Yeah, I know…'

'So, *Davo…*' Susanna said, with more than a hint of sarcasm, 'are you going to do it? Are you going to host this year's Winnies?'

'I don't know. I don't think it's for me,' said David.

'I think you should,' said Rachael. 'It's poetic, going back a year after winning. Like passing the baton.'

Carissa rolled her eyes.

'Well, they're pretty persuasive, these people,' said David. 'The figure is now three times what they first offered six months ago. But, you know what, it's just money. A huge amount of money, yes, but I have everything I need right here.' David cuddled his family. Then he subtly gestured towards a bandaged Michael in the next bed. 'Poor chap. Look at him.'

'What actually happened?' asked Rachael.

'He made a bad decision.'

The open curtain allowed Susanna to see the bound patient. She offered Michael a sympathetic, momentary smile. Michael was reminded of their wedding day, the way she'd looked at him.

Then it was gone.

'Imagine that,' said David. 'One bad decision, and, in an instant, everything you love is taken away from you.'

Michael could only stare at them. Susanna smiled once more at him before slowly closing the curtain between them.

And then Michael's bed was moving. His family disappeared out of sight. The bed rolled into the lift, and the doors closed behind Michael and his doctor.

EPILOGUE

'Uno!'

'What?' said Carissa, distracted away from her phone.

'Oh and pick up four,' said Rachael.

'Hang on,' said Carissa.

'And change the colour to–'

'*Hang on*, I said.'

'Hang on *what*?'

'You know you can't put that down if you have a blue, right?'

Rachael didn't reply, she just smiled.

'Or a seven.'

'I know the rules, Carissa.'

'I know you *know* the rules, doesn't mean you're following them though, does it?'

A phone buzzed. Carissa grabbed hers from the table only to find no new messages.

'That's me!' said Rachael, digging her mobile from her jeans.

Carissa stared at her little sister with a cocked head whilst Rachael took plenty of time to study the incoming message, before popping the phone back into her pocket without making a sound.

'Have you picked up?'

'What's the point?' said Carissa. 'You've already won.'

'You have to pick up four, first. And I will change the colour to–'

'Why? What's the point?'

'It's the rules, Carissa,' said Rachael. 'Yellow. Change the colour to yellow.'

'I know it's the rules but–'

'So pick up four then.'

'Oh my god you are so annoying sometimes.'

'I can't help the rules.'

'Okay, alright, Jesus, I'll pick up…One, two, three, four, there, happy?'

'Very.' Rachael carefully laid down the winning card. Carissa slapped her eight or ten cards onto the table and went back to her phone. Rachael collected the cards up and started shuffling.

'Carrie,' said Rachael, quietly, after a couple minutes.

Carissa didn't answer.

'Carrie,' said Rachael, a little louder.

Still nothing.

'Carrie!'

'Yeah, yeah, I'll play again,' said Carissa, eyes still on her phone.

'Right. Cool. Also…um…you remember that lock?'

'That lock?' repeated Carissa without looking up.

'The bathroom lock. The one at Aunt Zoe's.'

Carissa looked up.

'Do you remember what happened?' asked Rachael.

Carissa paused for a moment. 'Yeah, of course I remember.'

'Tell me.'

'Well, you were a silly little girl who got scared when she couldn't open the bathroom door and so to shut up your whining I talked you through unlocking it.'

'Carrie, I mean it.'

Carissa saw that her sister was getting upset.

'Jesus, I'm just kidding. What's wrong?'

'I need to tell you something,' said Rachael.

'Alright.'

'Okay…here goes…' said Rachael, taking a deep breath. 'I didn't touch the lock. I didn't slide the lock across. I never touched it. You told me to, but I didn't. I opened my eyes and looked at it, and, and...I saw it, Carrie. I saw it slide across all by itself. I know that sounds crazy but it's true. I promise, I never touched it. I never moved it. Well, at least… not with my hands, anyway.'

Rachael burst into tears. Carissa moved around to sit next to her. She put her arms around her sister like she had that day when the bathroom door finally opened.

'Rach, listen, that was years ago. You were only little, seven or eight or something.'

'But I–'

'And you were frantic, I mean, you were all hyperventilating and stuff. You know how you get.'

'Carrie–'

'I mean it's no wonder you can't remember what happened.'

'Carrie, stop!'

Carissa stopped. She looked away from Rachael.

'Carrie. Why won't you look at me? Carrie? You don't believe me, do you? This is why I didn't tell you before. I knew you wouldn't believe me. Just like Daddy didn't.'

'You told Dad?' asked Carissa, turning back.

'He just thought I was being silly, wanting to be like Damo and the others. But I'm not being silly. I'm not making this up. You have to believe me, Carrie.'

'Okay, okay. Just calm down. You're getting worked up again, just like that day. Let me think for a minute.'

'What's there to think about? You don't believe me, I knew it. You think I'm lying, and that I'm just–'

'I don't think you're lying,' said Carissa.

'Carrie?'

'I believe you, okay?' said Carissa.

'You do?'

'Yes. But I think we should wait until mum gets home.'

'What?'

'She'll be home soon.'

'Are you gonna tell her?'

'We'll tell her together'

'Do we have to?'

'Yes.'

'Why?'

'Because it's time we talked about it.'

'Time we talked about *what*? Aunt Zoe's?'

Carissa paused. 'About everything.'

'I don't understand. Do you think she'll believe me?'

'Of course she will.'

'But she might say the same as Daddy did. She might think I'm–'

'She'll believe you, Rach, trust me.'

'How can you be so sure?'

'Because,' said Carissa, 'she already knows.'

Printed in Great Britain
by Amazon

48019648R00168